THE GHOST

AND THE WEDDING CRASHER

HAUNTING DANIELLE

THE GHOST
AND THE WEDDING CRASHER

USA *TODAY* BESTSELLING AUTHOR
BOBBI HOLMES

The Ghost and the Wedding Crasher
(Haunting Danielle, Book 32)
A Novel
By Bobbi Holmes
Cover Design: Elizabeth Mackey

Copyright © 2023 Bobbi Holmes
Robeth Publishing, LLC
All Rights Reserved.
robeth.net

ROBETH
PUBLISHING, LLC

ISBN: 978-1-949977-74-5
A

Dedicated to Don, for never questioning this journey I chose to take and for encouraging me along the way. I love you.

ONE

Late Thursday afternoon, on the last day of January, Melinda Belworth stared out the picture window next to her desk and watched the snow fall. She glanced back at her computer monitor, her fingertips resting lightly on the keyboard, preparing to resume her typing when her landline rang. Moving her right hand from the keyboard to her telephone, she answered the call.

"Hello?"

"Hey, Linda. I was hoping you'd answer," came the male voice.

Abruptly, Melinda sat up straighter, her right hand clutching the headset while her left hand moved from the keyboard. "Charlie?" He was the only one who ever called her Linda.

"I've missed you."

"Charlie, I can't believe it's you. I've tried calling you a couple of times over the last few months, and it always went to voicemail."

A long sigh came from Charlie's end of the call. "You haven't heard?"

Melinda sat up even straighter. "Heard what?"

"It's a long story. I'm in Vancouver."

Hesitantly, she asked, "Washington or Canada?"

"Canada."

Melinda squealed. "You're here! Where are you? The same place?"

"No. I'm staying somewhere else. Please listen. I need your help."

Melinda frowned. "What's going on?"

"Babe, listen. First, I need you to understand I'm innocent. Don't believe what they tell you."

"What are you talking about? What do you mean innocent? You're scaring me."

"I was arrested in Frederickport, framed for something I didn't do."

"Oh, my god!"

"Listen. Promise me you won't google it. I don't need you worrying about me. And I know you. This will get you all worked up. I need to borrow some money so I can lie low for a while and figure this thing out. I need time to prove my innocence. When I see you, I'll explain everything. I'll pay you back. I promise."

"Where are you?"

Charlie gave her the name of a motel on the other side of town.

"How did you get up here? Don't tell me you broke out of jail."

"Like I said, I'll explain everything when I see you." Charlie then told her how much money he needed.

Melinda glanced at the wall clock. "I'll have to go to the bank, but there is no way I'll get over there before it closes."

"That's okay, you can bring it to me in the morning, after the bank opens."

"I want to see you. I could come over there now," Melinda offered.

"No. It's too late in the day, and I don't want you driving in this weather. Not at night. Anyway, I'm exhausted, and I just want to crash. We'll see each other in the morning, and I'll explain everything. Will you do what I ask?"

"Of course."

"And you promise, no googling? Let me explain everything myself."

"Whatever you say."

Charlie gave Melinda his room number, and they exchanged a few more words before ending the call.

Melinda hung up the phone and sat quietly at her desk, running the conversation through her head. Uncle Clement didn't like Charlie Cramer. She didn't understand why, and all he would ever say was, "There is something about that boy."

He was hardly a boy, Melinda thought, and he had a great job, one that took him traveling all over the world. She wished his travels brought Charlie more frequently to Vancouver, where she lived with her uncle Clement.

Melinda looked back at her computer and remembered what Charlie had asked of her: *don't google*. She continued to stare at the computer and then let out a sigh.

"Sorry, you really didn't expect me to wait until the morning to find out what sort of trouble you got yourself into." She reached for her mouse.

———

CLEMENT BELWORTH SAT COMFORTABLY in his wingback leather chair, its placement close to the stone fireplace, affording him the extra warmth of its raging fire while he read his novel. Those who might describe Clement would typically use adjectives like dignified and respectable, wealthy, or confirmed bachelor. He had recently celebrated his eightieth birthday.

As he turned a page, the door opened, and Melinda burst into his study. Clement had been her guardian since his brother and sister-in-law died in a car accident. Melinda had been six when her parents died. It had been twenty years since she had moved into his home.

"What's wrong?" Clement asked after noticing her troubled expression. He closed his book and set it on the end table.

"I think I'm in trouble," Melinda blurted.

"What's wrong?"

Hesitantly, Melinda approached her uncle. "Remember Charlie Cramer?" She took a seat on the empty chair next to her uncle.

Clement groaned. "The man is too old for you. And he's a traveling salesman."

"And he's a murderer," Melinda blurted.

Clement stared blankly at Melinda. "What?"

In rushed words, she told Clement about Charlie's phone call and then said, "I googled it."

"Of course you did. Who did he murder?"

"According to the articles I found, Charlie was arrested for two murders. The first was his old business partner. The murder happened ten years ago in Portland. And then a couple of months ago, he murdered the business partner's sister. The murder victims were twins. And when the police arrested Charlie right after the second murder, he was getting ready to murder someone else! He's a freaking serial killer!"

Clement's eyes widened at his niece's tone. "I take it you don't believe he's innocent?"

"No. I read the articles. No wonder he didn't want me to google it. He is guilty, Uncle Clement. And I promised to take him money tomorrow! He was probably going to kill me next!"

"You obviously won't take him that money."

"Of course not. But what do I do? If I don't show up, he'll be mad. He knows where I live! He might come here and kill us both!"

Clement reached over and took his niece's hand. "Calm down. He won't come here. Not if he's in jail."

"What are you going to do?"

"The only thing we can do." Clement gave his niece's hand a little squeeze.

MILES AWAY, in Frederickport, Oregon, Laura Miller stood alone in the rain. She cursed herself for not buying an umbrella before traveling to Oregon. She didn't understand what the deal was with these Oregonians who prided themselves on braving the elements without an umbrella. Did they like to get wet? It wasn't as if Danielle or her sister had grown up in Oregon. But they sure acted like it now. Neither one owned an umbrella. Fortunately, she wore a hooded rain jacket.

It hadn't been raining when Laura left Marlow House. The rain had started not long after turning down the cul-de-sac. Her plan had been to walk to the end of the cul-de-sac and then head back to Marlow House before nightfall and in time for dinner. Ahead was a house with a large, covered porch. She had driven down this street with Kelly several days earlier when looking for a house—this one specifically.

From what Adam Nichols had told Kelly, the house had been owned by an elderly man who passed away several years earlier and left the property to his nephew, who lived in London. Adam Nichols had initially contacted the new owner about selling the property. But the nephew wasn't interested. He also wasn't interested in putting the house in the rental program. But since that time, the house had remained empty. Adam had suggested Kelly drive by the property, and if interested, he would try contacting the owner again. Kelly didn't care for the neighborhood, so she told Adam she would pass.

Instead of walking home in the rain, Laura decided to keep herself dry on the guy's porch. After all, he was in London. He would never know. And then she could call her sister, and Lily could pick her up.

Laura rushed up the walkway and started up the porch steps just as the front door swung open. She stared into the startled face of a bearded man wearing wire-rimmed glasses.

"Lily Bartley?" the man blurted, his eyes fixed on Laura.

Laura grinned up at the man and removed the hood from her head, revealing blond curls instead of red hair like her sister's. "Lily's my sister. My name is Laura. I'm sorry, I didn't think anyone was here, and I wanted to get out of the rain for a minute. I'm sorry." Laura backed up. "I didn't mean to intrude. I thought the house was vacant. You know my sister?"

"You look just like your sister. At least, if I can believe the photos I've seen of her and her husband, Jon Altar. This is my house, by the way. I got into town last night. Sidney Corvin." The man took a step toward Laura and held out his right hand. "And you're welcome to take refuge on my porch."

Visibly relaxing, Laura smiled, walked toward him, and accepted his brief handshake. Now out of the rain, she asked, "So you don't know my sister?"

The man shook his head. "No. But I'm good with faces, and I remembered hers from an article I read on Jon Altar. And I know he lives in Frederickport. You said your name is Laura. I take it you live in Frederickport too?"

"I'm just visiting. Technically, I'm homeless."

The man arched his brows. "Homeless?"

Laura shrugged. "The company I worked for was bought up by a conglomerate. Their first order of business was to downsize."

"You lost your job and your home?"

Laura gave another shrug. "Don't feel sorry for me. I was ready to quit anyway, and I must admit they gave us a great severance package. So, I decided the universe was trying to tell me it was time to make some changes."

"And you decided to become homeless?" he teased.

Laura laughed. "Something like that. I sold my condo and broke the news to my parents that I was going to do what I've always wanted to do. Travel."

"How did your parents take that news?"

Laura grinned. "Mom took it better than Dad. Mom was a hippy in her younger years, so I think the idea of me seeing the world appealed to her."

He flashed her a grin. "Your first stop was to see your sister?"

"Something like that. I was planning to come up here anyway, even if I hadn't lost my job. One of my friends is getting married in March. And I'm going to be her maid of honor. Frederickport is my first stop. I plan to stay through the wedding, and then, well, I haven't exactly figured out where I'm going next."

"I take it you're staying with your sister?"

Laura shook her head. "No. I'm staying across the street at Marlow House. Do you know it?"

He smiled at Laura and nodded.

Laura looked up at the sky. "Hey, it stopped raining. I can walk back to Marlow House."

"I have a favor to ask you."

"What's that?"

"I would really appreciate it if you said nothing to anyone about seeing me here."

Laura frowned at his request.

"Oh, it's nothing nefarious. I just like my privacy. And ever since I inherited this place, a local Realtor, Adam Nichols, has been hounding me to list it."

Laura grinned. "I know Adam. Umm, is it true you live in London?"

He nodded. "Yes. And while I'm here, I would rather appreciate my privacy. There are some things belonging to my uncle I need to go through. That's who left me the house. And I'd rather do that without real estate agents knocking on my door. I imagine Nichols won't be the only Frederickport Realtor showing up on my doorstep if they know I'm in town."

Laura nodded. "Your secret is safe with me. I understand wanting privacy." She then let out a sigh.

"Why the heavy sigh?"

"Since you live in London, I was sort of hoping you might give me some pointers on where to stay. But I'll respect your privacy and won't come knocking on your door."

He stared at her, his expression unreadable. After a few moments, he broke into a smile and said in a conspiratorial whisper, "I would love to help you. I think I might enjoy the company. But only if you come alone and promise not to tell anyone I'm here."

Laura smiled up at him. "Deal."

Returning her smile, he said, "When you come back, please call me what my friends call me, Frank."

She arched her brows. "Frank?"

"Do I look like a Sidney?" he asked.

She smiled. "Not really."

"They named me after my uncle. While I'm honored he left me his estate, I never felt like a Sidney."

"Is Frank your middle name?" she asked.

Frank shook his head. "No. It's a long story."

TWO

Earlier that day, Officer Brian Henderson pulled the police car in front of Charlie Cramer's house in Frederickport, Oregon, and parked. Joe Morelli sat in the passenger seat and looked out the side window at the house. Cramer had inherited the property from his mother. He had not lived in the house full-time since leaving home after graduating from high school, yet he stayed there on his infrequent visits to Frederickport, providing it wasn't being rented.

Before his arrest in November, he'd discussed selling the property with Realtor Adam Nichols, yet he'd put the sale on hold after his arrest. That surprised Charlie's onetime friend, Joe Morelli, who assumed Charlie needed the money from the sale more than ever now to help pay for his legal defense. Although, if they did not capture him, there would be no need for a legal defense.

Brian turned off the ignition and sat in the vehicle. He stared up at the Cramer house. Since Charlie had broken out of jail while held over for his trial, they had been monitoring the property, should he try hiding out in his childhood home.

"I seriously doubt he would come back here. I bet he's miles away by now." Joe unfastened his seatbelt while Brian did the same.

Although neither officer expected to find Cramer hiding out at the house—after all, they had checked the property regularly, and they assumed the neighbors had noticed, and so might a fugitive staking out a potential hideout. They entered with caution.

After their last visit, Brian had asked, "What will happen to this place if they never find Cramer? Eventually, the money he deposited with Adam will run out. Then what?"

Joe had said, "Kelly and I discussed that the other night. One thing that could happen, his victims might sue his estate, and if he isn't here to fight it, he could lose the property by default." One of those victims was Brian's girlfriend, Heather Donovan.

Before entering the house, the officers checked the perimeter of the property, and nothing appeared out of order or disturbed. The house wasn't entirely dark when they entered. Plenty of sunshine streamed through the curtained windows, and like they had done on previous visits, they did not turn on any lights. Upon entering each room, they opened closets and checked areas where someone might hide.

Joe entered the master bedroom first and headed straight for the closet. When he opened the closet doors, he froze. "Brian!"

"What is it?" Brian asked when he stepped into the bedroom. He found Joe standing before an open closet.

Joe glanced at Brian and then pointed to the empty closet. "The last time we were here, a suitcase was sitting there. It's gone. Someone was here."

SOME PEOPLE in Frederickport referred to Brian Henderson and Heather Donovan as the odd couple. It wasn't just their age difference. Sure, Brian was old enough to be Heather's father, and while his two ex-wives had only been a few years younger than Brian, he had dated several much younger women after his last divorce. But Brian had earned a reputation as a cynical police officer with misogynist tendencies and not seen as someone who might be attracted to a quirky woman like Heather.

Some people felt Heather was a witch—the kind who rode

broomsticks. Others compared her to a vampire, because of her style of dress and makeup. While many saw Brian and Heather as an unlikely couple, a few people in their close-knit group understood the unusual circumstances that had drawn them together. Heather was also one of the four mediums who lived on Beach Drive.

When Brian got off work on Thursday evening, he and Heather had plans to head over to Marlow House after dinner to watch a movie.

DANIELLE MADE the popcorn before Heather and Brian arrived at Marlow House. She had prepared two bowls, one for her and Walt to share, and one for Brian and Heather. The two couples gathered in the living room, waiting for the movie to start while discussing what Brian and Joe had discovered at the Cramer house that morning.

"Charlie isn't in Frederickport, is he?" Danielle asked.

"I doubt it. I can't imagine why he'd come back here." Brian grabbed a handful of popcorn from the bowl in Heather's lap.

"To kill me, that's why!" Heather snapped.

Danielle flashed Heather a sympathetic smile before asking Brian, "Who do you think took the suitcase, and why? And are you sure there was really a suitcase in the closet?"

"It was there. I remember seeing it. We called Adam because we figured he might have moved it." Brian tossed some popcorn in his mouth.

"And he didn't?" Walt asked.

Brian shook his head. "Adam told us that after the last renters moved out of the house and before Cramer got into town, the master bedroom closet was empty. Adam assumes the suitcase was something Cramer brought when he was staying there before his arrest. He went over there and checked the house, and nothing else was missing."

"How did they get inside?" Danielle asked.

Brian grimaced. "I hate to say it, but it's possible we didn't lock it up the last time we checked on the property, because there was no sign of a break-in. And it's no secret; everyone in town knows the house is vacant. Could be some kids got in there one night and then grabbed the first thing they could easily carry off."

"Was the door locked when you were there today?" Walt asked.

"Yes. All the doors were locked," Brian said.

"So the burglars were considerate and locked the doors after they left?" Danielle asked.

"Or Charlie showed up and wanted his things and used his key to get in," Heather angrily suggested.

Brian smiled at Heather. "I seriously doubt Charlie had a key to his house when he broke out of jail."

"He might have a key hidden somewhere," Heather countered.

Brian shrugged. "Yeah, that is also possible."

"I think it's more likely some kids took the suitcase. I don't see Cramer coming back here," Danielle said. "What would be the point? If I were being charged with a capital offense, I'd be on my way to Canada. If he's caught up there and extradited, chances are they would take the death penalty off the table."

"There's a moratorium on the death penalty in Oregon," Brian reminded her. "I think the last time they executed someone in this state was 1997."

"I'll just feel better when he's captured," Heather grumbled.

They chatted a few more minutes about the fugitive before changing the topic of conversation. Heather asked, "So, is your houseguest watching the movie with us tonight?"

"No, she's across the street. Joe and Kelly are over there playing cards tonight," Danielle explained.

"I figured they might want to watch the movie," Heather said.

"I told Lily about it. They might turn it on. I don't know," Danielle said.

"From what I remember, it was pretty bad." Brian chuckled. The movie in question was a horror movie filmed in Frederickport back when Adam Nichols was still in high school. Danielle and some of her friends had only recently learned about the movie's existence when the local newspaper ran an article about the movie being aired on cable.

"Hey, the only reason I want to watch it, Brian says there's a bunch of scenes of Presley House," Heather said. Heather had inherited Presley House before moving to Frederickport. It had been vacant for years, and many believed it was haunted. The haunting was true. Unfortunately, the house burned down not long after Heather moved to town, and she lost the land because of unpaid taxes.

"Did they shoot any scenes inside?" Walt asked.

Brian shook his head. "No."

WHEN DANIELLE MADE the popcorn earlier, Walt had started a fire in the living room fireplace. The flames now danced and flickered. Max climbed up on the sofa and snuggled between Walt and Danielle. Walt held the bowl of popcorn in his lap. Earlier, they had turned the overhead light off when turning on the television, so the only illumination aside from the TV came from the fireplace.

They had been watching the movie for about a half an hour when Heather said what Danielle had been thinking. "This is horrible."

Danielle laughed. "Yeah. I'm thinking it was supposed to be a comedy, not a horror movie."

"I can't believe they made this, and here Walt's movie is still on hold," Heather said.

"According to Walt's agent, it might go forward after all," Danielle said.

Both Heather and Brian looked at Walt. "Really? You never mentioned it," Heather said.

Walt shrugged. "It's not a deal until it is. And we know what happened the last time."

"Well, next time, keep the crew from getting murdered." Brian snickered.

Heather frowned at Brian. "That's horrible. It sounds like something I would say. I think you've been around me too long."

Brian laughed.

Heather looked back at Walt. "Hey, isn't your new book coming out soon?"

"They're talking about this summer," Walt said.

"Why so long?" Heather asked.

Walt shrugged. "It's just the way it works."

Snowflakes fell from the ceiling. Heather glanced up and said, "Looks like Eva's here."

Marie Nichols arrived first, the vision of an elderly woman wearing a floral sundress and straw hat. She materialized in the middle of the room, blocking the television for everyone except Brian. Unlike the others, Brian was not a medium and could not see Marie.

The snowflakes whirled next to Marie, who glanced impatiently at the incoming spirit. "We're waiting, Eva."

The next moment the snowflakes vanished, and a woman bearing a striking resemblance to Charles Dana Gibson's Gibson Girl appeared by Marie's side. She was Eva Thorndike, onetime silent screen star and childhood friend of Walt Marlow.

Eva sighed. "You're so impatient, Marie."

"Umm, you guys are in our way." Heather waved her hand to where she wanted them to move. "I know this movie is crappy, but I don't want to miss seeing Presley House."

The next moment, the two spirits moved to the side and faced the television.

"Oh my, is that the terrible movie they filmed in Frederickport?" Marie asked.

"Yes, unless they made more than one terrible movie here." Danielle laughed.

"I remember when they filmed that!" Eva said. "I tried to give them some suggestions, but of course, no one could see or hear me."

"Have you seen Adam yet?" Marie asked.

"Adam?" Heather and Danielle chorused.

Marie chuckled. "Yes, he and his friends got hired on as extras. They had a lot of fun, but when the movie came out, it didn't turn out as they thought. Let's just say it was Adam's brief foray into acting. Although, one of his friends caught the attention of the director, and he had a somewhat successful, yet brief acting career."

"Why brief?" Danielle asked.

"Unfortunately, he started running with a wild crowd. I knew his parents. I remember at first they were quite proud, always talking about him and how well he was doing. But then they stopped talking about him. Adam told me later that he got involved in the Hollywood party scene and drugs, and you know how that can go."

"Is he still alive?" Heather asked.

Marie shrugged. "As far as I know. He got into construction or something. I never heard he died. His older brother still lives in town. I don't really know him. But his parents died years ago."

"You guys, we can talk about this later." Danielle looked at the television. "I want to see Adam's big acting debut."

"And I've no clue what anyone has been talking about," Brian mumbled to himself as he tossed more popcorn into his mouth.

THREE

Danielle had offered to babysit ten-year-old Evan MacDonald on Friday afternoon, as his older brother, Eddy, who normally watched him after school, had something else he needed to do that afternoon.

Lily had come over to Marlow House, with her son, Connor, to visit with Danielle and see her sister. But when she arrived, her sister wasn't there. Danielle told Lily Laura was taking a walk. Lily, holding her young son's hand, followed Danielle to the living room, where she found Walt sitting on the floor with Evan, playing with what appeared to be a wooden airplane. The toy flew around the room like a stunt plane, doing loops around Evan.

The moment they walked into the room, Connor spied the plane and giggled as he pulled free of his mother and reached for the flying toy. The next moment, it changed course and flew to Connor, who tried unsuccessfully to grab it from the air.

Walt and Evan laughed at Connor and then shouted a quick hello to Lily before turning their attention back to Connor, who enthusiastically clapped at the airplane before it hit the floor.

Lily stood quietly, still standing where she had been when Connor pulled away from her. She watched as her son lifted the toy like a bird he was about to free. Once again, the small wooden airplane took flight. Watching the plane circle the room, she asked, "That isn't a remote control airplane, is it?"

"Nope. Walt's making it fly," Danielle said with a snort.

Connor sat on the floor with Evan seconds before the plane landed beside them. Evan picked up the plane and handed it to Connor to inspect.

"What happens if my sister sees that? Heck, I could have been her."

"Nah, you rang the doorbell. Laura has a key," Danielle quipped.

Lily turned a frown to Danielle. "Seriously, how am I supposed to explain that to my sister?"

"The boys are just having fun. Stop being such a party pooper." Danielle grabbed Lily's right hand and led her to the sofa, where the two friends sat down while the boys remained on the floor with Walt.

Lily leaned back on the cushions. "I'm going to blame the hormones."

"How are you feeling?" Danielle asked.

"As long as I eat my dry Cheerios before I get out of bed, the morning sickness isn't too bad. But I'll tell you what, this is my last pregnancy."

Danielle, also sitting on the sofa, patted her own protruding belly and said, "This might be my last one too."

Lily glanced over to her son and watched as he handed Walt the toy airplane and said, "Fly, fly."

Lily let out a sigh and turned to face Danielle. "But seriously, Connor is saying quite a few words now. How am I going to explain this to Ian's parents when Connor someday tells them how Walt can make the airplane fly?"

Danielle shrugged. "You can say Connor has a great imagination."

"And then there is Marie. Connor adores Marie. I would hate Mom or June to find out Connor's favorite grandma isn't even his real grandma. Heck, she isn't even alive."

Danielle chuckled. "There is no reason to tell them she's Connor's favorite."

"That's actually the least of my worries. Honestly, Dani, I have been thinking about it a lot lately. Connor is too young to understand he shouldn't be talking about Marie around certain people. What are they going to think when he starts rambling on about her?"

Danielle studied Lily for a minute and smiled. "Remind them he's a lot like you. After all, they know you had an imaginary friend when you were his age."

Expressionless, Lily's gaze met Danielle's. She stared at her a moment before breaking into a grin. "You know, you're right. I had Rupert." Plus, Rupert, like Marie, had been a ghost.

"And it all worked out."

Lily let out another sigh. "I suppose."

"And trust me, Walt is being careful with the flying thing. He's behaving around your sister."

Lily studied Danielle. "You know, it really was super nice of you to let her stay at Marlow House. But I do feel it's asking too much. I know I asked if she could stay, but I thought it was going to be a couple of days for the shower and then again for the wedding. I had no idea she would freaking move in for two months!"

"Don't worry about it. And remember, Laura called and asked me before she showed up. She planned to rent something from Adam. But that's silly. It'll be more convenient for you two." Lily lived across the street.

"We really need a guest room, and now with the baby coming, our house is feeling even smaller. I don't want Connor to have to share a room with the baby, and Ian needs his office."

"You aren't thinking of moving, are you?" Danielle asked.

Lily shook her head. "No. Absolutely not, although June would love that. She believes Beach Drive is cursed."

Danielle chuckled. "Rather funny when you think about the property they bought. But in fairness, the Marymoor spirits have moved on. So what are you going to do?"

"Ian and I have been talking about adding on. We don't have the property to add out, but we could build up."

"A second floor? Over the garage?"

Lily shook her head. "No. We talked about it. While that would be the easiest, as far as us living at the house and adding on, Ian doesn't want his office so removed from our living space. After all, it's kind of nice to have him in the house when I go somewhere. And it'd be too far for him to watch the kids while working in his office."

"You know, you can always have June come over to watch the kids whenever you want to take off," Danielle teased.

Lily frowned at Danielle. "Oh, shut up."

Danielle laughed and then said, "You're actually considering adding a second floor to your house?"

Lily nodded. "Yeah. Ian's been talking to his father about it. He's coming over to see what can be done. Of course, June keeps saying it would be easier if we bought a bigger house. True, but I don't want to move."

Danielle's black cat, Max, strolled into the room, panther like, and let out a loud meow. In response to whatever the cat told Walt, Walt put his hand in the air, and the next moment, the wooden airplane landed on his palm.

"Laura's here," Walt announced as he handed the toy to Connor and walked over to a chair and sat down.

"See, we had it covered," Danielle whispered to Lily.

When Laura walked into the living room a few minutes later, she was not alone. Evan's father, Police Chief MacDonald, was with her.

"Look who I found walking up to the front door," Laura said.

They exchanged greetings from around the room, and Evan called out, "Hi, Dad! Do we have to go home now?"

"In a little bit. I need to talk to the adults first," MacDonald told his son.

A few minutes later, the chief sat in the chair next to Walt, while Laura joined her sister on the sofa with Danielle, and the boys remained on the floor by the fireplace. Evan pulled over the box of toy trucks and dumped them on the floor in front of Connor.

"What's going on, Chief?" Danielle asked after the adults all sat comfortably and the boys played quietly on the other side of the room.

"I have news on Charlie Cramer," the chief announced.

"Does it have something to do with the missing suitcase Brian told us about?" Danielle asked. Max had just jumped up on Danielle's lap and now curled up to take a nap. She absently stroked his back while sporadically rubbing his white-tipped ears between her fingertips as she listened to what the chief had to say.

"That's the guy who killed Joe's friend, right?" Laura asked.

"Yes," the chief said with a nod. "And no, it has nothing to do with the suitcase. They almost caught him, but he was nowhere near Frederickport."

"Where was he?" Walt asked.

"It looks like he made it all the way to Canada," the chief announced.

"Canada?" Lily blurted.

"Doesn't surprise me he headed that way," Danielle said. "That's where I'd go if I wanted to avoid the death penalty. And yeah, I understand Oregon hasn't executed anyone for a long time, but if I were Charlie, I wouldn't risk it."

"True. But I suspect his motive was more about escaping altogether," the chief said.

"Where was he in Canada? What happened?" Walt asked.

"He made it to Vancouver, Canada," the chief explained. "There's a young woman who lives in Vancouver. Cramer met her a couple of years ago, and whenever he's there on business, they'd hook up. Late yesterday afternoon, she got an unexpected call from him. She did not know he was facing murder charges. Cramer told her he had been arrested in Frederickport, but insisted they framed him, and he failed to mention it was for murder. He told her he needed to borrow some money so he could lie low. She was supposed to take it to him this morning at the motel he was staying at."

"Was she going to take it to him?" Danielle asked.

The chief shook his head. "He asked her not to google the arrest, said he wanted to explain everything himself, in person. Fortunately, when he called, it was too late for her to go to the bank to get the money, so it gave her time to think about it."

"She googled him, didn't she?" Lily asked.

"Yes. And she wasn't as enamored of him as he thought," the chief said.

"Charlie was pretty full of himself," Danielle scoffed. "Believing he had a chance with Heather."

"She told her uncle about the phone call and what she had read online. They called the police. But when they got to the motel, the room was empty, and the back window was open. Looks like he must have seen them pull into the parking lot, and he escaped out the back before they got out of their vehicles."

"Are they sure he was really there?" Danielle asked.

"From what I understand, they checked, and the phone call the woman received came from that room. The room was registered to a John Smith," the chief explained.

"Original," Laura scoffed.

"The guy at the motel's front desk couldn't recall much about the guest aside from the fact he had checked in a few hours earlier. He wore a big coat with the hood up, and the only thing the man from the motel noticed about his looks, he wore black horn-rimmed glasses."

"That's what Charlie wears," Danielle said.

"According to the guy at the front desk, Cramer didn't have a car."

"You mean John Smith," Lily snarked.

The chief flashed Lily a smile and then added, "Someone dropped him off. So unless that same someone picked him up, Cramer is on foot, and I don't know about you, I wouldn't want to be walking the streets of Vancouver, Canada, in January."

"He'd be better off turning himself in," Danielle said. "At least now, even if Oregon reverses the moratorium on executions, chances are Canada won't extradite him unless they get assurances the death penalty is off the table."

"True, but the guy is desperate, and I don't see him turning himself in. After all, he got himself all the way to Canada," the chief reminded her.

"I hope they warn the citizens of Vancouver," Walt said. "Cramer is a dangerous man. He won't last in the cold. He'll break into someone's warm house, even if it means killing the occupants."

FOUR

"That looks like a lot of work," Walt noted. He sat alone at the kitchen table, watching Danielle standing at the stove, frying chicken. As she did most recent days, she wore loose-fitting stretch pants and an oversized fleece blouse, barely concealing her notice-able baby bump. She hadn't bothered securing her long, dark hair into a fishtail braid that morning, but wore it in a high ponytail.

"I told you. I had a craving for fried chicken," Danielle reminded him as she turned battered pieces of chicken in the hot oil.

"We could have gone out for dinner. Lucy's has fried chicken," Walt said.

Danielle wrinkled her nose. "It's not the same. And I don't mind cooking."

"I'm cleaning up," Walt announced. He had already set the table for two and brought a bowl of macaroni salad and coleslaw out from the refrigerator, placing them at the center of the table. Danielle had prepared both dishes the day before. Walt had also set a basket of Heather's homemade sourdough bread and a butter dish on the table.

The pet door swung open, and Max entered the house. He let out a loud meow. Walt looked at the cat and asked, "Is she alone?"

Danielle glanced at Walt. "Is who alone?"

"Max said Heather is on her way to the back door. She's not with anyone." Without standing up, Walt focused his energy on the door. It unlocked and swung open.

"Wow, love the service here," Heather said from the now open doorway. She stepped into the kitchen and gave a sniff. "What are you cooking?"

By her outfit, it looked as if Heather had recently gotten off work. She wore a calf-length black skirt with heeled black dress boots, and a brandy-colored fleece jacket over a black formfitting blouse. That morning she'd fastened her long, jet-black hair into a tight bun atop her head. Over the day, hair tendrils had freed themselves and now framed her face. She had also trimmed her bangs that morning, so they no longer covered her dark brows but fell just above them.

Danielle, who was now plating the fried chicken, said, "Fried chicken. You want to eat dinner with us? We have plenty."

"No, thanks. I already ate." Heather removed her jacket, hung it over the back of an empty chair, and joined Walt at the kitchen table. She watched as Danielle carried the platter of chicken toward them. "I rode to work with Chris this morning, and when we got off, we stopped at Beach Taco."

Danielle set the platter of chicken on the table and sat down with Heather and Walt. "Didn't Chris take Hunny to work today?"

"Yeah, but they always let Chris bring Hunny in." Heather stood up and walked to the counter, helping herself to a glass from an overhead cupboard.

"Is that legal?" Danielle asked, now spooning servings of salad onto her plate while Walt helped himself to a piece of chicken.

Filling her glass with cold water from the refrigerator, Heather said, "It's not like Hunny goes into the dining room. The owner always lets Hunny stay in his office."

"How did Chris rate such treatment?" Walt asked.

"It might have something to do with the fact the Glandon Foundation purchased a bunch of gift certificates from the restaurant, which we gave away during one of our events. But Chris never asked for special treatment. It was something the owner insisted on after Chris made some offhand comment about how he'd stop by more, but he always had Hunny with him."

"Crafty of Chris." Danielle snickered.

"I don't think Chris ever said it to get something."

Walt gave a snort at Heather's comment before taking a bite of his chicken.

"So where is your houseguest?" Heather glanced around the room as if Laura might appear. She took a sip of the water and returned to the table with the glass and sat back down.

"She went over to Lily and Ian's. She's having dinner with them."

"Did Brian join you and Chris for dinner?" Walt asked.

Heather shook her head. "No. He had the late shift. But he called me about thirty minutes ago. It's why I came over. Guess what he told me?"

"Charlie Cramer's in Canada," Danielle blurted.

Heather frowned. "How did you know?"

"Edward was here about an hour ago," Walt explained. "When he picked up Evan, he told us."

Heather slumped back in her chair. "I wonder how he got all the way to Canada. Do you think he hitchhiked, or does he have someone helping him?"

Danielle shrugged. "I don't know. But did Brian tell you about him calling a girlfriend and trying to get her to bring him money?"

"Yeah, he did." Heather let out a sigh and shook her head. "To be honest, I don't really care how he got there. I'm glad he didn't come back here. He's not thrilled with me for getting him arrested. I've been a nervous wreck ever since I heard he escaped."

"There is really no reason for him to come back here," Walt said. "Unless he's into revenge, which that doesn't seem to be the case, considering where he ended up."

"I wish they'd found him," Heather grumbled.

"If they don't catch him soon, they might find him frozen to death, considering the weather up there right now," Danielle said.

Heather groaned. "I just hope if that happens, his spirit doesn't come back here. I really don't want to see the guy again." Heather helped herself to a chicken leg.

Walt flashed Heather a grin. "Thought you weren't hungry?"

Heather shrugged. "I didn't say I wasn't hungry. I said I had already eaten. But come on, this is Danielle's fried chicken. She makes the best." Heather took a bite of the chicken leg.

Danielle grinned. "Why, thank you. It's how my mom used to make it. First you roll it in a flour mixture with Mom's special mixture of herbs and spices, then dip it in buttermilk, and then roll it again in the flour."

"You really need to give me that seasoning recipe." Heather took another bite.

"You keep the sourdough bread coming, and I'll give you the recipe," Danielle said.

"Deal." Heather took another bite of chicken and then said, "Oh, I wanted to tell you, I had a chat with Olivia." Olivia was the new neighbor who had moved into Pearl Huckabee's house.

"I've seen little of her," Danielle said. "I think she's been keeping busy at the library."

"She has." Heather reached for two napkins. She placed what remained of the chicken leg on one napkin and used the second napkin to wipe her fingers. "It's been challenging for her. After all, the person who was supposed to be training her murdered the person Olivia was supposed to be replacing. But she's figuring every-thing out. Anyway, I stopped in the library this afternoon to pick up something for Chris, and we had a little talk. She had a long chat with Lily the other day."

Danielle nodded. "Yeah, Lily mentioned it. They talked about Lily and Chris's out-of-body experiences during their comas, and the similarities with what Olivia had been doing."

"From what Olivia told me today, I don't think we need to worry about her walking through our walls anytime soon," Heather said.

"Why do you say that?" Walt asked.

"Lily mentioned more than her and Chris's experience to

Olivia. She told her about her cousin's husband, and it got Olivia to thinking about how risky it was to willingly separate her spirit from her body. Olivia assumed her body would be safe at home while she took off exploring. She never considered the possibility of some spirit jumping into her body and stealing it and then leaving her wandering around like a ghost."

"Was anything said about me?" Walt asked.

"According to Lily, she said nothing to Olivia about you and your cousin's exchange," Danielle said.

"And I certainly didn't," Heather said. "She knows it's a possibility. But it's not just the thought of a rogue spirit taking over her body; she got to thinking how vulnerable her body is when she disconnects and leaves it. Anyway, she claims she won't be doing any more astral projections. At least, not for recreational purposes."

"I must admit, if I weren't so possessive of this body, especially after all I've been through, the allure of astral projection could tempt me. Imagine being able to travel wherever you want, exploring the world without being tethered to a body or spending countless hours on an aircraft traveling to your destination." Walt smiled wistfully.

Danielle studied Walt for a moment and then chuckled.

Walt frowned at Danielle. "What's so funny?"

"I was about to say a ghost can do all that. But then I remembered…" Danielle didn't finish her sentence.

Walt nodded. "Not all ghosts." They all knew what Walt meant. When he had been a ghost, he hadn't had the option of staying on this plane, he would have had to move on. There had been no exploring for him.

Heather frowned. "Which I really don't understand. Why can Eva and Marie stick around and go wherever they want, yet the minute you stepped out of the house, they expected you to move on to the next level?"

Danielle looked at Heather and smiled. "You know, we all have our own path. And I'd say the Universe knows what it's doing." Danielle reached over and took one of Walt's hands in hers.

Walt smiled at Danielle. "Yes, it does."

FIVE

On Saturday morning, Danielle sat at the kitchen table, sipping her juice while watching Walt pour himself a cup of coffee. She inwardly sighed, thinking how he always dressed stylishly, yet not as formally as when they had first met. Part of her missed the three-piece pinstriped suit he'd once worn. Yet if he started wearing a suit like that again, she imagined people would find it strange. Not only because those types of suits had long since gone out of style, but it would make them a strangely mismatched couple considering her casual manner of dress. The last month she had been dressing solely for comfort, looking more like someone getting ready to go to the gym or clean house. As her thoughts wandered, Walt turned from the counter and flashed her a smile before walking toward the kitchen table.

"What are you thinking?" Walt sat down and took a sip of his coffee, his gaze still on Danielle.

Danielle shrugged. "How handsome you are."

Walt grinned. "Thank you, but you outshine me."

Danielle laughed. "Yeah, right. I feel like a slob compared to you."

Walt scoffed, leaned over, gave Danielle a quick kiss, and then said, "Don't be silly. You're radiant."

"But I'd look better wearing one of those feminine dresses you like."

Walt shook his head. "You look utterly feminine now. You're beautiful, Danielle, no matter what you're wearing."

Danielle leaned back in her chair and flashed him a grin. "You know how to charm a lady."

"Good morning!" Laura called out as she entered the kitchen.

"Morning," Danielle and Walt chorused, turning their attention to Laura, who now poured herself a cup of coffee.

"What're your plans today?" Danielle asked.

Laura took her now full cup to the kitchen table and joined Walt and Danielle. She took a sip before saying, "First, I'm going to take a walk. Afterwards I'll head over to Lily's. Kelly's picking me up over there, and we're going over to her parents' house to finalize the menu for the wedding."

"I thought you liked to walk in the afternoon," Danielle said.

"I'm going to start walking in the morning. I have a lot to do today, anyway."

"Is Lily going with you and Kelly?" Danielle asked. It was a reasonable question considering the bride was not only Lily's sister-in-law, but Lily and Ian were paying for the wedding.

Laura shook her head. "No. Lily wanted to be involved, but since the morning sickness kicked in, even reading the menu makes her want to throw up."

"I don't remember her having it this bad with Connor." Danielle took another drink of her juice.

"Heather walks every morning. If you want a walking partner, I bet she would be happy to have the company," Walt suggested.

"True. But she gets up pretty early. And she also walks on the beach. Jogging on the sand is not my thing. I prefer a relaxing walk. And I won't be alone. Sadie is coming with me." Laura took another sip of coffee.

Danielle smiled. "Sadie? She makes good company."

"Yeah, I asked Ian last night if it would be okay if I took her with me when I take my morning walks." Laura glanced at the wall clock. "I'd better get going." She stood up.

"No breakfast first?" Danielle asked.

Laura shook her head. "No, Kelly and I are going out to brunch before we go to her parents'."

———

"I DON'T THINK Laura would ask Heather to go walking with her," Danielle told Walt after Laura left Marlow House. "Even if Heather agreed to walk later and not on the beach."

"I'm not sure about that. She seems more friendly toward Heather compared to the last time she was here."

"You know why that is, don't you?" Danielle asked.

Walt shook his head. "No, why?"

"The last time Laura was here, she was trying to get Chris's attention."

"She's still doing that," Walt reminded her.

"True. But when Laura was here for Connor's birthday, she didn't know about Brian and Heather. At least, not until Connor's party. She thought she was competing with Heather for Chris's attention."

"Heather is Chris's employee, friend, and neighbor."

"And there are no romantic relationships with employers, friends, or neighbors?" Danielle scoffed. "Heather was often Chris's plus one. Like when we all had dinner at Pearl Cove the last time Laura was here. But since Laura doesn't have her sights on Brian, Laura obviously no longer sees her as competition. Which makes it easier for her to be less snarky with Heather."

Walt frowned at Danielle. "Do you like Laura?"

"Well, sure. She's Lily's sister."

"And if she weren't Lily's sister, would you still like her?" Walt asked.

Danielle considered the question a moment before answering, "I'd still like her, but I probably wouldn't have been as open to having her stay here until Kelly and Joe's wedding."

"WHAT ARE YOU CARRYING?" Lily asked her sister when she walked into her living room with Ian. Lily sat on the sofa, drinking hot chocolate and still wearing her pajamas, while Connor played with plastic dinosaurs on the floor. Sadie, the golden retriever, trailed behind Ian and Laura, her tail wagging.

"It's an umbrella," Laura announced, holding the closed umbrella briefly over her head for Lily to see.

"An umbrella? Seriously? What if the neighbors see?" Lily teased. "And where did you get that thing?"

"Kelly gave it to me."

Lily let out an exaggerated sigh and glanced briefly at the window. "It's not even raining."

"It's Oregon, it will."

After Laura left with Sadie on a leash a few minutes later, Lily said, "My sister is such a wimp. She already has a hooded rain jacket. She's going to look silly with that umbrella."

LAURA WORE DENIMS, boots, and a rain jacket over her pullover sweater as she walked down the sidewalk of Beach Drive with Sadie, carrying her umbrella. On a leash, Sadie walked in front of Laura, but did not pull on the lead.

When they reached the intersection by the pier, Laura paused a moment. When she walked yesterday, she hadn't taken the same route that she had taken on Thursday. Therefore, she hadn't seen Frank again.

"Perhaps I should turn down this way. Maybe I'll run into that cute guy again. What do you think, Sadie?"

Sadie glanced back at Laura when she heard her name.

"But you won't tell anyone, will you?" Laura asked with a grin.

When Laura and Sadie reached the cul-de-sac, she paused a moment, second-guessing if she should walk by Frank's house again. After a moment of deliberation, she realized Frank did not know if this was her normal walking path or not. After all, he had only recently come to Frederickport. Confident in her decision, she started down the street.

Laura glanced up at the sky and then at the umbrella; she muttered under her breath, "If it starts raining, I would have been smarter to come without an umbrella. After all, it would give me an excuse to take refuge on his porch again."

She walked down the street, seeing no activity in the neighborhood. All seemed quiet. She continued on her way. As she passed Frank's house, she heard a male voice call out, "You have a dog?"

Laura stopped walking and turned to face Sidney's house. She found him standing on his front porch, smiling down at her. She smiled back and reversed course, walking to his front steps with Sadie.

"It's my sister and brother-in-law's dog."

"I wondered if I might see you again," Frank said when she reached his porch.

"I usually walk in the afternoon, but I started walking in the mornings."

"Does your sister ever join you?" he asked.

Laura shook her head. "No. My sister's pregnant, and I don't think she's up to it."

Frank walked down his front steps and gave Sadie a greeting pat while the dog curiously sniffed his hand.

"You kept my promise, didn't tell anyone I was here?" he asked.

"Of course." She flashed him a grin.

"Would you like to join me for a cup of coffee?"

"I'd love one."

Ten minutes later, Laura sat with Frank on his front porch, each drinking a cup of coffee. Before Laura had sat down on one of the Adirondack chairs, Sidney had insisted on wiping it down with a towel to remove any moisture. She appreciated the considerate gesture.

"So tell me, what's it like to stay at Marlow House?" Frank asked. "I remember my uncle telling me about that place. He used to say it was haunted."

Laura laughed. "Sometimes it feels that way. But it's a beautiful house. While it's a bed-and-breakfast, I'm the only one staying there. I have the only bedroom downstairs, which is nice, because it's more private."

"The hosts' room is upstairs?"

"Yes. Walt and Danielle used to have their bedroom on the third floor, which is technically the attic, but they moved to a bedroom on the second floor. Danielle's pregnant, and they're setting up one bedroom on the second floor as a nursery. I honestly don't know if they will ever reopen as a full-time B and B. She's having twins."

"Twins. Wow, that's going to keep her busy."

"No kidding."

"I assume she doesn't work outside the home if she runs a B and B?" he asked.

Laura shook her head. "No, she doesn't. And her husband works from home. He's a writer. His office is in the room that used to be their bedroom in the attic."

"Ahh, he's a writer like your brother-in-law," he said.

A bark from Sadie interrupted their conversation. The dog stood yet did not try running off the porch. Instead, she watched, with tail wagging, while a man from down the street walked their way with a schnauzer on a leash.

"Morning, Sidney!" the man called out, giving the pair a wave as he walked by Sidney's house. Frank returned the hello and a wave.

"One of your neighbors?" Laura asked.

Frank nodded. "He lives a few doors down."

"I thought you didn't want anyone to know you're here."

Frank shrugged. "Obviously, my neighbors know. But I don't think any of them are real estate agents."

Sadie was still standing, watching the man with the schnauzer continue down the street, when a vehicle pulled up in front of the house and parked. Laura, who had just finished her coffee, decided it was time to continue on her walk when she noticed the man from the vehicle now walking toward Frank's front porch.

"I should really get going. Thanks for the coffee," Laura said, now standing.

"Hey, Sidney," the man called out from the foot of the steps.

"Morning, Hal," Frank called back.

Laura started down the stairs with Sadie. She exchanged a hello nod with the man called Hal as she passed him.

"IS IT SMART TO GET A GIRLFRIEND?" Hal asked. The two men stood together on the front porch, watching as Laura disappeared down the street with the golden retriever.

"Not a girlfriend, Hal. Guess who she is?" he asked.

"Looks like trouble to me."

"It's Lily Bartley's sister."

"Holy crap," Hal cursed. "Are you freaking insane?"

"And guess where she's staying? Marlow House."

"You're nuts! What are you thinking?"

"Relax, Hal. This might be what we need to pull this off."

"Or to get us both thrown behind bars."

"Have some faith. Everything is falling into place. And this, it's like having inside information."

"What if she wants you to meet her sister?"

"That will not happen. Trust me, Hal. I have this under control."

SIX

"How was your walk?" Lily asked when Laura returned Sadie on Saturday morning. Lily had changed out of her pajamas and now wore stretch pants and a sweatshirt. Ian was in his office working, and Connor had fallen asleep on the living room floor, surrounded by plastic dinosaurs. Lily had left him there to doze and led Laura into the kitchen.

"I enjoyed it."

"I see you didn't need the umbrella." Lily snickered.

"I like to be prepared."

Lily took a seat at the breakfast bar and asked Laura if she wanted something to eat.

"Remember, Kelly is picking me up for brunch, and afterwards we're going over to her parents' to discuss the menu with her mom. Are you sure you won't come with us?"

Lily shook her head. "I'd love to. But I don't want to ruin your brunch by puking."

Laura giggled and asked, "Is it really that bad?" She took a seat at the breakfast bar next to her sister.

"I doubt I would puke. But I seriously can't handle the smell of most food right now. As for helping select the menu options, I don't want to think about food right now. But can I ask you a favor?"

"What?"

"Make sure they pick out some good stuff. Do a lot of different appetizers. If I'm lucky and get over this morning sickness before the wedding, I can enjoy the food." Lily laughed.

Laura laughed with her sister, and when they quieted down, Laura asked with a serious tone, "Are you okay with me being Kelly's maid of honor and all?"

"Sure, why wouldn't I be okay with it?"

"For one thing, she is your sister-in-law, not mine."

"Ian said she felt uncomfortable choosing between her sisters-in-law."

"Yeah, but I always assumed you and Joe's sister would be one of her bridesmaids," Laura said.

"Kelly never discussed her bridesmaids and groomsmen with me. I assumed she was having them." Lily shrugged. "But now she says she's not." Since changing the wedding venue to Pearl Cove instead of Ian and Lily's house, Kelly had announced there would be no bridesmaids or groomsmen, only the maid of honor and best man.

"Oh."

Lily studied her sister's face for a moment and then asked, "Are you having second thoughts about being the maid of honor? I thought you wanted to?"

Laura shrugged. "It's just that when I mentioned to someone back home about how my first stop was Oregon, and about the wedding, they thought it was weird I was going to be your sister-in-law's maid of honor."

"Hey, I'm glad you and Kelly get along so well. I understand my marrying Ian has been an adjustment for her."

"She sometimes feels a little left out. And I get it. I sometimes get jealous of your relationship with Danielle. It's hard when we grow up thinking of our siblings as our best friends, and then one day, they have a new best friend."

"Aww, Laura, you will always be my bestest friend." Lily leaned over to Laura and gave her a hug.

"Better friend than Ian?" Laura whispered.

"Bestest girlfriend."

Laura laughed and returned her sister's hug.

LAURA MILLER and Kelly Bartley sat in a booth across from each other at the Clam Shack. The server handed them each a menu, took their drink order, and left the two women alone.

Kelly looked over her menu at Laura. "This is the first time I've been here. I've been trying to get Joe to come since it opened last month. But he keeps saying he'll come after they get all the kinks out."

"Yeah, I kind of get that. Sometimes coming to a restaurant right after it opens isn't a good idea."

"You'll be the guinea pig." Kelly laughed. "Although so am I. If I like it, I'll get Joe to come."

"I'm surprised your mom didn't join us."

Kelly cringed. "I sorta didn't tell her. Maybe not mention it when we go over there?"

Laura grinned. "No problem."

"I love Mom, and I'm glad they moved to Frederickport, but sometimes she can be a little overwhelming."

"Hey, I get it."

Kelly peeked over her menu at Laura. "I'm excited you're going to be here for almost two months. Any chance you'll stay? Frederickport is a nice place, and it would give you a chance to get to know Chris better."

Closing her menu and setting it on the table, Laura shrugged. "Nothing's going to happen between me and Chris. Hey, would be nice, but I don't think I'm his type."

"I don't know about Chris's type. But if you think about it, both Chris and Joe had a thing for Danielle. I don't get it." Kelly shrugged.

"That's okay. Because you ended up with Joe, and I met an interesting guy, and he lives in London." Laura grinned at Kelly.

Kelly arched her brow. "Do tell."

"Promise not to say anything to anyone. He doesn't want certain people to know he's in town." Laura then told Kelly what Frank had told her.

"So he's cute?"

"Real cute. He has a beard, sorta. Not a long one. More manicured. Kinda sexy. I never really liked beards, but it looks good on him."

"Sexy Brit accent?"

Laura sighed. "No accent. From what I understand, he's an American living abroad for business."

Their conversation stopped when the server showed up with their beverages. She took their food orders, picked up the menus off the table, and left them alone again.

"You didn't answer my original question," Kelly asked.

Laura frowned. "What was that?"

"Have you considered staying in Frederickport? It's not like you have a condo to go back to anymore. Frankly, I can't believe how fast you moved."

"Me either. I didn't expect my neighbor to actually buy my place. Or that he would really pay cash. I just figured he was being a braggart. Whenever he'd see me in the hall, he'd ask me how I was doing and then say something like, *remember, if you decide to sell your place, come to me first. I'll give you a good price and pay cash. You don't have to worry about paying a commission.*"

"Were you surprised when you asked him to buy it, and he did?" Kelly asked.

"Yeah, I was. I was also shocked how fast escrow closed. Selling my condo ended up being the easiest part of the move. Taking all my crap to my parents' house for the yard sale was a major pain. But if I'm traveling, do I really want to pay storage for a bunch of furniture?"

"Aren't you afraid of traveling Europe alone?"

Laura shrugged. "A little. My mom has a friend in Italy; she contacted her. So I'm staying with them for part of the time. And hey, I have a new friend from London."

Kelly grinned.

"What about you and Joe? Still thinking of buying a house?"

"Not right now. I confess, I'm a little jealous that Adam and Mel found something. But they have more money than Joe and me, and I'm burned out at looking at houses, and everything is so expensive. Joe's place is nice, but I really wanted to start our marriage in a new house that was both of ours."

Laura reached across the table and patted Kelly's left hand. "You guys will eventually find the perfect place."

Kelly smiled wistfully at Laura and then glanced down at her hand Laura had just patted. Now staring at her engagement ring, she frowned.

"Kelly, you need to tell him."

Kelly glanced up at Laura and fidgeted with her ring. "I can't tell Joe I hate my engagement ring."

"It's a beautiful diamond."

Kelly groaned and slumped back in her seat. "Yeah, I know. But this setting is horrendous. I keep finding myself subconsciously hiding my left hand when I meet new people. I hate it when Joe wants me to show off the ring. He doesn't even notice the expressions I get."

"Guys can be clueless."

"He loves his grandmother and was honored she gave him the ring. The fact it fit me perfectly, he saw as a sign."

"I thought he said you could change the setting if you wanted?" Laura asked.

"He did. But I could tell he didn't want me to. He seemed so happy that it fit me perfectly." Kelly picked up the Bloody Mary the server had brought her and took a drink.

"You still have time to change the setting. After all, if I could sell my condo in less than a month and get it closed, you should be able to get a new setting in time for the wedding. Tell him that while you love the ring, after wearing it this long, you realize it isn't your style.

That perhaps you could do what he originally suggested and have it reset."

"He didn't suggest I get a new setting. He said I could if I wanted."

"He won't remember how he originally said it. But he'll probably remember he said you could if you wanted. I'm sure he'll be fine with it. He loves you."

Setting her cocktail on the table, Kelly looked at her engagement ring. "I know. But I love Joe too. And I don't want to hurt his feelings."

Laura was about to say something when she noticed someone walk into the restaurant. In a whisper, she said, "That's the guy who visited Frank when I was there this morning."

Kelly glanced to where Laura was looking and spied a man walking to a table on the other side of the restaurant. "I've met him once. Joe knows him. They attended school together."

"He's one of Joe's friends?"

Kelly turned back to Laura. "Not really. We ran into him once at the theater, and Joe introduced us. The guy mentioned he went to high school with Joe. I don't remember his name."

"I think it's Hal."

"Oh, that's right. Hal something. Joe later told me Hal is some kind of handyman who looks after houses where the owners aren't full-time residents, but don't rent out their properties. He grew up in Frederickport and knows a lot of people."

"I bet that's why he stopped at Frank's. Hal probably watches the house for Frank when he's in London."

Kelly shrugged. "It would make sense, especially since your friend doesn't live here full time."

"Umm… I forgot to mention. You are the one who initially told me about Frank."

Kelly frowned at Laura. "What do you mean?"

"Remember when we were driving around the other day looking at houses?" Laura reminded her.

Kelly arched her brows. "That guy from London?"

"And what Adam told you was correct. This is Frank's first time in Frederickport."

Kelly giggled. "Adam is the Realtor he's trying to avoid?"

Laura nodded.

"Sort of hilarious it's Adam. I get it. Adam can be persistent. Which is kinda funny, had I been interested in that neighborhood, he'd be trying to contact the guy."

"Remember, you can't tell anyone about him," Laura reminded her. "I haven't even told Lily."

"How come?"

"Knowing Lily, she would want to meet him, and she is not the best secret keeper."

Kelly chuckled.

"And I promised him I would keep his secret so he could enjoy a quiet visit here without local Realtors badgering him."

"Hmm... perhaps I should reconsider his house."

"Oh, stop!"

Kelly laughed. "Don't worry, I'll keep your secret as long as you keep mine."

"Which secret is that?"

"That I hate my engagement ring."

SEVEN

Friends from Beach Drive met up at Pier Café for dinner on Saturday evening. The group included Walt, Danielle, Brian, Heather, and Chris Johnson, aka Chris Glandon.

The last one had just sat down at the table when Chris asked, "Aren't Lily and Ian joining us?"

Danielle passed around the menus that had been sitting in the center of the table and said, "Smells are really getting to Lily these days."

"Another reason never to get pregnant," Heather scoffed as she opened her menu.

"How are you feeling these days?" Brian asked Danielle.

"The morning sickness has passed. I'm actually feeling pretty good. A little less energy than normal."

"That sounds about right; you are growing two humans inside you," Chris reminded her.

Heather wrinkled her nose at Chris and said, "Ew. I'm not sure I like how that sounds."

Walt chuckled at the comments, but instead of saying anything, leaned over and kissed Danielle's cheek.

"Why? It's the truth." Chris shrugged.

Their conversation ended when Carla stepped up to the table to take their order. Once again, she had changed her hair color, this time sporting solid burgundy. After taking their drink order, Heather said, "I like that new color. It goes really well with your complexion."

Carla grinned at Heather. "Thanks. I might keep this for a while. You're the second person today who complimented me on it."

Heather shrugged. "It looks great."

After giving Heather another grin, Carla turned her attention to Brian. "Any news on Charlie Cramer? I read on Facebook that he was spotted in Canada. Did they catch him yet?"

"Not that I've heard," Brian said. Under his breath he muttered, "It was on Facebook?"

"How did he get over the border so easily?" Carla asked.

"I'm curious; who do you think helped him get to Canada?" Heather said.

Carla looked at Heather. "Someone helped him?" Instead of waiting for Heather's reply, she turned her attention back to Brian and asked, "Does he have an accomplice?"

Brian shot a brief scowl to Heather and then looked back at Carla. "As far as we know, he's alone. They captured the other prisoners who were with Cramer when he escaped."

"But he got away? Sounds like someone helped him," Carla said.

Heather nodded. "Yeah, that's what I think."

After Carla left their table to get the drink orders, Brian told Heather, "You really shouldn't encourage Carla."

"What? Telling her I like her hair color? I do."

Brian rolled his eyes. "Not that."

"Yeah, I knew what you meant. But what's the big deal expressing my opinion that someone is probably helping Cramer?"

"Because it's Carla," Brian began.

"And Carla will end up telling everyone in Frederickport that someone is helping Cramer get away," Chris answered for Brian. "And before long, there will be wild speculation spreading through town."

Brian gave Chris a nod. "Chris gets it." He turned back to Heather.

Heather shrugged. "I don't."

"You're dating the officer who arrested Cramer," Walt reminded her. "Will Carla see that as your opinion or inside information?"

"I still don't see what the big deal is," Heather grumbled.

"Perhaps we should change the subject and talk about something more positive," Danielle suggested. "Like Adam and Melony's bridal shower next week."

"Since when did guys start attending bridal showers?" Brian asked. "No one ever threw me a shower when I got married."

Heather reached over to Brian and patted his hand. "That's because you're old. Keep up, old man."

Instead of being insulted, Brian chuckled.

"They do it sometimes now," Danielle said. "I sort of like the idea."

"Melony almost nixed the shower altogether. Not sure why, maybe because she's been married before. But when I suggested having a coed shower, she liked the idea," Heather said.

"Yeah, she liked the idea of forcing Adam to go," Walt said with a laugh.

Danielle gave Walt a playful swat and said, "Oh, hush. It's going to be fun."

———

JOE PARKED his vehicle in the pier parking lot and turned off the ignition.

"I feel kinda spoiled going out twice in one day," Kelly said as she unfastened her seatbelt.

"You should," Joe teased.

"I wish Ian and Lily had agreed to come with us," Kelly said.

"Laura told you Lily didn't want to go to lunch with you guys because the smells bother her," Joe reminded her. "And they are worse down here."

"I suppose I understand. But I wish Ian would join us. No

reason for him to stay home because Lily can't go. It's not like she's actually sick."

"She is pregnant with his child."

"I know but—"

Joe cut Kelly off by asking, "If you were pregnant, would you want me to go to dinner with Lily and Ian if you were home with morning sickness?"

Kelly scrunched her nose at Joe. "When you say it that way, I suppose I understand. But... well, if I had morning sickness my entire pregnancy, I wouldn't expect you to always stay home because I had to."

Joe grinned at Kelly. "Okay. I might remind you of that someday."

A few minutes later, the pair walked up the pier toward Pier Café when they noticed a group of five people coming their way. It was Walt and Danielle's dinner party, who were just leaving the restaurant.

When Joe and Kelly and the group met, they all stopped a moment on the pier and exchanged greetings before Joe and Kelly continued on to the diner and the others headed home.

"SOMETIMES THIS ALL seems so bizarre to me," Joe told Kelly fifteen minutes later as the two sat in a booth in Pier Café, waiting for their food order to be delivered.

"What do you mean?" Kelly asked.

Leaning back on the bench, Joe looked across the table at his fiancée. "I remember how Danielle and Brian disliked each other. Hell, he was convinced she murdered her cousin, and then he was certain she killed Stoddard."

"You've said that before. Many times. And as I've reminded you before, you thought she killed Cheryl, too. Of course, you once thought I might have killed Peter Morris."

"I never really thought you killed Morris. Anyway, Brian and

Chris seem rather chummy these days. There was a time." Joe shook his head.

"Yeah, I remember all that. I thought it was pretty funny when we all figured out who Chris Glandon was. Of course, you and I weren't together back then, and I remember my brother had been trying to get an interview with him. And now that he's one of his good friends, he's kept Chris's secret."

The next moment, the server brought their food. When they were alone again, Joe said, "I understand Chris and Heather are hosting Mel and Adam's wedding shower."

"Yeah, I imagine that's one reason it's a coed shower." Kelly picked up her burger, about to take a bite. She paused and looked at Joe. "You didn't want your sister to do a coed shower, did you?"

Joe shook his head. "No. It should be a girl thing. But what does Chris co-hosting have to do with it?" Joe picked up the nearby ketchup bottle and removed its lid.

"Not only are they having it at the Glandon Foundation offices, I bet Chris is paying for everything. Heather probably couldn't afford to do it on her own. Truth be told, I bet Heather's arranging it, but Chris is paying for everything. Which is okay. Chris can afford it." Kelly took a bite of her burger.

"Not sure about that. Heather could afford it." Joe turned the ketchup bottle upside down and held it over his plate before giving it several taps on the bottom of the bottle.

"What are you talking about?"

"Think about it, Kelly. She is Chris's personal assistant. Do you honestly think Chris, considering his generosity, doesn't pay his employees well? Especially his personal assistant. And while Heather might be a little different, from what I hear, she does a good job for him."

Kelly set her burger on her plate and frowned at Joe as she wiped her mouth with a napkin. "Really? I never looked at Heather as someone who would make much money."

"I have a feeling she makes damn good money. Probably more than the two of us combined." Joe recapped the ketchup bottle and set it on the table.

They continued to eat their dinner. The conversation shifted to their own wedding plans at Pearl Cove, and Kelly's recent lunch with Lily's sister, Laura.

"Can I tell you a secret?" Kelly asked.

Joe looked up from his plate. "Sure. What?"

"It seems Laura met some guy on her morning walks. She's only talked to him a few times, but it sounds like she finds him attractive."

"More attractive than Chris?" Joe asked with a snort.

"Unfortunately, that's probably never going to happen. Anyway, Laura is leaving after our wedding. But this guy, he lives in London. So who knows, maybe they'll start something here and pick up with it over there." Kelly flashed Joe a grin.

"Laura met some guy from London in Frederickport? Who is this guy?"

"Remember when Adam gave me that last list of houses to drive by? This guy's house was on the list. He arrived in Frederickport a few days ago. It's his first time here. He inherited the house from his uncle. It's on Sand Dollar. I didn't care for the neighborhood. Anyway, one reason he doesn't want anyone to know he's in town, Adam has been hounding him to put the house in the rental market or list it. He doesn't want to be bugged while he's here."

Joe chuckled. "I know who you're talking about."

"You do? You've met him?"

Joe shook his head. "No. I knew his uncle. And I remember he left the house to his sister's son. The sister had already passed away, and the nephew was pretty much his only living relative. But he lives in London. Has some job over there. I thought for sure he would put the house on the market, but then Hal mentioned he was going to be the caretaker for the property."

"That's right, Hal! Laura and I saw him at brunch today. I didn't say hi to him. Doubt he would remember who I am. But Laura recognized him. Said when she was leaving this guy's house, Hal had just arrived, and the London guy called him by name."

"You mean Sidney?" Joe asked.

"You said you never met him."

"I know they named him after the uncle, the one who owned the property. And the uncle's name was Sidney."

"He doesn't go by Sidney. He introduced himself to Laura by that name, but said he goes by Frank."

Joe frowned. "Frank?"

Kelly shrugged. "I imagine there's a story behind the name, but he didn't say what it was. As for your friend Hal—"

"I wouldn't call Hal a friend."

"Old high school friend?"

"Honestly, back in high school, I'm pretty sure Hal sold drugs. Not the crowd I ran in."

Kelly's eyes widened. "Why isn't he in jail? Why do people let him take care of their houses?"

"Back then, I wasn't on the Frederickport Police force; I was a teenager," Joe teased.

Kelly rolled her eyes. "I know, but still."

"Hey, back in high school, the rumor was he was selling drugs. And it could have been nothing but a rumor. We didn't run in the same crowd; it's just what I heard. He moved to Portland after graduation but moved back to town about ten years ago to help his parents and take over his dad's business. He seems to have straightened himself out."

EIGHT

"Good morning," Laura greeted on Sunday morning as she entered the kitchen of Marlow House. She found both Walt and Danielle sitting at the table. Walt read the newspaper while sipping coffee, and Danielle surfed on her smartphone with a half glass of orange juice sitting next to her.

Both Walt and Danielle looked up from what they read and chorused, "Good morning."

Laura walked to the coffeepot, picked up a clean mug Walt had already set on the counter for her, and paused a moment. She glanced at the table. "I didn't think anyone read the newspaper anymore."

Walt smiled. "I've always enjoyed the morning newspaper."

"But you can get so much more on your phone," Laura said.

"It's not the same," Walt argued.

"Sometimes I think you were born at the wrong time," Laura told Walt.

"You've no idea," Danielle muttered under her breath and resumed surfing on her phone.

Walt watched as Laura filled her cup with coffee. "Why do you say that?"

Turning toward Walt, Laura shrugged. "Lots of things. The way you dress, for example."

Walt arched his brows, and Danielle peeked up from her phone, curious to see where this conversation was going.

"You think I dress old-fashioned?" Walt sounded more amused than offended.

"Oh, no." Laura walked to the table with her mug of coffee and sat down with Walt and Danielle. "Not at all. In fact, I like the way you dress. But it seems all the guys these days dress super casual unless they're at work or going out somewhere. I never see you in jeans and a T-shirt. For example, I can't ever imagine you wearing a baseball hat backwards."

"I should hope not."

Danielle gave an unladylike snort to Walt's indignant response.

"And I've noticed how you always open the door for Danielle. Even the car door. It's kind of old-fashioned. But nice." Laura sipped her coffee.

"I agree; it is nice." Danielle reached over to Walt, gave him a pat, and then picked up her glass of juice and took a sip.

"Thank you, I think," Walt muttered.

"Are you walking today?" Danielle asked.

"Yes. I probably shouldn't have coffee before I walk, but I could really use the caffeine. To be honest, I sorta wanted to stay in bed." Laura took another drink of her coffee.

"I know the feeling," Danielle said. "I'm always tired these days."

"You have a legit excuse. I'm just being lazy."

"What did you end up doing last night? Did you go over to Lily and Ian's?" Danielle asked.

Laura shook her head. "No. Lily told me she was turning in early. So I took up your offer and made myself a sandwich from the cold cuts in the refrigerator. Then took a shower, washed my hair, and climbed into bed and watched an old movie."

"You could have come to the diner with us," Danielle reminded her.

"I appreciate the offer. But you said Chris was going to be there."

Walt cocked a brow. "And you didn't want to see Chris?"

"Oh, it's not that. I didn't want Chris to see me!"

"Why is that?" Danielle asked.

"My hair was a mess. I should have washed it the night before. I certainly didn't want Chris to see me looking like that!" Laura cringed at the thought.

―――――

AFTER LAURA FINISHED HER COFFEE, she said goodbye to Walt and Danielle, visited the bathroom, grabbed her jacket and umbrella, put on her shoes, and headed across the street to get Sadie. Fifteen minutes later, she was walking down Frank's street. To her delight, she found Frank sitting on his front porch.

"Are you joining me for coffee?" he asked when she reached his house.

Laura accepted his offer. Ten minutes later, she sat in the same chair she had used the day before, a cup of warm coffee cradled between her hands, and Sadie curled up by her feet.

"I doubt you'll need that umbrella," Frank teased.

"It's possible I've discovered the secret to stopping Oregon's rain. Simply carry an umbrella."

Frank laughed.

"Can I ask you a question?" Laura asked.

"Sure." Frank sipped his coffee, his gaze never leaving Laura.

"Yesterday, a guy you called Hal came to visit you. I saw him later at a restaurant I was at with a friend."

"You did?"

"Yeah. I didn't talk to him or anything. My friend Kelly Bartley, she recognized him. Her fiancé, Joe, went to school with him."

Frank silently listened, his gaze never leaving Laura.

"Kelly mentioned he's like a caretaker. So I kind of wondered if he's the caretaker for this house. If that's how you know him since you just got here, and you said you had never been here before. I'm just curious." Laura paused a moment, shrugged, and added, "Okay, I'm nosey."

Frank chuckled. "Yes. My uncle was friends with Hal's parents. And when my uncle got older and needed help, he hired Hal to help him out. After I inherited the place, Hal got ahold of me, asked me if I wanted him to take care of the property when I wasn't here. So I hired him. Honestly, I was a little reluctant to have a stranger watch over the house. But I gave him a chance because my uncle obviously trusted him. And by the way the place looked when I arrived, it seems he's doing a good job."

"When are you going back to London?"

Frank shrugged. "I'm not sure yet. Early March. Maybe sooner."

"I'm leaving in March."

"Ahh, starting your world travels?" Frank grinned. "Where is your first stop?"

"I haven't put my itinerary together yet. I know some places I'll be going. Like London." Laura grinned sheepishly and took a sip of coffee.

Frank returned her grin. "If I'm back when you get to London, then you'll have to let me show you around."

"I'd like that."

"So would I. But I imagine you have a lot you intend to do here first. Didn't you say you're going to be in a wedding?"

Laura nodded. "Yes. My friend Kelly, she's getting married. She's actually my sister's sister-in-law. But we kinda hit it off when my sister got married. We've kept in touch and hang out when I come up to see Lily."

"You said you were staying at Marlow House, not at your sister's?"

"Yes. My sister doesn't have the room. And Marlow House is right across the street from her place. It's got plenty of room, and technically, it's a bed-and-breakfast."

"I remember reading some things about Marlow House. After I inherited my uncle's estate, I'd occasionally do internet searches on Frederickport. I was curious about the place. A while back, I came across some wild stories. One about some priceless necklace found at Marlow House, and something about gold coins."

"Actually, they found the gold coins at the house my sister lives in. Lily wasn't living in the house back then. At the time, the house was owned by the grandmother of Adam Nichols. You know, that Realtor you're trying to avoid."

"Adam Nichols's grandmother got the gold coins?"

Laura shook her head. "I don't really understand it all. But the coins actually belonged to the Marlow estate, which Danielle inherited. The whole thing is rather bizarre, because she married some distant relative of the Marlows who left the estate to some relative of Danielle's. I know it's kind of hard to follow." Laura laughed.

"No kidding. And the necklace?"

"They call it the Missing Thorndike. It once belonged to Eva Thorndike, who was a silent screen star back when the original Walt was alive. Oh, did I mention Danielle's husband shares the same name as this distant relative, and he looks just like him? Danielle has a portrait in her library of the Walt Marlow who left the estate to her great-aunt. He looks like her husband's twin. It's bizarre."

"I imagine she got a pretty penny for the necklace and gold coins. Makes one wonder why she bothers running a bed-and-breakfast."

"I have to agree. But she never sold the necklace or gold coins. Lily said they had a buyer for the coins once, but it fell apart. I think that's when someone stole the coins."

"Someone stole the gold coins?"

"Yeah, but they got them back. I don't know the details of that."

"Where are they now?"

"From what I understand, Danielle keeps them in a safe-deposit box at the local bank. Both the coins and the necklace. Not sure if she plans to sell them eventually or keep them." Laura shrugged.

"Interesting." Frank took a sip of his coffee.

"Thing about Danielle, she's not really that materialistic. Sure, she has a beautiful house and stuff, and Walt has that really cool Packard, but according to my sister, she's not into buying a bunch of stuff for herself. Lily says when Danielle finally sells the gold coins, she'll probably donate the money. She's already donated a lot of her inheritance."

Laura took the last drink of her coffee and glanced at the time on her smartphone. She stood up. "I should probably head back. My brother-in-law will think I stole his dog."

Frank stood and took the mug from Laura's hand. "I hope you stop by again. I'll have the coffee on."

"That would be nice."

———

FRANK WATCHED as Laura and Sadie walked down the street, away from the house. After a few moments, he carried the two coffee cups inside. Twenty minutes later, he had just finished making himself some breakfast when he heard a knock on the door and a voice call out, "It's Hal."

Frank got up from the table, walked to the door, and let Hal in. The caretaker followed him back to the kitchen.

"Coffee's on. Help yourself," Frank said as he sat back down at the table to eat his breakfast.

"Have you worked out the timeline yet?" Hal poured himself a cup of coffee.

"We have to wait for your brother to get here."

"Yeah, I know. But after that," Hal asked.

"I'm not sure. It depends on what my new little friend tells me." Frank stabbed some scramble eggs with his fork.

"Did you see her again?"

"Yeah." Frank shoved the bite of scramble eggs into his mouth. Still chewing his food, he said, "She was here a little while ago. No reason to go into this blind when we have an insider willing to give us what we need."

"What did you find out?"

"Basically confirmed what we already knew. Marlow still has the necklace and gold coins. Both of which are in her safe-deposit box at the local bank."

"Now what?"

"I keep courting my little friend. But once your brother gets here, we need to put everything in place so we can move fast when the opportunity arises. As soon as we get our hands on that necklace and gold, we need to move fast. Did you find a place to keep our hostage yet? We can't do it here."

"I'm still looking," Hal said. "I don't want to use a property I'm managing."

Hal's cellphone rang. He looked at it. "That's my brother, ready?"

NINE

Melinda's best friend once called her predictable. She didn't find insult at such an observation because her friend had a point. Yet she felt it was more about consistency than predictability. Melinda believed her routine provided order. She started each day bringing a cup of hot tea to her desk, where she would then turn on her computer and surf through her favorite social media sites. After finishing her tea and catching up on current events, she would join her uncle in the sunroom for breakfast, prepared by a member of his household staff. While the routine might deviate some, such as when she was off with friends, her mornings pre-breakfast remained consistent, even if it was a laptop she surfed while enjoying her morning tea, instead of her home desktop.

On Sunday morning, Melinda had just turned on her computer and had not yet taken a sip of tea when the landline rang. Instead of answering the phone, she stared at it. People rarely called the landline. Even her uncle used his cellphone instead of the landline. Yet Charlie had called her on it the other day, not her cellphone, and she couldn't help but wonder if the caller might again be Charlie. If so, what would she say to him? What would he say to her?

The phone continued to ring. She stared at it. Finally, she picked up the phone's receiver and put it by her ear. Hesitantly she said, "Hello?"

"Why did you do it, Melinda?"

"Charlie?" she whispered into the phone.

"You turned me in."

"No, I didn't," she lied.

"Did you get the money?"

"I would have," she lied again. "But before I even left for the bank the next morning, it was all over the news that the police had gone to that motel looking for you. What was the point? I didn't know where to take the money."

One fact the news stories did not report was how Charlie had contacted Melinda for money, which was why they raided his motel room. Nor did they report how they had traced the call placed to her landline, verifying the call had come from the motel room.

"Don't believe what they said on the news about me. I told you they framed me. I didn't kill anyone. I'm innocent."

"Who would frame you?" she asked.

"The actual killer, of course. I wouldn't have killed my best friend. And I certainly wouldn't wait years to kill his sister. She was my friend too. Killing her makes no sense. I'm innocent."

"What do you want me to do?" she asked.

"I want you to get me that money and bring it to me."

"Where? Where do you want me to bring it to?"

He didn't respond.

"Charlie?"

"I'm still here."

"Where do I bring the money?" she asked.

"You won't be able to get it out of the bank until Monday. I'll call you Monday morning and tell you where to meet me."

"Okay."

"I hope I can trust you, Melinda."

WHEN MELINDA WALKED into the sunroom a few minutes later, she found her uncle sitting at the table, drinking his orange juice while reading his morning newspaper. Marian, a member of the household kitchen staff, scurried around, arranging small platters of food on the table.

Clement glanced up from his newspaper and smiled at his niece. "Good morning, Melinda." He closed his newspaper and handed it to Marian.

"Good morning, Uncle." Melinda walked to Clement, gave him a perfunctory kiss on the cheek, and then took a seat at the table.

"Will there be anything else, sir?" Marian asked.

Clement surveyed the table a moment and then looked up at Marian. "Everything looks fine. You can leave."

Melinda picked up a cloth napkin, arranged it on her lap, and then looked to the doorway to see if Marian was out of earshot. She was. Melinda looked at her uncle and whispered, "He called me again. Charlie."

Clement arched his brows and set his glass of juice on the table. "And?"

Melinda repeated her conversation with Charlie and then said, "This scares me."

"As it should. First thing we do, I'm calling the police and see if they can find out where the call came from this morning. Perhaps it came from another motel. At least it will give the police his general location."

"What happens if they don't find him by Monday? Will the police want me to make a show of taking him the money so they can catch him?"

"That's too dangerous. I won't allow it. If they want to, an officer can go in disguise. But I see no reason for an untrained civilian like you to get that involved. My first concern is keeping you safe. But they may want you to talk to him on the phone if they haven't apprehended him by then and he calls."

SUNDAY AFTERNOON, Laura sat alone in the kitchen of Marlow House, surfing on her cellphone while eating a cinnamon roll from Old Salts Bakery, when Sadie came charging through the pet door, her tail wagging.

Laura, who had been propping her feet on the chair next to her, immediately put her feet on the floor as Sadie excitedly rushed to her and gave her a quick sniff before racing from the kitchen through the open doorway into the hallway. The next minute, Ian walked through the kitchen door from the side yard.

"Sadie sure makes herself at home," Laura observed.

"She does. Sadie and Walt have a special relationship."

"What I find weird is how Sadie never touches Max's food," Laura said.

"She wouldn't dare." Ian laughed.

The next moment, Walt and Danielle walked into the kitchen, Sadie by their side.

"Thanks for letting Sadie hang out," Ian said.

"I still don't get why Sadie can't stay home. It's not like you're going anywhere," Laura asked.

"I enjoy Sadie's visits." Walt reached down and scratched the top of the golden retriever's head.

"It's my mom. She gets—for the want of a better word—nervous when Sadie's around Connor."

Laura frowned. "Why? Sadie is great with kids."

Ian shrugged. "Mom's always had this aversion to dog hair and germs. Thinks dogs are unsanitary and have no place around babies."

"Really? I've seen her around Sadie and Connor before. I kind of noticed she wasn't a dog person, but do you really need to make Sadie leave when she comes over?" Laura asked.

"Normally I wouldn't. But my dad is coming over so we can discuss the home renovations, and I don't feel like being constantly interrupted with my mother's *Ian, you should wash that ball, it was in Sadie's mouth,* or *let me change Connor's pants, they have dog hair on them.* This seemed like the easiest solution."

"And Walt's right, we love having Sadie," Danielle said.

As if on cue, Max sauntered into the room. Tail wagging, Sadie watched the black cat approach her, and didn't resist when Max rubbed along either side of her.

"Obviously, Max loves her too." Laura laughed.

"I have to say, those two have come a long way," Walt noted.

Ian looked at Laura. "You going over with me?"

Laura stood up. "Sure. I'm curious to hear all your ideas."

They exchanged a few more words, and then Ian and Laura left out the kitchen door, heading to Ian and Lily's house across the street.

"Are they still going over to Ian's parents' for Sunday dinner?" Walt asked. He sat down at the kitchen table and removed the cover from the cake pan while Danielle grabbed a couple of plates and forks. She walked to the table as Walt cut two slices of double fudge chocolate cake.

"As far as I know." Danielle walked to the refrigerator and removed a gallon of milk. "Frankly, I think Lily wanted just John to come over so they could discuss their ideas. But June insisted on coming too."

A few minutes later, as Walt and Danielle each ate a slice of double fudge chocolate cake, Walt glanced down at Sadie, who stared at him.

"You know you can't have chocolate," Walt reminded her.

Sadie continued to stare.

"Have you been enjoying your long morning walks with Laura?" Walt asked.

Sadie cocked her head slightly.

"Really? I saw when Laura got back. Oh?"

Danielle looked up from her cake. "What is Sadie saying?"

"According to Sadie, they don't walk that far because Laura has a friend she stops and visits. They spend more of their time visiting with this guy on his front porch than walking."

Danielle cocked her brow. "Some guy?"

"I'm assuming it's a guy, considering Sadie said the person had fur all over his face."

"They sit and talk? Where?"

"I don't know what street. From what Sadie conveyed, the front porch of what I assume is his house. They have what is probably coffee."

Danielle grinned. "That's interesting. I don't think she's mentioned anything to Lily about meeting someone."

"Sadie doesn't like him," Walt announced.

Danielle's grin quickly faded. "She doesn't? Why not?"

Walt shrugged. "Something about how he smells off."

The kitchen door opened while someone yelled, "Knock, knock!" It was Heather. She stepped into the house carrying a freshly baked loaf of homemade sourdough bread.

"Hey, Heather!" Danielle spied the bread. "Awesome. We finished the last loaf this morning."

While Heather carried the bread into the kitchen, Sadie greeted her, tail wagging. Heather set the bread on the counter and leaned down to pet the golden retriever. She glanced back at the table. "Is that double fudge chocolate cake?"

"Grab yourself a plate," Danielle said.

Heather grinned, quickly washed her hands at the sink, and after drying them, eagerly snatched a small plate from the cupboard and a fork from a drawer. She took them to the table and sat down while Walt cut her a slice.

"I thought you were keeping your doors locked?" Heather watched as Walt placed the slice of cake on her plate.

"Ian was just here a little while ago, dropping Sadie off, and we left it unlocked for him. We must have forgotten to lock it after he and Laura left," Danielle said.

"I saw Ian's parents pulling up to their house when I was walking over here."

"Yeah. John and Ian are brainstorming about remodeling ideas for their house."

"Oh, not to change the subject, but did you hear the latest on Charlie Cramer?"

"No, what? Did they catch him?" Danielle asked.

Heather looked up from her cake. "Brian has a late shift, so he went into work about an hour ago. The chief was getting off the phone when Brian walked into his office. He had been talking to his contact in Canada. The chief had called them, checking to see if there was any word on Cramer. I think the guy might have told him more than he was supposed to."

"What did he tell him?" Danielle asked.

"Charlie is still in the Vancouver area. He called the woman again, the one who was supposed to give him money. They traced his call again, and it came from a pay phone a few miles away from where the woman lives."

"I take it they didn't capture him?" Walt asked.

"Unfortunately not. Apparently, he didn't realize she was the one who turned him in. Supposedly, he's calling her tomorrow and letting her know where to bring the money."

"Why wait until tomorrow?" Danielle asked.

"She has to get the money out of the bank. Oh, and I'm not supposed to know any of this. So don't tell anyone." Heather took a bite of her cake.

TEN

When Ian returned from Marlow House with Laura and something was said about Ian's parents coming over, Marie Nichols decided to leave after they arrived. She wasn't a fan of Connor's paternal grandmother, June Bartley. And when she realized Ian had taken Sadie over to Marlow House because June had issues with the dog around Connor, she almost wanted to stay and tweak June's ear. But she was an adult—or at least she had been when she had died—so she would behave herself. Plus, she didn't want Connor to catch her doing something so naughty as tweaking his grandmother's ear—even though she deserved it.

However, when Ian and Lily began discussing the reason for his parents' visit, she stayed. They were considering adding a second bedroom onto their house, and since Ian's father, John, was a retired general contractor, he could help. Marie held an affinity for the house—and not just because she loved its occupants. Marie had sold the property to Ian and Lily before her death. It had been her first childhood home. The property had stayed in the family even after Marie and her parents moved out. For many years, it had been a rental, with Ian as its last tenant.

Happy the house had gone to a family who deserved it, she was naturally curious to learn their plans, and wondered how they would ever add an extra bedroom. Because of that, she stayed despite finding June annoying.

WHEN JUNE AND JOHN ARRIVED, they found Lily and Laura already in the living room, with Laura on the floor, playing dinosaurs with her nephew. June greeted the pair and gave her grandson a kiss before taking a seat on the sofa. When sitting down, she did not know Marie was already sitting there. Fortunately, she did not sit on the ghost.

June glanced around the room and then looked at Lily. "Did you lock Sadie in a bedroom? I hope not Connor's. Now that you have a bed in his room, you know that dog's going to be jumping on it." While Connor was still in a crib, they had recently added a twin bed to the room to get Connor used to the bed before they transitioned him from the crib. And while they did not want Connor and the new baby to share a room—nor did they want Connor to feel the new sibling had kicked him from his crib—they worried they might be too optimistic about how quickly they could add on, and so decided one option was to add the twin bed now, get Connor used to the new bed, and then before the baby arrived, he could start sleeping in the bed, and the baby would move into the crib. They considered this plan B.

"Sadie sleeps with us. And we're still alive." Lily found her mother-in-law's concerns more amusing than annoying.

June winced at the comment yet said nothing.

Laura almost gave a snort at her sister's sassy comment yet resisted the temptation. Instead, she made her version of a dinosaur noise while waving a plastic pterosaur overhead, making it fly. Marie smiled at the play, thinking of the times she too made the pterosaur fly, yet when she made it fly—no hands held it.

Connor had the same thought and dropped the dinosaur in his hand. He looked at his aunt, said, "No, no!" and demanded she hand over the plastic pterosaur.

She complied, bemused her nephew had dropped the toy he had been playing with and now wanted the one she held. Once she handed it to the child, he held out his hand, holding the pterosaur to the sofa. "Gamma! Gamma! Fly!"

June beamed at her grandson. "Oh my, look at that! He wants me to make it fly!" Getting up from the sofa, she tried taking the pterosaur from her grandson, but he quickly snatched it away from her, now clutching it at his chest.

"Give it to Grandma, and I will make it fly," June cooed. Once again, she tried taking it.

Connor pushed June's hand away and yelled, "No! Gamma Marie. Gamma Marie fly!" With his free hand, he pointed to the sofa. Only he could see Marie. Lily knew Marie was there, but like Laura and June, she couldn't see the ghost.

"What is he talking about?" Laura asked.

"Oh dear," Marie muttered, seeing Connor now crying. Marie moved from the sofa and placed herself between the child and the startled grandmother. "Don't cry, Connor. Remember, flying is our secret. Grandma Marie must go now. You need to be a good boy."

Connor stopped crying and looked up into Marie's face. He sniffled and wiped his face with the cuff of his shirt. Laura and June continued to stare at Connor and his peculiar behavior.

"I'll be back later. You be a good boy and play with your grandma June and aunt Laura." The next moment, Marie vanished. Connor started crying again.

"Why is he so upset?" Laura asked.

"I think he needs a nap," Lily said. "Come here, Connor." Lily outstretched her hands. Dropping the pterosaur, Connor stood and waddled to his mother. He climbed onto her lap, burying his face in her blouse. She began rocking him while gently rubbing his back.

"I don't understand what that was all about. Why did he call me Grandma Marie?" June returned to the sofa and sat down, wearing a confused frown.

"I don't think he was calling you Grandma Marie," Laura said. "It was like he was talking to an imaginary friend." Laura froze a moment and then looked at her sister. "Rupert? Does Connor have an imaginary friend like you did?"

Lily smiled weakly. "Umm… I think he might. But hey, I survived having an imaginary friend."

Laura stood up and walked to the sofa, sitting down with June. "Why Grandma Marie? Or more accurately, Gamma Marie? Rupert's a better name for an imaginary friend."

"I don't know why Connor needs an imaginary grandmother. He has me," June said with a pout.

"I'm still trying to figure out the Marie. Seems like an odd choice for a kid who's not even a year and a half," Laura said. "Although I could never figure out how you came up with a name like Rupert."

After a moment, Lily said, "It's probably my fault."

Both Laura and June looked to Lily, who continued to rock Connor.

"Umm, you know, Adam's grandma Marie Nichols sold us this house," Lily began.

"I remember meeting Marie at your wedding," Laura said. "Wasn't she murdered a couple of months afterwards?"

"Please don't talk about M-U-R-D-E-R around Connor. He is just a baby. Anyway, Marie lived to a ripe old age. Over ninety, I believe."

"Still, she never met Connor. So why would she have anything to do with his imaginary friend?" Laura asked.

"When Marie was a baby, Connor's room was hers. I often talk about her to Connor when I tell him stories. I tell him how nice Marie was, and that she was like an extra grandma to Dani and me. And how she is probably here, looking after him, keeping him safe." Much of what Lily said was actually true.

"I certainly hope when telling these stories, you never mention she was M-U-R-D-E-R-E-D," June said.

"Umm, no. I can honestly say I have never talked about that with Connor," Lily said.

The topic changed when Ian and John returned to the living room to discuss their ideas for the home addition.

AFTER LEAVING Lily and Ian's, Marie popped over to Marlow House. She found Walt, Danielle, and Heather sitting at the kitchen table. By the crumbs and frosting smeared on the plates before each person, Marie surmised they had just finished eating double fudge chocolate cake.

"Is that your lunch?" Marie asked. She sat on the empty chair at the table.

"No. Afternoon snack," Danielle said.

"I can remember substituting cake for dinner a few times when I was alive." Marie grinned.

"I'm surprised you're over here," Walt said. "Ian and John are going over the addition plans for the new house. I thought you'd be over there listening in."

ACROSS THE STREET, John sat on the sofa with his wife while Ian sat in a chair across from them, with Lily sitting next to Ian in the rocker, Connor still on her lap.

They had just discussed the various options for adding onto the house. The easiest one and most affordable involved adding a second floor to the garage for Ian's office. The second option involved adding a second floor to the house, and instead of adding one room, they could add an office and an extra bedroom and bathroom.

"I thought they only needed an office for Ian?" June asked. "They should just add a room over the garage."

"I don't really want to do that," Lily said. "Ian would have to go outside to go to his office. It's not convenient."

"I agree," Ian said. "It would be a pain if I wanted to watch the kids and work."

"Lily's a stay-at-home mom, so that shouldn't be a problem," June said. She was about to say more but decided not to when Ian flashed her a reproving glare.

"I understand Ian and Lily wanting better access for the office," Laura said. "But wow, two rooms instead of one, and a bathroom?"

"If Ian wants to build a second floor on the house and go to all that trouble, he might as well add another room. It will give them a guest room," John said.

"Is the septic tank big enough?" Laura asked.

"Adam told us they replaced the septic tank a few years back, and according to him, it's to code for a four-bedroom house," Lily explained.

"The house would be a four bedroom. The office won't be considered a bedroom," John explained.

Connor fussed. "I think he's hungry," Lily said.

Ian stood up, picked Connor off Lily's lap, and set him on his feet.

Lily stood and looked at Ian. "I need to go to the bathroom. Can you make Connor a sandwich?"

"I can do that," June offered.

Lily smiled at her mother-in-law. "Thank you. There's some egg salad in the refrigerator, and the bread's in the pantry, in the bread box."

"I'll pick up the toys," Laura offered.

"I'd love to look at those old floor plans Adam gave you," John told Ian.

"They're in my office."

While Ian and John headed to Ian's office, Lily went to the bathroom, and Laura stayed in the living room, gathering up all the toys off the floor. June took Connor by the hand and led him to the kitchen while telling him she was giving him something to eat.

Once in the kitchen, June moved the highchair before putting Connor in it. When looking for the bread, she turned her back to Connor. With her back to her grandson, she failed to notice how he kept kicking the counter, making his highchair tip back and forth.

It happened so quickly. They had stepped into sight of the highchair at the same time: Lily, Laura, and Ian. It was Lily and Laura's simultaneous and horrified, "*Connor!*" that sent June twirling around from the pantry in time to see her grandson falling backwards, still strapped into the highchair.

Later, Lily would tell Danielle how she felt it was slow motion, with Ian racing to save his son while knowing he would never make it. And then, as the highchair was about to crash on the floor, it miraculously stopped in midair and returned to its original position, standing upright, with Connor still strapped into the chair.

Marie.

ELEVEN

Marie hadn't lingered at Marlow House. She returned to the Bartleys', curious if they were discussing the home renovations. But when she arrived in the living room, she found only Laura, who busily gathered up Connor's toys, putting them in the nearby toy chest.

Unbeknownst to Laura, after she finished the task and started toward the kitchen, the ghost of Marie Nichols walked by her side. Laura's reaction to seeing her nephew falling backwards in his highchair was to scream—the same reaction as her sister, who had also stepped into the area. Marie's reaction was different.

It took less than a minute for Marie to regret her handling of the situation. Instead of stopping Connor's highchair from falling backwards by momentarily freezing it inches above the floor and setting it upright again, as if it had never fallen, she should have simply cushioned the fall with her energy and allowed the chair to fall backwards to the floor. Everyone would be happy Connor was unscathed, and they might forget how the chair had appeared to slow down before hitting the floor. Her solution proved more difficult to ignore. In Marie's defense, it had happened so fast, she didn't have time to consider all the options.

Marie soon realized any discussion on the home renovation was on hold. Both June and Laura kept repeating—with slight variations —*Did you see what happened?* While Lily, who obviously realized what had happened, was more annoyed with her mother-in-law for moving Connor's highchair, something she had asked June not to do several other times. Somehow, John had missed seeing the chair fall, and wasn't sure why everyone was shouting.

During the mayhem, Connor seemed quite happy and kept slapping the tray of his highchair, as if he wanted another wild ride. Afraid the child would look at her and call out, Marie felt it best if she left.

A few moments later, she stepped through the front wall of the Bartley home as her grandson drove up in front of Marlow House and parked. Melony was with him. Marie followed Adam and Melony into Marlow House.

WHEN DANIELLE OPENED the front door for Melony and Adam, it surprised her to find Marie standing behind them, wearing a sheepish grin. The ghost waved at Danielle.

"Hi, guys," Danielle greeted. She opened the door wider, making room for Adam and Melony to enter. As the couple walked by her, she flashed Marie a questioning frown.

"I'll explain later," Marie muttered as she followed Adam and Melony to the parlor.

Five minutes later, Adam and Melony sat in the parlor with Walt and Danielle, discussing the details of the upcoming wedding. When Danielle had first seen Marie standing with Adam and Melony, she initially assumed Marie had simply seen her grandson drive up and decided she would rather eavesdrop on Adam's wedding plans as opposed to the remodeling plans of her old house. Yet by Marie's comment, she suspected there was more to her return to Marlow House.

"You said your parents aren't making it to your shower, but are they coming to the wedding?" Danielle asked Adam.

Adam shook his head. "No. When I gave Dad the date, he said they had other plans."

"I raised a putz," Marie muttered. "Not coming to his own son's wedding. What is he thinking?"

Melony reached over and patted Adam's knee. "They never liked me. I led their innocent boy astray."

Walt gave a snort. "Somehow I don't see that." With a grin, Melony winked at Walt.

The topic shifted back to the wedding plans, and after a few moments, it shifted again when Adam asked, "Hey, did you hear Charlie Cramer is in Canada?"

"Yes. The chief told us the other day," Danielle said.

"Did you hear someone broke into his house?" Adam asked.

Danielle shook her head. "No. I didn't hear that."

"That house belonged to Cramer's mom," Adam said. "He had it in my rental program and, before his arrest, intended to list the property."

Danielle nodded. "I remember."

"After his arrest, he asked me if I'd manage the property until his release. The way he talked, it sounded like he didn't expect to be locked up long."

"Which he wasn't," Walt reminded him.

Glancing at Walt, Adam chuckled and then said, "True. I wasn't that optimistic and told him he needed to deposit money in an account to cover expenses during his incarceration. After he escaped, the police department monitored the property in case he came back. Well, the other day, when Brian and Joe checked, they discovered a suitcase was missing from one of the bedroom closets. I remember it was there when I last checked on the house."

"What else was missing?" Danielle asked.

Adam shrugged. "Nothing. Just the suitcase. I never opened it, so I don't know what was inside. I assume it was Charlie's. Remember, at the time of his arrest, he was only visiting. His tenants had recently moved out."

———

WHEN LAURA RETURNED to Marlow House late Sunday afternoon, she found Walt and Danielle in the parlor with Adam Nichols and his fiancée, Melony Carmichael. Adam and Melony sat on the sofa, with papers scattered on the coffee table before them, while Walt and Danielle sat in the chairs facing them.

So frazzled over what she had seen at her sister's, Laura had failed to notice Adam's car parked in front of the house when crossing the street. She barreled into the room, looking for Walt and Danielle, and then froze abruptly when she realized they were not alone. "Oh, I'm sorry. I didn't realize you had anyone in here with you."

Danielle waved her in. "That's fine. You okay? You look a little out of sorts."

Hesitantly, Laura stepped into the room. "You can't imagine what just happened at my sister's!" In rushed words, Laura told them about the incident with Connor's highchair.

"You said it just stopped?" Adam asked. "And floated over the floor?"

Walt and Danielle exchanged quick glances and then looked at Marie.

Marie smiled weakly at the pair and gave a shrug. "What was I to do? I couldn't let the poor child get hurt. Why would June move the highchair where she did? Connor has a habit of pushing at the counter with his feet."

"I swear. You can ask Lily and Ian. It was the most bizarre thing I have ever seen. In fact, if June hadn't freaked out so much, I might wonder if I imagined the whole thing."

"How is that even possible?" Melony asked.

Laura shook her head. "It isn't. To be honest, Lily's reaction was also bizarre."

"How so?" Adam asked.

"June and I kept asking how that was possible. How could the highchair fall over and then stop right before it hit the floor and right itself? How is that possible? But while we kept asking that question, Lily got snippy with June for moving Connor's highchair. If I were Lily, I'd wonder how the highchair practically picked itself up off the floor." Laura sat down on the end of the sofa next to Melony.

"There has to be a logical explanation," Melony said.

"I can't imagine what that might be," Laura said.

"I have a theory," Walt said.

They all looked at Walt.

"Umm, what's that?" Danielle suppressed a giggle.

"It's possible to push an object and instead of it falling over, it rocks back and forth. It's obvious Connor sent his highchair rocking back and forth, and fortunately for him, when it rocked back, it stopped."

"That's not what happened!" Laura insisted. "I was there. The back of the highchair was about a foot from the floor before it stopped. It just stopped. And then it righted itself."

"It sounds like it happened awful fast," Walt said. "And I imagine it was a horrifying sight, seeing Connor falling backwards. So vulnerable and knowing it was impossible to reach him in time. I imagine your mind might have been playing tricks on you."

Laura let out an exasperated sigh and stood up. "That's not what happened." The two couples watched as Laura marched toward the open doorway. "I have to go to the bathroom." Laura left the room.

Adam chuckled. "You might have made her mad."

"Her version of the story sounds far more interesting than what probably happened," Walt said.

"Or perhaps her version was accurate," Melony suggested.

They all looked at Melony.

Walt smiled at her. "Why do you say that?"

"Like the cliche says, truth can be stranger than fiction," Melony whispered.

"You're talking about what we saw at the Marymoor site?" Adam asked.

Melony nodded. "Someone or something used that pipe like a baseball bat. Perhaps the same type of someone or something stopped Connor's highchair from falling."

Adam glanced to the open doorway where Laura had exited.

Marie looked at Walt. "Don't you feel guilty trying to gaslight poor Laura like that?"

Walt gave Marie a shrug.

"Sometimes I ask myself if we really saw what we think we saw that day," Adam said.

"Do you feel the same way about that croquet set you claim attacked you in our attic?" Walt teased.

"I'd rather not think about it at all," Adam grumbled.

Laura marched back into the parlor. "Okay, this is really bugging me. I know what I saw!"

"We believe you," Melony said.

Laura froze in her steps. She looked at Melony. "You do?"

"Adam and I know from personal experience that sometimes there isn't always a logical explanation. Sometimes you must step back and consider explanations you never imagined possible."

"What do you mean?" Laura asked. She walked back to the sofa.

Melony shrugged.

Laura sat down, her gaze fixed on Melony. "Come on, what did you see? What thing that you never thought possible?"

Melony shrugged. "Let's just say I believe in the possibility of ghosts—or spirits."

"My mom believes in ghosts. And… well… I sort of do too." Laura's hands fidgeted. "I… I've never discussed this before except for with Lily." Laura looked at Walt and Danielle. "But you probably know. After all, you were there."

"What are you talking about?" Melony asked.

"I witnessed something when I was here for Connor's birthday. It was over at June and John's property."

Adam and Melony exchanged glances.

"Walt and Danielle were there. They didn't know I was. But I saw things I can't explain. And I try not to think about it."

Adam chuckled. "Welcome to the club. Mel and I witnessed things there, too."

Laura looked at Adam. "You did?"

"Inanimate objects that didn't stay inanimate?" Adam asked.

Laura nodded.

"Perhaps some friendly spirit intervened on Connor's behalf. Maybe he has a guardian angel," Melony suggested.

Laura considered Melony's words. After a few moments of silence, she looked at Adam. "And I know who it is!"

"You do? Who?" Adam asked.

"It's your grandmother, Marie Nichols!" Laura insisted.

"Oh my," Marie muttered as Walt and Danielle sent her a questioning gaze.

"My grandmother?" Adam chuckled. "Why do you say that?"

"Did you know Connor has an imaginary friend?" Laura asked.

Adam shook his head. "Umm, no. I didn't know that."

"And guess what he calls this imaginary friend?" Laura asked.

Adam shrugged. "No clue."

"Marie. More accurately, Grandma Marie. Although how Connor says it, it sounds more like Gamma Marie."

Adam smiled sadly. "While I imagine Grandma would have loved Lily's son to call her Grandma, she never got to meet him. She died before he was born."

"But Connor's bedroom used to be your grandma's nursery when she was a baby," Melony reminded him.

Laura looked at Melony and grinned. "Exactly!"

"Oh dear. Laura and Melony figured it out," Marie muttered while Walt and Danielle exchanged quick glances.

Adam leaned back on the sofa and chuckled. "You're suggesting my grandma is haunting Lily and Ian's house and is Connor's guardian angel?"

"It's the most reasonable explanation," Laura insisted.

Adam arched his brows at Laura. "The most reasonable?"

Melony nudged Adam. "Oh, come on, isn't it an interesting idea?"

Laura looked at Walt and Danielle. "What do you think? Danielle, I know you believe in the possibility of such things."

"I suppose anything is possible," Danielle said.

TWELVE

Hal pulled up Surf Drive on Sunday afternoon and parked his car in front of the vacant house. One street over was Beach Drive, and the ocean beyond that. Just as he got from his vehicle, he heard a male voice call out, "Hey, Hal! How you doing?"

Hal turned to the voice and spied the neighbor Ernst Girbau, from one house over, walking toward him. "Hey, Ernst. Figured you would be in Palm Desert by now?" Ernst and his wife typically spent the winter months in a warmer climate.

When Ernst reached Hal, he said, "We're taking off tomorrow. Got a little late start because we had some doctor appointments." Ernst then pointed to the house between him and the house Hal had parked at. "Did you hear what happened to Old Miss Barry?" Miss Barry was the elderly woman who lived alone in the house next door to the Girbau house.

Hal shook his head. "No, did she die?"

"Heck no, she's too mean for that. Broke her hip, though. Landed her in rehab for a couple of months at Seaside Village. Wife and I visited her yesterday. Wanted to check on her before we go. I suggested she call you. Figured she'd need someone to check on her house while she's in rehab. She doesn't have family, and we're going to be gone. I told her you watch Bosman's house." When mentioning Bosman, Ernst momentarily pointed to a house behind Hal's parked car. "But she's too darn cheap, said her house has been standing this long without a man looking after it. She's not having anyone watch it." Ernst shook his head.

"Maybe she has security cameras and plans to monitor it herself. Pretty common these days."

Ernst let out a snort. "Funny you say that. I offered to pick up a camera and hook it up for her before I left. She made it perfectly clear she didn't want a surveillance camera anywhere on her property. Insisted that's how the government spies on you. And then I found out she doesn't have internet, so we couldn't hook it up anyway, and she doesn't own a cellphone."

Hal looked over at Miss Barry's house and noticed her large garage. "What does she keep in that big garage?"

"If you're thinking someone might steal her car when she's gone, that's not a problem. She doesn't drive. Garage is empty. Has a few yard tools in it. That's all."

Hal glanced across the street at the only house facing Miss Barry's. He remembered no one lived in that house full time. It was now an Airbnb. He looked back to Ernst and said, "I imagine she probably has friends who will look in on it for her, like you do when you're at Palm Desert."

Ernst shook his head. "Nah. She's been a recluse for years. I haven't seen anyone at her house in over ten years. Pays to have her groceries delivered and won't let them step foot in her house. Good thing she broke her hip when out getting her mail. My wife found her. Had she broken her hip when she was in the house, she probably would have died."

DANIELLE SAT on the living room sofa, a fleece throw over her lap and her stockinged feet propped on the coffee table as she read a book. Her cat, Max, slept curled up by her side on the cushion while Sadie napped on the floor beneath her feet. Across the room, Walt knelt in front of the fireplace as he used the brass poker to adjust the logs before adding another.

Danielle looked up from her book and asked Walt, "How about Mallory?"

Pausing a moment, Walt glanced at Danielle. "Where did you get that name?"

"A character in the book I'm reading."

"I don't think you want to give our daughter a name that means ill-fated."

"Seriously? It does?"

Walt nodded and turned back to the fire.

"Scratch that one. I need to pick up a baby name book with meanings," Danielle muttered under her breath.

"Good evening!" came a familiar voice. Walt and Danielle glanced toward the open doorway and saw Chris walking into the room, his pit bull, Hunny, trailing beside him. During the warmer summer days, Chris's weekend attire went from beach bum to GQ and back again. Tonight it looked as if he was about to hit the slopes, or at least one of the cozy bars at some high-priced ski lodge.

"Hi, Chris!" Danielle greeted.

"I thought I locked all the doors." Walt stood and brushed his hands together, removing any ashes.

"You did. I have a key." Chris flashed Walt a grin and walked straight to Danielle. He leaned over the sofa and kissed her forehead. "Evening, little Mama."

"I won't be little for long." Danielle chuckled.

Now standing behind Danielle, his hands resting on the back of the sofa, Chris asked in mock seriousness, "Walt treating you well? If he isn't, I can take you away from all this. I'll even raise the twins as my own."

The next moment Chris flew off the floor and across the living room as if doing a superman impression, flying circles around the room without the wires, while Hunny and Sadie looked up and started barking. Max woke up, wondering what all the commotion was.

Instead of a terrified scream, Chris laughed like a teenager on a rollercoaster ride. By the time he landed safely on his feet, Walt was already sitting on the chair facing Danielle.

Danielle flashed Walt a dry expression. "You do realize Chris only says those things so you'll make him fly."

Walt shrugged.

"Dang, Walt, that was a good one!" Still grinning, Chris sat in the chair next to Walt.

Danielle shook her head and muttered, "I don't know about you two."

While running his fingers through his hair to bring it back to order after his brief flight, Chris said, "I take it Laura isn't here?"

"Why do you assume that?" Danielle asked. "She's in her room and will be here any second."

"I don't think so. Walt just flew me around the room."

Danielle shrugged. "True. She's over at Ian's parents' for Sunday dinner."

"Ahh, that's why Sadie is here," Chris observed.

"I don't think you're going to have to worry about Laura trying to get your attention anymore. I think she's found someone else," Walt said.

Chris arched his brows. "Really? Anyone we know?"

"No one is supposed to know about it. The only reason we know is because Sadie told Walt," Danielle said.

Chris looked over at the golden retriever and chuckled. "You little gossip." Danielle then told Chris about what Sadie had conveyed to Walt. After the telling, they discussed Laura's stay in Frederickport, her friendship with Kelly, and then the conversation shifted again.

"Joe's grandmother is also joining them for dinner tonight," Danielle said. "She's in town, staying with Joe's parents until after the wedding. His parents went out tonight and didn't want to leave her alone, so Kelly asked June if it was okay if they brought her. From what Lily told me, it will be the first time Kelly meets her."

"Umm, is this the same grandmother who gave Joe her engagement ring that he gave to Kelly?" Chris asked.

Danielle nodded. "The same one."

"I hope Kelly doesn't do something drastic, like poison the poor woman." Chris let out a snort.

"Why would she do that?" Danielle asked with a half laugh.

"Come on now, you've seen that ring. I think Joe's the only one who doesn't realize how hideous that thing is," Chris said.

"I have to give Kelly credit. She puts on a good show. I don't think she's ever said anything to Joe about how she really feels about it. The only reason I know is because she's talked to Laura about it," Danielle said.

"And of course, Laura told her sister," Walt said.

"And Lily told Danielle," Chris finished for Walt.

"Exactly." Walt laughed. "Hard to keep a secret on Beach Drive."

Chris grinned at Danielle. "Be honest, the only reason you chose Walt over Joe, you saw the ring."

Walt rolled his eyes. "I'm not giving you another ride."

Chris let out a sigh. "You're no fun."

Danielle chuckled.

"I talked to Adam before I came over here. He told me he and Mel were over here completing their plans for the wedding," Chris said.

"Yeah. I still can't believe his parents aren't coming to the wedding. I get why his brother can't, since he's working out of the country. But his parents?" Danielle shook her head.

"You ready to be best man?" Walt asked.

"Yeah. Seems I'm always the best man, never the groom." Chris shrugged. He had been Walt's best man.

"You know how to fix that, don't you?" Danielle asked.

"Yeah, but you won't marry me," Chris teased.

Danielle rolled her eyes, and Walt said, "Marlow House airport is closed."

"Fine," Chris said with faux disappointment. No longer teasing, he said, "Seriously, I'm looking forward to this wedding. I think Mel is the best thing that ever happened to Adam."

Danielle nodded. "I agree. When I first met Adam... well, let's just say Mel brings out the best in him."

"In other news, Adam also told me someone broke into Charlie Cramer's house," Chris said.

"Adam told us," Walt said.

Chris shook his head. "Wild all this stuff about Cramer in Canada. Hope they catch the guy. I know Heather will be happy when he's back behind bars."

HE SAT on the side of the bed and stared at the suitcase. Taking it from the house had been risky. But it would have been riskier had he done it himself. Had it been him, he would never have removed the suitcase from the closet. After all, he only needed one thing from it. He would have removed it and then left the suitcase behind so no one would notice it had gone missing.

His partner had argued that since he was the one taking the risk, he intended to grab the suitcase and get out of there, to avoid leaving fingerprints behind. He reminded his partner that he would be wearing gloves, but then his partner gave more reasons for taking the suitcase instead of simply removing the item.

First, it would take more time to locate the item from a full suit-case. He wanted to get in and out of the house as quickly as possible. After all, the police had been stopping by and checking on the house. And if someone caught him going through the suitcase, he wouldn't be able to talk himself out of an arrest by claiming he just wanted to check the house out because he understood the owner was facing murder charges, and he figured he could get a good price on the house if the guy needed money to pay his legal fees. He would tell the person he wanted to see if the house was worth buying, and he wasn't hurting anything. It wasn't like anyone was living there. While it was a lame excuse, it was one he felt he could pull off if caught inside the house.

His partner also said he worried he would not place the suitcase exactly where it had sat in the closet. What if someone noticed the suitcase had been moved? After all, the police had been checking the house, along with the Realtor hired to manage the property.

Perhaps the Realtor had taken an inventory of the house, including what was inside the suitcase. If they noticed someone had tampered with the suitcase, and then checked its contents, it would send up red flags when they found the item missing. He had to admit, his partner was correct in that regard. A random thief would not break into a house and bother taking something from a suitcase when it would be easier to carry out the suitcase. Not to mention, the item taken could lead back to him.

So far, there had been no news on a break-in or missing suitcase. But that didn't mean the authorities weren't aware it had gone missing.

He stood up from the bed, walked to the suitcase, picked it up, and carried it to the open closet. Before placing it inside, he said, "I hope you don't turn out to be the one mistake in all this."

THIRTEEN

After Ian showed his father the old floor plans given to him by Adam, John wanted to take them home and study them, as he had several ideas on how they might add a second floor. John was still looking at those floor plans when they had returned from Ian's office. Because of that, he'd failed to witness his grandson's high-chair toppling over. But he heard his daughter-in-law and her sister scream Connor's name. By the time he had looked at Connor, the highchair was already standing upright, and John questioned the commotion.

His wife and Laura had kept going on and on about how the highchair had picked itself up before hitting the floor, yet by the way both Ian and Lily acted, it sounded more like Connor had kicked the counter and almost tipped his chair over. Lily had expressed her annoyance with his wife for moving the highchair, yet June was more interested in discussing what she and Laura claimed to have seen. Obviously, June and Laura were imagining things and over-reacting.

They left earlier than he intended. June had claimed she needed to get home to get Sunday dinner started, yet he suspected it annoyed her that only Laura seemed to find anything unusual about the highchair incident. He understood his wife often overreacted.

During the ride home, his wife kept asking, "How did you not see what happened back there?" After the third time asking the same question and ranting on about how she couldn't fathom Ian and Lily's reaction, he told her to calm down; she was imagining things and overreacting.

John regretted suggesting she calm down.

IAN PICKED UP HIS SISTER, Kelly, on the way to his parents' house late Sunday afternoon. Joe, who worked that day, planned to pick up his grandmother after he got off work, and intended to meet the others at his in-laws' house for dinner.

Laura and Kelly sat in the back seat with Connor in the car seat, while Lily sat in the passenger seat up front. On the drive to June and John's rental house, Kelly and Laura chatted about the high-chair incident. While Kelly hadn't been there when it happened, her mother had already called her and told her all about it. Laura's version of the story was the same as June's.

Kelly leaned forward in the passenger seat and asked Lily, "Did it really almost hit the floor and stand back up on its own?"

"You don't believe me?" Laura asked. "You don't believe your mom?"

"It almost tipped over. That's why I screamed. But I must have missed what Laura saw," Lily lied.

Kelly looked at her brother. "How about you?"

"Do we need to talk about this?" Ian asked. "I'm just grateful Connor didn't get hurt."

Kelly sat back in her seat. "I told Joe, and he just laughed and asked me what you guys were all drinking."

"Hey, I know what I saw. Both your mom and I saw it," Laura insisted.

AFTER ARRIVING AT IAN'S PARENTS' house, Lily greeted her in-laws and then took Connor's hand and led him into the living room to find the basket of toys June kept for him.

Still standing in the entry hall, June immediately brought up the subject of the highchair to Kelly, as she hadn't seemed to believe the story when she'd told her over the phone. But now Laura was here to back up her version of events. Not wanting to get into this discussion again, John immediately left, making the excuse he needed to make cocktails for their guests. Ian, who also wished to avoid the conversation, offered to help his father, leaving Laura alone with Kelly and June.

"Maybe you and Laura should skip the cocktails tonight," Kelly teased.

"I don't find that funny," June snapped.

"Come on, Mom, you have to admit the story is really out there," Kelly said. "It probably just looked like it almost fell from where you were standing."

"Laura was across the room from me." June looked at Laura. "Weren't you, Laura?"

Laura nodded and started to say something, but Kelly cut her off with, "I know, Mom. She already told me. But please, can we not talk about this when Joe gets here with his grandmother? This is the first time any of us are meeting her, and I don't want her to think Joe is marrying into a crazy family."

"Crazy family?" June snapped. "You don't believe me? You don't believe Laura?"

"It's not that. But can we not discuss this when Joe gets here?" Kelly asked.

Laura reached out and touched June's wrist. "Walt suggested Connor probably sent the highchair rocking back and forth when he kicked the edge of the counter. And it looked like it was about to fall but then rocked back into place." Laura didn't believe any of that, but she also didn't want to share her theory that the ghost of Marie Nichols had picked the highchair off the ground and set it upright. Had she said that, instead of Joe's grandmother worrying he was marrying into a crazy family, Ian's mother would worry his son had married into a crazy family—hers.

"Fine. We won't talk about it again tonight. But I know what I saw." June turned abruptly and marched to the kitchen, leaving Kelly and Laura standing in the entry hall.

GIANNA MORELLI STOOD JUST over five feet. In her younger years, she had measured in at five three, but ninety-five years had taken a toll on her height, yet fortunately not her mental acuity. She had been a willowy young girl, and the passage of time, womanhood, and a love of cooking Italian cuisine had not rounded out her figure. Those who knew her attributed her trim figure—despite the delicious meals she prepared and enjoyed—to her high energy. That high energy carried her well into her elderly years, and unlike many women who made it to her age, she didn't use a walker, yet she did use a cane.

After being introduced to Joe's grandmother, Lily and Laura stood off to one side and watched as June showed Gianna to a comfortable chair. Gianna had requested to sit near Connor, wanting to watch the boy play.

"Wow, I'd like to look as good as that at ninety-five," Laura whispered.

"No kidding. According to Joe, she's sharp. Doesn't miss a beat."

"Too bad she didn't have as good a taste in jewelry as she obviously has in clothing. That's an adorable dress," Laura whispered.

JUNE HAD JUST GONE to the kitchen to check on dinner. John stood at the breakfast bar, making cocktails, and then handed each one to Ian to deliver. Connor played with his toys on the floor while Kelly stood nervously with Joe in front of his grandmother.

Gianna sat regally in the recliner, reminding Lily, who stood across the room with Laura watching, of a queen at court.

"So this is the woman who has captured my favorite grand-child's heart?" Gianna asked, critically eyeing Kelly up and down.

"It's so nice to finally meet you, Mrs. Morelli," Kelly said nervously.

Gianna continued to study Kelly while occasionally glancing at Joe and then back to Kelly. "Do you know why he is my favorite?"

Kelly swallowed nervously and shook her head. "No, ma'am."

Gianna smiled wistfully and looked at Joe, who stood quietly beside Kelly before her. "Did he tell you they named him for my Joseph?"

"Yes, ma'am." Kelly knew they had named Joe for his grandfa-ther Joseph, who had died thirty years earlier. Gianna had never remarried.

"Joseph was a good man. A good husband. A good father. But he worked too hard and died too young." Gianna turned her gaze back to Kelly and said, "Joseph, please leave us. I wish to talk to Kelly alone."

"Umm… yes, Grandmother." Joe looked sheepishly at Kelly, noting her uncomfortable expression, before leaving her alone with his grandmother.

Gianna pointed to the floor before her. "You have young knees, dear. Can you please sit down here so I'm not looking up?"

Kelly smiled weakly, but dropped to her knees, sitting in front of Joe's grandmother.

"Do you love him?" Gianna asked.

Kelly's eyes widened. "Yes, I do."

"I understand you're living with him already."

Once again, Kelly swallowed nervously. "Yes."

Gianna let out a deep sigh. "In my day, girls did not live with men if they weren't married. It wasn't done."

Kelly smiled weakly.

"Let me see your hand. Your left hand," Gianna demanded. Hesitantly, Kelly presented her left hand to the woman.

Gianna leaned forward and took Kelly's left hand in hers. She studied the engagement ring that had once been hers. After a moment, she looked at Kelly's face. "My husband, he picked this ring himself. The first time I saw it was when he proposed. I loved him very much."

Kelly had no words; she simply smiled back.

"Did Joseph tell you how none of the grandchildren ever lied to me? Not that they were such angels that they wouldn't try, but knew I could always tell when someone was lying?"

Kelly frowned. She wasn't sure where this conversation was going, and Gianna continued to hold her hand. "Umm, no. He never mentioned that."

Gianna smiled at Kelly. After a moment, she asked, "Tell me, do you think it is a beautiful ring?"

Kelly's eyes widened.

"Is it a beautiful ring?" Gianna repeated.

"I love Joe!" Kelly blurted.

Gianna dropped Kelly's hand and laughed. "Joseph!" she called out.

Joe quickly rushed to his grandmother's side. Confused, Kelly looked from Gianna to Joe.

"Yes, Grandmother?"

Gianna pointed at the ring. "Joseph, take the ring."

"Excuse me?" Joe muttered.

Kelly's eyes filled with tears.

Still looking at Joe, Gianna shook her head at her grandson. "You're just like your grandfather."

"I don't understand?" Joe said.

Kelly told herself she would not cry. Instead, she removed her ring and handed it to Joe.

Confused, Joe took the ring but looked from Kelly to his grandmother.

"I love you, Joseph, but like your grandfather, you have horrible taste in jewelry. When I gave you that ring to give to Kelly, I expected you to have the stones removed and the gold melted down and made into something beautiful. I didn't expect this poor girl to be saddled with that hideous ring like I was!"

Kelly blinked away the tears, not comprehending what she heard.

Joe frowned at his grandmother. "Did Kelly tell you the ring is hideous?"

"Of course not, you foolish boy. She was willing to live with that thing because she loves you."

Joe turned to Kelly. "Is that true? Do you think it's an ugly ring?"

"Don't answer that," Gianna snapped.

Unbeknownst to Kelly and Joe, June had returned from the kitchen, and she, along with the rest of the dinner party, had been silently eavesdropping. The only one in the room who seemed oblivious to the conversation was Connor, who busily explored the new toys his grandmother had purchased.

Gianna looked around the room and called out, "Everyone who thinks the engagement ring my grandson gave Kelly is hideous, raise your hand."

It was silent for a moment. But then Ian raised a hand, followed by June, Lily, Laura, John, and finally, Kelly.

FOURTEEN

"Dog delivery service," Lily called out when she knocked on the kitchen door of Marlow House on Monday morning. Not waiting for the door to open, Sadie rushed through the pet door. A moment later, Laura unlocked and opened the door for her sister. Lily handed her the leash. It hadn't been hooked to Sadie's collar.

"Thanks, but I was going to pick her up." Now holding the leash, Laura stepped aside so Lily could enter the house.

"That's okay. I was in the neighborhood." Lily walked over to the table where Walt and Danielle sat eating breakfast. They both greeted her.

Laura rolled her eyes at her sister's comment and shut the kitchen door.

"Did Laura tell you what happened last night with Kelly's ring?" Lily asked as she took a seat at the table.

"She did." Danielle grinned. "I've never met Joe's grandmother, but I like her."

"She was a crack-up," Lily said. "And when she asked everyone who thought the ring was hideous to raise their hand, I thought for a moment no one was going to do it. Because, while it was hilarious, it was still awkward. But you gotta love my dear husband; he was the brave one. Raised his hand first, and then we all followed. Poor Joe, he seemed genuinely confused, but I suspect Kelly earned some major brownie points with the grandmother for loving her favorite grandson enough to put up with that ring."

"No kidding," Danielle agreed.

"Although, I do kinda wonder if Kelly planned to lose the ring after they were married." Lily snickered.

"Lily!" Laura scolded.

Lily shrugged. "Hey, I wouldn't have blamed her."

"That's a nice size diamond," Laura reminded her. "I can't imagine losing something that expensive on purpose."

"Yeah, a nice size diamond in a gawd-awful setting. All I can say about the grandfather, while he wasn't cheap, he had no taste," Lily said.

Laura chuckled. "You are horrible."

"And nothing I'm saying is untrue," Lily said.

"I'm glad it worked out this way for Kelly," Danielle said.

"What are your plans today?" Walt asked Lily.

"I'm joining Laura on her walk."

"Want something to eat first?" Danielle asked.

"No, you can't go with me," Laura said.

Lily frowned at her sister. "Why not? You prefer walking alone?"

"I won't be alone. Sadie will be with me."

"Seriously? You don't want me to go?" Lily pouted.

Laura walked to Lily and placed her hands on her sister's shoulders. She leaned down and quickly kissed Lily's cheek and said, "Of course I would love for you to go. But it wouldn't be a good idea. It's not like I'm leisurely walking. Sadie likes to run. So pretty much I jog."

Lily wrinkled her nose. "Jogging? Seriously?"

"That's something you can't just jump into without building up your stamina. And you must admit, Lily, you haven't been moving much. You're not in shape to start jogging. It could hurt the baby."

Lily let out a sigh. "Yeah, I know I haven't been moving much. That's why I thought it might be a good idea to walk with you. I didn't know you were jogging. Isn't that why you didn't want to go with Heather in the morning because she jogs?"

Laura shrugged. "I don't enjoy jogging on the beach. It's too hard running on the sand. And I really don't want to get up as early as Heather does during the week."

While Laura and Lily talked, Walt glanced down at Sadie, who stood by his side, resting her head on his knee. Their eyes met. They silently communicated while the three women chatted. Finally, Laura said, "I should probably get going. Come here, Sadie."

"Enjoy your walk," Walt told Laura as she hooked the leash on Sadie's collar.

After Laura and Sadie left, Lily said, "I almost get the feeling she really didn't want me to go. And not because she was worried about me."

"Your instincts are correct." Walt sipped his coffee.

Furrowing her brows, Lily looked to Walt. "What do you know?"

"He's been talking to Sadie," Danielle said.

Lily turned to Danielle. "What do you know?"

Danielle shrugged. "I haven't had a chance to tell you, but from what Sadie told Walt the other day, your sister has met someone."

"What do you mean met someone?" Lily asked.

"On her walk," Danielle explained. "Some guy who lives a few blocks from here. She stops by his house and has coffee and talks with him on his porch. At least, I assume it's coffee. I don't think Sadie knows."

"I can't believe she didn't tell me!" Lily scowled.

"And I asked Sadie this morning if they've been running on the walk. And she said no. In fact, they spend more time visiting with her new friend than they do walking," Walt said.

"Why, that rat!" Lily stood. "I'm going to join my dear sister on her walk! I knew something was off when she said she was jogging. Laura does not jog or run."

"No, you're not." Walt used his energy to gently push Lily back into her chair.

"Hey? Did you just push me?" Lily snapped.

"It was barely a nudge. Let your sister have a little fun. It's harmless. And Sadie promised to keep an eye on her," Walt said.

Lily let out a sigh and slumped back in her chair. "Well, poop."

"By the way, we heard about the highchair incident," Danielle said. "Marie told us, and then your sister said something. Surprised you didn't call and tell me."

"I really didn't have the chance. We were pretty much with Ian's family all day. But it scared the crap out of me! I was certain Marie had already left because of how Connor acted. I had gone to the bathroom, and June offered to give Connor lunch. Never expected her to move the highchair where she did. And I've told her many times that if she puts Connor in the highchair, she can't have it where his feet reach the counter, because he tries to kick it. It would be nice to teach him not to do that, but the kid isn't even two."

"Fortunately, Marie got back in time to stop him from getting hurt," Danielle said.

"Yeah, that created an entirely new problem." Lily groaned.

Walt told Lily the theory he'd suggested to Laura.

Lily shook her head. "I understand why she didn't buy it. It's the same theory John had, because he didn't see the chair fall. It all happened so fast. But if you would have seen the position of the chair when Marie stopped it, no way would anyone think it was rocking."

"Laura didn't accept it," Walt said.

"She came to the conclusion Marie Nichols haunts your house. And that she's Connor's guardian angel," Danielle explained.

Lily arched her brows. "Wow. The truth."

"And she shared that theory with Adam and Mel," Walt added. "They were here last night."

"Yeah, I saw Adam's car. What did they say?" Lily asked.

"Considering what they saw on your in-laws' property, it doesn't seem as farfetched to them as it might have a year ago," Danielle said. "And Laura mentioned something about what she had seen there."

"She did? Wow, that surprises me. Since she and I talked about it, we never again discussed it."

Danielle frowned at Lily. "Never?"

Lily shook her head. "No. While she seemed to accept every-thing, I think she wanted to forget about it. But now, after yesterday…"

"YOUR DOG certainly seems interested in our conversation." By his tone, Frank found this amusing.

Laura looked down at Sadie, who sat by her side. Since Laura and Sadie had joined Frank on his porch fifteen minutes earlier, the golden retriever showed no interest in napping by the chair, as she had during previous visits. Instead, she sat quietly by Laura's side, watching the pair and turning her head to watch whoever talked.

"She is acting a little weird today," Laura agreed.

"Look! She did it again. She turned her head to look at you." At that moment, Sadie turned to look at Frank again. Frank laughed.

Laura smiled. "She is a smart dog. I'm just glad she can't talk."

"And why is that?" Frank grinned.

"Lily doesn't need to know all my secrets. And I promised to respect your privacy. Because if I don't, you might not let me have coffee with you. And frankly, our talks are a lot more fun than walking."

"I'm glad you feel that way. I've been enjoying it too. And I'm looking forward to showing you around London."

"I'm getting excited about starting my adventure! Especially now that I know I'll have a tour guide in London."

"So tell me, what are your plans for the next few weeks? I imagine the wedding planning is keeping you busy."

"Did I mention there are two weddings?"

"Two?"

Laura nodded. "Yes. That Realtor you're trying to avoid, Adam Nichols, he's getting married at Marlow House in two weeks."

"You're kidding?"

Laura shook her head. "Nope. He's a good friend of Danielle. Which is one reason I've been so careful not to tell my sister about you. She would say something to Danielle, and Danielle might let it slip to Adam."

"And he's getting married at her house?"

"Yeah. His grandmother was a good friend of Danielle. In fact, she owned the house my sister lives in. She sold it to Ian before she died." Laura paused a moment and then said, "I think Marie is haunting the house."

Frank laughed.

"No, I'm serious." Laura then told Frank what had happened to the highchair.

AN HOUR after Laura and Sadie continued on their walk, Hal showed up at Frank's house carrying a grocery bag.

"Good, you went to the store," Frank said when he opened the door for Hal and let him in the house.

"I got everything you asked for."

Frank took the bag and headed to the kitchen, Hal following behind him.

"Was your girlfriend here this morning?" Hal asked.

Frank set the bag on the kitchen counter and began unloading the groceries. "Yes, she was. And I have to say, the girl is a little out there."

"Do you think she's going to be helpful?"

"Oh yeah. She has no problem sharing everyone's business."

"What do you mean she's out there?" Hal asked.

"She's convinced Marie Nichols's ghost haunts her sister's house."

Hal laughed. "Sounds like a demonic possession to me. That old busybody tried to get one of my friends fired from their job at the theater back in high school. When I heard someone killed her, I didn't cry any tears."

"Sounds like her ghost is a guardian angel who protects small children."

"Yeah, right," Hal said with a snort.

"Anyway, it will be at least two weeks before we can make our move."

"We have to wait for my brother anyway," Hal reminded him. "But what's the holdup on your end?"

Frank told Hal what Laura had told him about Adam's wedding. "It's not just the wedding, but there is going to be a lot of activity on Beach Drive for the next couple of weeks. We don't need that many people around. The other wedding is in March. We should plan on pulling this off right after Nichols ties the knot."

"I agree, we don't need an audience," Hal said.

"No kidding. And guess who is giving away the bride?"

"Who?"

"The freaking police chief," Frank said.

"Seriously?"

Frank nodded. "Sounds like he won't be the only cop hanging around."

"We don't need a crowd when we grab Marlow. And we certainly don't need any cops."

FIFTEEN

C anadian authorities had determined the phone call Charlie
Cramer made to Melinda on Sunday came from a pay phone
in a little pub several miles from the motel where he'd made the first
call. They obtained security footage of a man they believed to be
Charlie Cramer entering the pub shortly before the time of the
second call. He was of a similar height, body type, and while he
kept himself bundled up with a scarf wrapped around his neck and
covering the lower part of his face, and a hood pulled up over his
head, his black horn-rim glasses were visible. The bartender told the
detective he remembered seeing him yet did not recognize him or
see him again. Considering the cold weather, the bartender never
questioned the man's bundled-up attire as suspicious.

Authorities continued to be on the lookout for Charlie near the
pub, motel, and surrounding areas since he seemed to stay in that
vicinity. Unfortunately, they had not yet tracked him down. When
Monday rolled around, several detectives sat with Melinda as she
waited for Charlie to call.

Melinda fidgeted nervously at her desk, waiting for the landline
to ring. She glanced over at the detectives, who quietly chatted
amongst themselves. She worried Charlie had seen police scouring

the area around the pub or talking with the bartender. If he noticed that, he would know she had called the police. Until the police had him in custody, she did not want to anger him and become his next victim. She worried he might be bold enough to show up at her home and exact revenge for her betrayal.

The landline rang. The detectives stopped talking. Nervous, Melinda looked at the detectives.

"Take a deep breath. Remember what we told you. Answer the phone," one detective said.

Melinda nodded at the officer and then looked at the phone. After taking a deep breath, she exhaled, picked up the telephone's handset, and put the receiver by her ear. "Hello?"

"Did you get the money?" Charlie asked.

"Yes," Melinda lied. Actually, she had gone to the bank that morning, per the detective's instructions. While she hadn't withdrawn the requested amount, she had gone to one of the private offices with a teller, making a show of withdrawing funds. Had she withdrawn the amount Charlie requested, she would not want those funds counted out at a front teller. They worried Charlie or an accomplice might stake out the bank, verifying Melinda had followed his instructions and withdrawn the money.

Charlie then told Melinda where to meet him. She repeated the location and address.

After she hung up, she looked at the officers and said, "That's nowhere near the pub or motel."

As one officer called in Charlie's location, the other officer told Melinda, "No, it's not. We have people in the vicinity of the motel and pub ready to move in. But we'll get him."

TO THEIR NEIGHBORS, it looked like Melinda driving away from her house. The driver of Melinda's vehicle was a female officer disguised to look like her. In the back seat two officers hid under a blanket, while several unmarked police cars kept a close eye on the vehicle.

While Charlie had asked Melinda to meet him in a warehouse an hour from her home and forty minutes from where they initially believed he was hiding out, authorities were optimistic they would capture him this time. They already knew Charlie had called from a pay phone near the warehouse. Their only concern was Charlie might not return immediately to the warehouse, considering he would expect Melinda's drive to take an hour to reach him. If he became suspicious of unmarked vehicles driving in the neighborhood, he might bolt again.

Forty minutes before Melinda's car was to arrive at the destination, the first unmarked vehicle to reach the warehouse approached cautiously, intending to just drive by, on the lookout for the suspect lingering outside the designated meeting.

But as they approached the warehouse, the ground shook, and to their utter surprise, the windows of the building exploded. The warehouse was on fire.

OFFICER BRIAN HENDERSON sat with Joe Morelli in the break room at the Frederickport Police Station late Monday afternoon. Their shift started in fifteen minutes, and they were each having a cup of coffee before going on duty, while Joe told Brian about his dinner the night before at his future in-laws'.

"I had no idea Kelly thought the ring was ugly," Joe said.

Brian laughed. "What I find funny is that you could imagine she didn't think it was ugly."

Joe frowned. "You think it's an ugly ring, too?"

"Come on, Joe, are you seriously telling me you looked at that ring and saw something beautiful?"

Joe shrugged. "It has a nice diamond. And Kelly seemed happy when I gave it to her."

"Of course, because she wants to marry you. What did you expect her to do, tell you the ring was horrid and that she didn't want it?"

"It's not horrid."

"It's horrid."

"Why didn't you ever say anything to me?" Joe asked. "You're going to be my best man. Why didn't you tell me?"

Brian shrugged. "You don't go telling someone their heirloom engagement ring is ugly. Not unless they ask you for an opinion. And even then, it's not necessarily a good idea."

"After I proposed and gave Kelly the ring, I told her she could have it reset if she wanted."

"Yeah, I bet after you went on about how it was your grand-mother's engagement ring and sucked her into all that sentimental crap."

Joe shrugged.

"And I remember you going on to me about how the ring fit her perfectly, like it somehow proved she was the right one for you. I imagine you said something like that to her, too."

"Guilty." Joe let out a sigh. "Yeah, I suppose I didn't really give her an opportunity to tell me what she really thought about the ring. And if I'm totally honest, I did sort of think it was an ugly setting. But I figured women like all that gaudy stuff."

Brian laughed.

"Now I need to figure out where to take it to have it reset."

"Just let Kelly pick out the setting."

"I will."

"You might talk to Walt and Danielle. I know they used that jeweler in Astoria to make their gold bands."

The discussion on engagement rings ended when Police Chief MacDonald walked into the room.

"Good, I was hoping I'd find you two here," MacDonald said.

"What's up, Chief?" Brian asked.

"Hold on." The chief walked to the coffeepot, poured himself a cup of coffee, and then returned to the table and sat down with Brian and Joe. He took a deep breath, exhaled, and then looked at Joe and said, "Your old pal Charlie Cramer is dead."

"Dead? What happened?" Joe asked. "In Canada?"

The chief nodded.

"Did it happen when they tried to arrest him?" Brian asked.

"No." The chief took a quick sip of coffee and then said, "They were on their way to arrest him." He then explained everything that had happened that morning until the explosion.

"They found his body?" Joe asked.

"They found a body, which they assume is his. The explosion sent his glasses across the room and miraculously survived. They believe they're the same glasses he was wearing when they broke out of jail."

"What happened?" Joe asked. "What caused the explosion?"

"Apparently, your friend didn't make a wise choice when choosing a hideout. That section of the warehouse housed highly flammable and explosive material. They're not really sure yet what caused the fire, but they suspect it was an electrical shortage. Something sparked. They're not even sure why he was in that area of the building, since it appears he had been sleeping in another section of the warehouse."

"Are they sure it's his body? I keep wondering if he had an accomplice, considering he made it all the way to Canada. I find it hard to believe he made it all that way without help. Maybe it was his accomplice, and he's still out there," Joe said. "Of course, if those are Charlie's glasses they found, and he's still alive, it shouldn't be hard to find him, since he can't see a thing without his glasses."

"The bartender who saw him, and the person who checked him into the motel, both claimed he was alone. Unfortunately, the body was burned beyond recognition, and they may not get reliable DNA for a positive identification, and I don't know the status of dental records. Aside from the glasses that seem to be the same ones Cramer was wearing when he escaped, they found a duffel bag in another section of the warehouse. It looks like that might have been where he was sleeping. The duffel bag contained some clothes, along with a used toothbrush. So if they can't get DNA from the body, they might get it from the toothbrush."

Twenty minutes later, after the police chief returned to his office, he received a second call from the Canadian authorities. After the call ended, the chief called Brian and Joe into his office.

"What's up, Chief?" Brian asked as he and Joe stepped into the room.

"It looks like those glasses were Cramer's," the chief announced.

"Did they already verify it was his prescription?" Joe asked.

The chief shook his head. "No. But Cramer's fingerprints were on the glasses. And whatever prints they lifted from items from the duffel bag they found, those were Cramer's too. No one else's."

FRED STEIN always kept baggies in his pocket when walking his dog. He prided himself on being a responsible pet owner. He hadn't had to pull one out yet, but the way Fritz kept sniffing as they walked down the street, it was only a matter of time. Ahead, Fred spied his neighbor Sidney Corvin standing on his front porch. He waved at Sidney as his schnauzer, Fritz, tugged on the leash. The neighbor waved back.

A few minutes later, Fritz stopped to do his business. As Fred waited for his dog to finish, he glanced back at Sidney's house and noticed Hal Kent had just parked in front of Sidney's house. Fred knew Hal. He had been taking care of the property since before the elder Sidney Corvin had passed away before leaving the property to the nephew. Fred turned back around and pulled a baggie from his pocket.

HAL FOLLOWED Frank into the house and closed the door behind him.

"I've been waiting for you to call." Frank led Hal into the kitchen.

"I figured you'd want to hear this in person." Hal watched as Frank opened the refrigerator, grabbed two beers, tossed him one, and kept one for himself.

Frank motioned to the kitchen table. "I hope it's good news." The two men sat down.

Hal took a swig of his beer before saying, "Charlie Cramer is dead."

Frank didn't respond immediately. Instead, he took a sip of beer and chuckled.

Hal arched his brow. "Not the reaction I expected."

"This really isn't news I should be happy about. But we had no choice. You sure?" Frank took another sip of beer.

"My brother said it's all over the news in Vancouver. Found his body burned to a crisp in a warehouse."

Frank cringed. "Poor guy." He took another swig of beer.

"From what I heard about him, couldn't have happened to a nicer guy," Hal said.

Both men laughed.

SIXTEEN

C onfident Charlie Cramer was dead, Brian didn't wait until he got off work on Monday to give Heather the news. He understood she worried Cramer might return to Frederickport and finish the job he had started when Brian arrested the man.

Brian expected Heather to be relieved at the news of Cramer's death, but she said, "Damn. I hope he doesn't show up here."

"I assumed you'd be happy," Brian said.

"I'd be happier if they had arrested him. I'd rather have him behind bars than worry about him showing up again in my living room."

"At least this time, if he does, he can't hurt you," Brian gently reminded her.

There was a long silence. Finally, Heather asked, "Do you seriously see me as an innocent?"

Brian chuckled and then said, "In many ways, yes."

While Brian called Heather, Joe called Kelly. After getting off the phone with Brian, Heather immediately called Danielle and then Chris. Danielle called Lily to give her the news, but Kelly had just gotten off the phone with her brother, so Lily had already been informed.

ON TUESDAY MORNING, Ian and Connor left to have breakfast with the boys at Pier Café. The boys included Walt and Chris. Meanwhile, Lily took Sadie over to Marlow House for her sister to take on her daily walk. Unbeknownst to Lily, Marie tagged along. Marie had stopped by Lily's house earlier that morning to visit Connor, but when she realized the boy was going to breakfast with his dad, she knew she couldn't tag along. After all, the two friends Ian was meeting were mediums, and it would be awkward for her to barge in on their guys' breakfast. It wasn't like she could discreetly eavesdrop without them knowing. She could conceal herself from the mediums, yet that would be a betrayal of their trust.

"Good morning," Lily greeted when Laura opened the kitchen door for her. Sadie had already entered through the pet door. Lily handed her sister the leash.

"Morning, Lily," Danielle called out from the table. When she saw Marie enter with Lily, she gave the ghost a welcoming nod.

"Morning, Dani; how you feeling?" Lily joined her friend at the table.

"Good. Especially now, knowing Charlie Cramer is no longer a threat."

"I agree," Lily said.

"How's the morning sickness?" Danielle asked.

Lily shrugged. "I haven't puked for a few days, so that's good."

Marie cringed. "I really wish you girls wouldn't use words like puke." The ghost spied an empty chair already pulled out from the table. She sat down.

Danielle smiled at Marie, yet reserved comment.

"I've been thinking about Marie," Laura announced as she promptly sat down on said ghost.

Marie immediately stood, her body moving through Laura's. "I hate when someone does that." Disgusted, Marie took a seat in an imaginary chair on the other side of the table.

Laura gave a shiver. "Wow, that was kinda weird."

"What?" Lily asked, oblivious to what had just happened.

"Right when I mentioned Marie, this icy chill went through my body. It was creepy." Laura shivered.

"It's your own fault for sitting on me," Marie grumbled.

"If Marie is haunting Beach Drive, perhaps you sat on her, and she passed through your body," Danielle suggested.

Lily looked at Danielle. When Laura looked away from Danielle, Danielle gave Lily a nod. Lily arched her brows and glanced around the room, wondering where Marie had ended up.

Laura laughed. "Don't be silly. Anyway, I never said Marie haunted Beach Drive. I said she's haunting her old house."

"Really?" Lily muttered.

Laura looked at Lily and grinned. "We should have a seance at your house. Or get a Ouija board. Yes, a Ouija board."

"That might be fun," Marie said.

"I'm not sure about that," Lily said.

"We could invite Adam and Melony," Laura suggested.

Marie shook her head. "No. That's a bad idea."

"We have enough drama in our lives right now," Lily muttered.

"It would be fun. Unless, of course, that Charlie Cramer dude came through," Laura said.

"Oh please, don't be summoning that spirit," Danielle groaned.

Laura laughed and stood. "You guys crack me up. But seriously, consider it. It could be fun. And who knows, Marie might really come through. Might be a nice wedding present for Adam. Didn't you tell me they were close?"

Lily glared at her sister. "Laura, go on your walk."

"You're grumpy when you're pregnant." Laura laughed again.

"THAT WAS INTERESTING," Danielle muttered after Laura left with Sadie. "Although, I do wonder why you haven't told your sister the truth."

"Do you want me to?" Lily asked.

Danielle cringed. "Not really."

Lily smiled. "That's what I thought."

"It's just that you can never predict how someone will deal with that information. When I was a child and told my family I could see ghosts, Cheryl used that information against me. Had I been able to convince her I was telling the truth, I'm not sure it would have been different. I understand Laura is not Cheryl, but if you tell the wrong people, anything might happen."

"I do recall liking your cousin when Adam first showed an interest in her. Thought there might be a future for them," Marie observed. "But she turned out to be something of a tart."

Danielle glanced to Marie and silently raised her brows.

Marie shrugged. "I suppose she improved with death, from how you speak of her."

"If I'm honest, it's not just because you'd rather I not say anything," Lily said. "It's because of Kelly."

Danielle turned her attention back to Lily. "What do you mean?"

"Ian doesn't want to do anything to hurt his sister. He's happy she found someone. Ian's never seen Kelly this happy with a guy. And he likes Joe. He likes the way he treats his sister."

"What does this have to do with telling Laura?" Danielle asked.

"Even if I swore my sister to secrecy, Laura would share this information with Kelly," Lily said.

"And Kelly would share it with Joe," Danielle added.

Lily nodded. "We all know how Joe is. There is no way anyone could convince him any of it was true. Ian understands this better than most because it was so difficult for him to accept. But he also knows his sister would believe it—if he told her it was all true. And that would inevitably blow up her and Joe's relationship. He wants his sister to be happy. He doesn't want to do anything that destroys that happiness. And frankly, it's better for my marriage if Kelly is in a happy relationship. Imagine if she and Joe broke up over this."

Danielle cringed. "Yeah, I could see how Kelly might end up relying on Ian for emotional support."

"And if us telling Kelly the truth ended her relationship with Joe,

Ian would feel guilty, and Kelly would end up being more of a pain than she already is. And please, do not tell Ian I said that."

"I promise."

"But maybe you should tell Adam and Mel. They seem to accept the possibility of spirits, especially after what they experienced at my in-laws' property," Lily said.

"No. No. No. Do not tell Adam and Melony!" Marie insisted.

Curious, Danielle looked to Marie. "It seems Marie does not want her grandson to know."

"Really?" Lily looked to where Danielle looked, assuming that was where Marie had ended up. "Why?"

Marie let out a sigh. "I imagine it would be easy to convince Adam and Melony that I'm still here. But I don't want to do that to them."

Danielle frowned at Marie. "What do you mean?"

"I know my grandson. While part of him would like to know I'm still here, looking over him, another part of him would hate it. To put it in words he might use—it would creep him out. Think about it. Unlike you, he can't see me."

"Lily can't see you either, and I don't think it creeps her out."

"What are you talking about?" Lily asked. Danielle repeated Marie's words for Lily.

"Of course it doesn't creep me out. I like knowing Marie is still here."

Marie let out a sigh and shook her head. "Girls, you know I respect your privacy. I would never barge in on—well, when you're being intimate with your husband. At least... not intentionally."

"Ahh, and how Adam's mind works, he would always wonder if his grandma was there, watching." Danielle snickered.

"It's better I not put that thought into the dear boy's head. My son and daughter-in-law left Adam with enough issues; I don't need to add to them."

WALT, Chris, and Ian sat in a booth at Pier Café. Connor sat next to them in a highchair, and Ian sternly reminded his son to keep his feet away from the table's edge. He didn't want another incident like the one that had happened on Sunday, and while Walt was nearby to catch him, he didn't need Carla repeating the same story his mother had been telling.

"You guys heard about Cramer?" Carla asked when she came to take their order.

"What did you hear?" Ian asked.

"That he's dead. That will save taxpayers some money."

"Where did you hear that?" Ian asked.

Carla frowned at Ian. "What, you don't think it's true?"

"I didn't say that. I just didn't realize it was common knowledge," Ian said.

Carla grinned at Ian. "You get your inside scoop from your sister, who gets it from Joe. And I have my own source." Carla took their order.

When Carla left the table, Chris asked, "I wonder who Carla's dating from the station." Walt and Ian chuckled in response.

Chris leaned back in the booth and gave a sigh. "Heather is rather freaked out about all this."

"I thought she'd be happy," Ian asked.

"She doesn't want to see him," Chris said.

"You think his spirit will come back here?" Ian asked.

"Very likely," Walt said.

"At least we won't be surprised if he shows up," Chris said. "And this way, we'll know it's a ghost. Imagine if he popped up in Heather's living room and she didn't know he was dead."

"Oh, I hadn't considered that," Ian said.

Their discussion stopped when Carla returned to the table with Connor's juice. After she left, Chris said, "I wonder how Adam will handle Cramer's house. Does Cramer even have a will?"

"I bet Eden Langdon challenges his estate," Ian said.

"Heather and I discussed that," Chris said. "I'm surprised Cramer didn't have Adam list the house so he could use the funds for legal counsel before someone brought a civil suit against him.

Fortunately for Eden, Cramer didn't sell the house and spend all the money on lawyers."

"Is Heather considering suing his estate?" Ian asked.

Chris shook his head. "No. She said she didn't want his money. And that if anyone should have it, it's Eden, because Cramer destroyed her family."

"That sounds like Heather," Walt said.

SEVENTEEN

As the coffee brewed, Frank set two mugs on the counter. One for him and one for Laura. He went to use the bathroom before she showed up. After using the toilet, he stood in front of the mirror, washing his hands in the bathroom sink. He grabbed the hand towel, and while drying his hands, he looked into the mirror. He paused a moment and turned his head to the left and then to the right, inspecting his face. Tossing the hand towel back onto the counter, he opened the medicine cabinet and grabbed a tube of mascara. Closing the medicine cabinet door, he removed the lid from the mascara and set it on the counter.

Frank leaned into the mirror and carefully brushed the mascara wand over his beard. When done, he stood back from the mirror and again inspected his face, turning it from side to side. It amazed him how a little makeup made his beard appear longer and thicker.

TEN MINUTES LATER, Frank sat with Laura on the front porch. She sipped the cup of coffee he had given her. Sprawled out a few feet away, the leash still hooked to her collar, yet not secured on the other end, Sadie watched the humans, giving the impression she attentively listened to their conversation.

"How are the plans for the wedding going? Or should I say weddings," Frank asked.

"They're moving along. Way more drama than I expected when I came up here. And not wedding drama. One thing I've learned since coming to Frederickport, this certainly isn't a boring little town." Laura laughed and took another drink of coffee.

"How so?" Frank asked.

"My friend, the one whose wedding I'm in, one of her fiancé's old high school friends died in a fire yesterday."

"I'm so sorry. Was this in Frederickport?"

Laura shook her head. "No. This was in Canada. Near Vancouver. And he wasn't really Joe's friend anymore. At one time they were close. In fact, Kelly, my friend who's getting married, had hoped Joe would ask him to be his best man. But well… the friend turned out to be a serial killer."

Frank arched his brows. "Serial killer?"

Laura nodded. "Yeah. About ten years ago, he murdered his business partner. No one suspected he was the killer. Police said it was a robbery at their bike store. And this past Thanksgiving, he killed his business partner's twin sister."

"Do two murders make someone a serial killer?"

Laura shrugged. "Well, he was getting ready to kill a third person, one of my sister's neighbors, Heather Donovan. But Heather's boyfriend, who is a cop, showed up at her house, ended up saving her, and arrested the guy. He was in jail waiting for his trial, but then he escaped, made it all the way to Canada. He was hiding out in a warehouse. It caught fire. And the rest is history. At least for him." Laura took another drink of coffee.

"Are they sure it's him?" he asked.

"They're pretty sure. I don't know all the details."

"How does your friend's fiancé feel about all this? Now that his old friend is dead?"

Laura considered the question for a moment, the coffee mug resting on her lap as she absently fiddled with its rim. "I think it's been hard on Joe. I suspect there's a part of him that kept hoping that during the trial they would find out something to prove the guy really hadn't committed the murders. That there was some misunderstanding with Heather. To make it even more confusing for Joe— not sure confusing is the right word—the arresting officer, Heather's boyfriend, is the guy Joe asked to be his best man. They work together. Not sure I mentioned it, but Joe is a cop, too."

"Interesting." Frank sipped his coffee.

"And then there was the drama with the engagement ring." Laura told Frank about Kelly's ring and what had happened on Sunday evening.

"I can see what you mean about the drama."

"Anyway, as for the weddings, the next two weeks, it's all about Melony and Adam's wedding."

"Yes, the Realtor I'm trying to avoid."

Laura laughed. "Yeah."

"So what are the wedding plans for this week?"

"Saturday is a shower for Adam and Mel. It's a coed shower. I'm not really close to Adam and Melony, but I'm going, mostly because, well, I'm here." Laura shrugged.

"Are they having it at Marlow House?"

"No. Heather and her boss are hosting it over at the Glandon Foundation offices."

"Sounds like everyone on your street is going to the shower."

"It feels like that. Except, of course, for Connor."

"Connor?" He frowned.

"Yeah, my nephew. He's going over to his grandparents'. Then next Thursday is the bachelor and bachelorette parties. They're having the bachelor party a few doors up from my sister's at Chris's house. Us girls are having our party down the street at Heather's. And then they have the rehearsal on Friday and the rehearsal dinner at an Italian restaurant in town. I don't remember the name."

"Do you get to go?" he asked.

"Everything but the rehearsal dinner. I'm going to everything else, mostly because I'm staying with Walt and Danielle, and I'm Lily's sister. Heck, about everyone on Beach Drive will be there. And then the wedding is at Marlow House on Saturday."

They chatted a few minutes more about Laura's agenda for the two weeks, and then Frank changed the conversation to his Frederickport house and what he intended to do to the property.

"Are you planning to start using the house? Rent it out? Sell it? Move here?" Lily asked.

"With my job, I can't move here. But I needed to come and go through my uncle's things. I kept putting it off. When I told Hal I was coming, he told me I should wait until summer."

"He has a point."

"I may eventually sell the property, but I know I don't want to rent it. And maybe I'll take Hal's advice and come back in the summer."

"You could make good money renting."

Frank shook his head. "To be honest, I don't like the idea of strangers living in my house. And I don't need to rent it. I've been talking to Hal about what I need to do to keep the house in shape. One thing he recommends I do is get security cameras, since the house is empty most of the time."

"That's a good idea."

"I have no idea what kind I should get. Have you ever had them?"

Laura shook her head. "No. But our condo had them around our property. But that was the association's thing."

Frank nodded. "I imagine Marlow House has them around the property, but I don't imagine they have them inside. I think that would be awkward with B and B guests." Frank laughed.

Laura smiled. "Actually, they don't have any security cameras on the property. In fact, I think my sister said the only security cameras she knows of in the neighborhood are a couple of doors down at Chris Johnson's house."

"Really?"

They chatted about security cameras for a few minutes more before Laura changed the subject. "Can I ask you a question?"

"Sure. What?"

"How did you get Frank as a nickname? You said it was a long story. I have time."

Frank set his coffee cup on the table and studied Laura for a minute. Finally, he said, "I'll make you a deal."

"What?"

"When you come to London and you let me show you around, I'll take you out to dinner, and I'll tell you then."

"What happens if we don't see each other when I get to London?" she asked.

Frank smiled at Laura. "If you want to hear the story about my nickname, then you'd better meet me in London."

———

FRANK SAT on the front porch and watched as Laura walked the dog down the street. He held two empty coffee mugs, one in each hand. When she was a few doors down the street, she turned and gave a last wave. Lifting one hand, he gave her a salute-like wave with a mug. After she turned back around and continued down the street, he stood up, juggled the two mugs to hold them in one hand, and walked into the house, closing and locking the door behind him.

He took the mugs into the kitchen and set them in the sink. From the kitchen, he walked into the living room and picked up his cellphone from the coffee table and took a seat on the recliner. He called Hal.

"Did your friend show up?" Hal asked.

"Yes."

"Did you get anything today?"

"She's most accommodating. We can check out Marlow House on Saturday night."

"I thought you said it was going to be grand central on Beach Drive this week," Hal said.

"Yes. But on Saturday, they're all attending a wedding shower over at the Glandon Foundation offices. We can go through the house then."

"Do we really need to go through the house first? Isn't that kind of risky?" Hal asked.

"I think it's riskier not being as prepared as possible. And we don't have to worry about security cameras. They don't have them."

EIGHTEEN

Walt returned from Pier Café and found Danielle, Lily, and Marie still sitting at the kitchen table.

"How was breakfast?" Danielle asked as Walt shut the door behind him.

"More important, how was Connor?" Lily asked.

Walt chuckled. "Both were good." He walked to Danielle, who remained seated at the table, stopped, and dropped a quick kiss on her lips.

Lily stood. "I should probably go home. Ian has some work to do."

"I'll go with you and help with Connor," Marie offered.

Danielle conveyed Marie's message to Lily.

LILY HAD to admit Marie made a terrific nanny. Considering Lily's current lack of energy and sporadic bouts of morning sickness, it was nice having someone around to keep Connor occupied. When she had come home a few minutes earlier, Ian and Connor were already in the living room. Ian had little to say about his breakfast aside from the fact Connor had behaved himself and Carla hadn't changed her hair color. He went off to the office, leaving Lily with Connor and Marie.

Another perk of a caretaker ghost, Lily could stretch out on the sofa and lose herself in a novel without constant interruptions. When Laura, Kelly, or her mother-in-law offered to keep Connor occupied so Lily could take a break, there was a constant barrage of questions. Since she could neither see nor hear Marie, that was never an issue.

Sprawled out on the sofa, a book in hand, Lily found it impossible to focus on the story. It wasn't because of Connor, who played nearby with his dinosaurs and Marie. It was because her thoughts kept drifting from the book's plot to her sister and the man Laura had befriended and kept secret.

Lily glanced from the open book to the living room window and spied Laura crossing the street with Sadie. She sat up.

"Marie," Lily said quickly, "I have a favor. Laura will be walking in here any minute with Sadie. From what Sadie told Walt, Laura met someone on her walks. A man. And she stops each morning and has coffee with him on his porch. But she has said nothing to me about it. Can you ask Sadie if she visited him this morning?"

The next moment, a plastic *Tyrannosaurus rex* floated into the air and then dropped to the floor. Lily smiled. "Thanks, Marie."

"HOW WAS YOUR WALK?" Lily closed her book and set it on the coffee table, her eyes on Laura, who unhooked the leash from Sadie's collar.

Laura shrugged. "It was a walk."

Now off a leash, tail wagging, Sadie greeted Connor with a sniff to his ear and then nosed Lily.

Laura walked to her nephew, gave him a morning kiss, and ruffled his rusty curls. He handed her a plastic brontosaurus. She took it, held it in front of Connor, and made a growling sound. Connor laughed, and Laura handed the toy back to her nephew.

She sat down on the recliner facing Lily and did all that without moving through Marie, who had been sitting with the boy.

"Meet anyone interesting?" Lily asked with faux innocence.

Laura frowned at her sister, leaned back in the chair, and crossed her legs. "Like who?"

It was Lily's turn to shrug. "I don't know. Anyone?"

MARIE, who had been silently observing the exchange, focused her attention on Sadie, who now lay by the sofa, watching Connor.

"Sadie, we need to talk," Marie told the dog. Connor was the only person in the room who could hear Marie's words. The dog looked at Marie. Their eyes met.

After a few minutes of silence, Marie turned to Connor and, before vanishing, said, "Connor, Grandma Marie needs to leave for a bit. Be a good boy for your mom."

WHEN MARIE POPPED into Marlow House's kitchen a few minutes later, she found the room empty. She left the kitchen and began moving through the rooms on the lower floor. When she reached the library, she found Max on his back, stretched out on the sofa.

"Max, are you supposed to be on the furniture?" Marie chided.

Not getting up, the cat leaned his head back until he could see Marie. From his vantage point, she was upside down. He meowed.

Marie chuckled. "Okay. Where's Danielle and Walt?"

The cat silently conveyed Walt had retreated to his attic office to work, while Danielle was in the parlor.

"Thank you." Marie vanished. Max closed his eyes and resumed his nap.

DANIELLE SAT at the parlor desk, her right hand on the computer mouse while she focused on the computer's monitor.

"Whatcha doing?" Marie asked as she suddenly appeared in front of the desk.

Danielle jolted from the unexpected arrival and then let out the breath she had just inhaled. "Dang, Marie, you scared me!"

"I'm sorry. I had no idea you were afraid of ghosts." Marie chuckled.

Danielle rolled her eyes. "Funny."

"What are you doing on the computer?" Marie asked.

"I'm looking at baby names," Danielle said.

"Ahh. In my day we picked out a boy's and a girl's name. Because, of course, we didn't know what we were having until the baby was born. And here you're doing the same thing." Marie chuckled. "Twins, so exciting!"

"Yeah, says everyone who isn't the person going through the pregnancy or labor," Danielle grumbled.

"Posh, you're as thrilled as Walt."

Danielle shrugged. "I am. But it doesn't mean I'm not fully aware of how the pregnancy and labor are more complicated—and possibly dangerous."

"You're going to be fine," Marie insisted.

"And how challenging it is raising twins."

"Be grateful you're having a boy and girl," Marie said.

"Yeah, I always wanted to just have two kids, a boy and a girl."

"I don't mean that. But if you had identical twins, look at all the trouble identical twins can get into, playing tricks on their parents and teachers, trading identities. And imagine if you got them mixed up when they were babies. They could each grow up going by the wrong name."

Danielle chuckled.

"Oh, I almost forgot why I popped over here. Can you call Lily for me, please?"

LILY SAT ON THE SOFA, listening to her sister ramble on about Kelly's engagement ring and how she was going over to her house later to surf for setting ideas.

"After Joe's grandmother was so cool about the ring, Kelly started feeling guilty about wanting to have the diamond reset. She thought maybe she shouldn't change it and look at it as a symbolic symbol of their love."

"Symbolic symbol? Isn't that redundant?" Lily snorted.

Laura rolled her eyes. "You know what I mean."

Lily did, because Ian had already told her all this, but she let Laura ramble on.

"But the grandmother pulled Kelly aside and told her she really wanted Kelly to transform the ring into something pretty. It was what she had always wanted to do, but she didn't want to hurt her husband's feelings. And since Joe hadn't chosen that setting, there really was no reason for him to have his feelings hurt if Kelly wanted it reset. And the fact Kelly wore the ring without saying anything was enough of a romantic gesture, according to his grandmother."

Lily's cellphone rang. She leaned toward the coffee table, picked it up, and looked to see who was calling. Before answering, she said, "It's Dani."

"I have a message from Marie," Danielle said after Lily said hello.

Lily's gaze flashed over to Laura, who had moved to the floor to play with Connor. "Is she there?"

"Yes. She told me to tell you she had a nice talk with Sadie," Danielle said.

"And?"

"Laura stopped there again this morning. While Sadie is not a terrific judge of time, she thinks they were there even longer this morning."

"Interesting." Lily studied her sister, who now sat on the floor, her back to the sofa, as she played with her nephew.

AFTER LAURA LEFT for Kelly's, Lily called Walt.

"Yes, Lily," Walt answered his phone.

"I have a favor to ask you. I know you told me not to interfere with Laura's secret boyfriend."

Walt chuckled. "I'm not sure I'd call him her boyfriend. Sadie told me they have only been talking, no touching."

"Yeah, I know. But I would kind of like to know who this guy is. I mean, well, you never know about people. What if he turns out to be some psycho, and one day Laura doesn't come back from her walk?"

"She has Sadie with her," Walt reminded her.

"See, I have to protect Sadie, too. Remember that time you let Sadie go on a walk with some B and B guests? How did that turn out? If it weren't for a helpful ghost, Sadie would be a ghost dog now."

Walt groaned. "Okay, what do you want me to do?"

"Laura isn't here. She's with Kelly. I was wondering if you could pick Sadie and me up in the car. Connor can stay with Ian. And Sadie can give you directions to this guy's house, and we can just drive by and see where it is. Laura doesn't have to find out, and the guy doesn't have to know we drove by. We can just take a little car ride."

LILY SAT in the passenger seat of Danielle's Ford Flex while Walt drove the car and Sadie stood on the back seat, her head shoved between the two front seats, as she gave directions to where Laura's mystery man lived.

"Thanks for doing this, Walt," Lily said.

"No problem. I hope Laura doesn't come back early and run into us."

Lily giggled. "Yeah, I would need to come up with a story about why you're driving me and Sadie around in a car."

"And we don't have Danielle to come up with a story," Walt reminded her.

Lily giggled again.

"And if we told them the truth, they wouldn't believe us," Walt said.

"Even if they would, I wouldn't tell them the truth. I don't want Laura to find out I'm spying on her. But sometimes Laura doesn't use the best judgment with people."

Walt interrupted Lily by asking Sadie, "Up here?"

Sadie gave a bark, and Walt turned left.

"Remember, your sister plans to travel through Europe by herself," Walt reminded her.

"Honestly, I don't understand why my mom is okay with that. Dad doesn't like it at all."

Sadie barked again. Walt turned into a cul-de-sac.

"It must be on this street," Lily said.

Walt slowed down but kept driving.

Sadie barked.

"There it is," Walt said. "The house with the big front porch."

Lily looked at the house as they drove by. She noticed someone standing in the window, looking outside. "Someone's in the house. I wish he would come outside so I could see what he looks like."

Walt drove to the end of the cul-de-sac and turned around. When he drove by the house again, he didn't see anyone standing in the window. They continued home.

HAL PICKED up his cellphone and looked to see who was calling before answering. "What's up?"

"Guess who just drove by?" came the familiar voice.

"Who?"

"I'm pretty sure it was Walt Marlow."

"The Packard?" Hal asked.

"No, the car Danielle Marlow drives. But I think her husband was driving it today. And guess who was sitting in the passenger seat?"

"Who?"

"Lily Bartley. Can't miss that red hair. There was a dog in the car. I'm pretty sure it's the same dog Laura brings over with her. After all, it's her sister's dog she walks with, so it must be Lily."

"Where were they going?"

"I don't know. They drove down the street, turned around, and left."

"What do you think they were doing?" Hal asked.

"Not sure, but I don't like it."

NINETEEN

On Wednesday morning, Lily walked Sadie over to Marlow House for her sister. As with the previous days, Sadie entered through the pet door before Laura opened the door, and Lily walked inside. Walt and Danielle sat at the kitchen table, eating breakfast.

"Morning, guys," Lily greeted as she walked toward the table.

"I can come get Sadie," Laura said as she took the leash from Lily and shut the kitchen door. "You don't have to bring her over here every morning."

"Hey, I need my exercise too." Lily sat down at the table with Walt and Danielle. Lily spied a plate of Old Salts cinnamon rolls sitting on the center of the kitchen table. Without asking permission, she reached over and snatched a roll.

"You sure you feel up to eating that?" Walt teased.

"Actually, it looks good." Lily tore the roll in half.

"Seriously," Laura said, "it's silly for you to walk over here to bring me Sadie when I can simply pick her up when I start my walk."

About to pop a piece of cinnamon roll into her mouth, Lily eyed her sister. "Do you honestly believe the reason I'm coming over here every morning is to bring you Sadie?"

Confused, Laura looked at her sister. "Why else?"

Walt chuckled. "I think it has more to do with what's in your sister's hand." Walt turned to Lily and smiled. "Glad to see you're doing better and can eat cinnamon rolls again."

"Hopefully this won't make me puke," Lily said before shoving a piece of the sweet roll into her mouth.

"Don't let Ian's mother see you eating that. I suspect she'd have something to say about you eating all that sugar," Laura said.

"My mother-in-law always has something to say."

Walt stood up and walked to the counter. He removed a glass from the overhead cabinet and then walked to the refrigerator and retrieved a carton of milk. After filling the glass with milk, he walked to the table and set the glass before Lily.

Lily looked up at Walt and smiled. "Is that for my mother-in-law's benefit, giving me something healthy with this sugar?"

Walt smiled at Lily. "No, it is strictly for your benefit. Cinnamon rolls are better with a cold glass of milk."

Lily grinned at Walt and picked up the glass of milk and took a sip.

"Or coffee," Danielle grumbled.

"The smell of coffee still bothers me," Lily said.

"Danielle, I read somewhere pregnant women can have coffee," Laura said.

"Chocolate," Danielle and Lily chimed at the same time.

Laura frowned, looking from Danielle and Lily.

"I think what they're trying to tell you, while pregnant women can have caffeine, they should limit the amount of caffeine," Walt explained. "And I don't think either Lily or Danielle want to eliminate chocolate from their diet."

"And it is weird," Lily said. "Even when my morning sickness is at its worse, chocolate is one thing that appeals to me. And it doesn't make me feel sick to eat it."

"That is weird," Laura muttered.

Lily looked to Walt. "Are you going to walk home with me?"

Walt glanced at the clock. "If you plan to stick around for another fifteen minutes, yes."

"Ahh, the Zoom meeting," Danielle said.

"What Zoom meeting?" Laura asked.

"Walt and Ian have the same agent," Lily explained. "And he wants to have a Zoom meeting with them. I must admit, I'm curious to find out why."

"I should probably get going." Laura stood and hooked the leash on Sadie's collar.

Lily looked at her sister. "Have fun."

"I'll try." Laura opened the door.

"If you meet anyone interesting, I want to know all about it," Lily called out as her sister walked through the open doorway. Laura shut the door behind her without responding.

"That really bugs you, doesn't it?" Danielle asked.

"Yes, it does." Lily took another bite of the cinnamon roll. After she swallowed the bite, she said, "I noticed she didn't take her umbrella today."

"She probably just forgot it," Danielle said.

"Good morning, everyone!" came a familiar voice. "I saw Laura leaving, so I thought I would stop in and say hi."

"Morning, Marie," Danielle greeted.

"Hi, Marie, wherever you are." Lily pulled the remaining half of the cinnamon roll in half.

"Were you talking about anything interesting?" Marie sat on the empty chair at the table. "The gruesome death of Charlie Cramer, perhaps? By the way, has anyone seen him? Eva and I visited the cemetery last night, and there has been no sign of him."

"They haven't buried him yet," Danielle reminded her. "And we weren't talking about Cramer. I was teasing Lily about how her sister's secret friend is bugging her."

"Have you found out anything about him?" Marie asked.

"We found out where he lives." Walt proceeded to tell Marie about their car ride yesterday with Sadie.

"That sounds like Sidney Corvin's house," Marie said.

"You know him?" Danielle asked.

"Yes. I've known him for years. He died a couple of years after I did. I ran into him at the cemetery before he moved on. From what I recall, he was rather annoyed," Marie said.

"What is Marie saying about him?" Lily asked.

Danielle gave Lily a little shushing wave and asked Marie, "Annoyed, why?"

"Sidney left his estate to his nephew, his sister's boy. His sister and all Sidney's family were already gone. From what Sidney told me, his nephew didn't even bother having a funeral for him or coming to Frederickport after he died. The nephew lives in London. And instead of a funeral, the nephew sold the funeral plot Sidney had purchased for himself, and had his uncle cremated, and the ashes put out to sea. As I said, Sidney was not happy. He regretted not being more specific about his last wishes in his will."

"Who lives in the house now? If the nephew sold his uncle's funeral plot, he probably sold the house," Danielle said.

Marie shook her head. "Not sure. I once overheard Adam talking to Leslie about contacting the nephew to see if he wanted to sell the property or put it in the rental program. I don't know whatever happened. But you could ask Adam. He probably knows who lives there now."

LAURA HADN'T RETURNED from her walk, and Walt had gone across the street with Lily. Danielle sat on the parlor sofa with Max by her side. Max napped as she silently read through her to-do list for the upcoming wedding, checking off what had already been done.

Chief MacDonald would walk Mel down the aisle—or more accurately, down the stairs. The chief and Mel's friendship had begun before he had moved to Frederickport. She had been a close friend of the chief's deceased wife. Mel was the only one Danielle knew who ever called the chief Eddy.

Adam had asked Chris to be his best man, and to everyone's surprise, Mel had asked Heather to be her maid of honor.

According to Chris, Mel and Heather had gotten close after working together on several charity events. After Heather and Brian's unlikely match, Danielle told herself Mel and Heather's friendship shouldn't surprise her, because often the most likely of people can become close friends. After all, look at her and Adam.

She glanced up from what she had been reading when she heard the front door open and then close. A few moments later, Walt walked into the parlor.

Danielle set the papers she had been reading on the coffee table and looked up at Walt. "So what was the Zoom call all about?"

"It was interesting." Walt walked to the chair across from the sofa and sat down.

"Good interesting?" Danielle asked.

"It sounds like *Moon Runners* might make it to the big screen after all," Walt said.

"That's incredible, but why did Ian need to be part of the call?"

"They've arranged an interview for Ian and me. Together."

Danielle arched her brows. "Why?"

"My next book is coming out in June. They have new investors interested in going ahead with the movie. There is even talk of Seraphina taking the role." Seraphina was the actress originally cast as the leading role in *Moon Runners* before the film's major investor went on a killing spree.

"Really? Would she want to?"

"Apparently."

"I still don't get what Ian has to do with this."

"It's all about promotion. They want to interview Ian and me together. How the famous Jon Altar helped launch my career. How we're good friends and neighbors. Ian's on board with it."

"Wow. Where and when is this interview taking place?"

Walt cringed. "Soon. New York. If it was just one interview, they could probably come here. And they don't want virtual interviews."

"Gee, I don't think I could go with you. Not sure I want to fly that far, being pregnant."

"No, I don't want you to. And even though Lily's pregnancy isn't as far along, Ian doesn't feel comfortable with Lily flying, not with her unpredictable morning sickness."

"When do they want you to come?"

Walt cringed again. "That's the thing; they want us there by February 18."

"Right after Adam's wedding?"

"Yes. We'd only be gone a week. I told him I would talk to you about it, but if you don't want me to go, I won't."

"Don't be silly. You should go."

"I hate leaving you alone right now."

Danielle laughed. "Me alone? Anyway, Laura is here, so I won't be alone. I know Marie will be more than happy to help Lily with Connor. I have Heather practically next door, and Chris down the street. We'll be fine."

They both stopped talking when they heard the front door slam.

"Sounds like Laura is back," Danielle said.

A few moments later, Laura walked into the parlor.

"How was your walk?" Danielle asked.

Laura began removing her raincoat. "I forgot my umbrella, and it started to rain."

"At least you had a raincoat," Danielle said.

"Yeah, that's what Lily told me." Laura looked to Walt. "Is it really true you might go to New York right after Adam and Mel's wedding?"

Walt smiled. "Ian told you?"

"No. Lily did. She said it wasn't a sure thing yet because you wanted to talk to Danielle first."

"It's a sure thing. So it will be just you and me alone for a week." Danielle glanced down at Max, who had just woken up. "And Max."

"Does that mean we get to have wild parties while the guys are gone?" Laura teased.

Danielle chuckled. "I imagine by then I'll be exhausted after all the wedding activities."

"I feel a little better knowing you'll be here," Walt told Laura. "I hate for Danielle to be alone right now."

"Oh, I'll be fine," Danielle scoffed. "But I'm also glad Laura is here."

"What about Lily? You think she should be alone with Connor right now? Maybe she and Connor should come over here and stay when Ian's gone," Laura suggested.

"You can ask her," Danielle said.

After Laura left the room and was out of earshot, Walt said, "Lily won't want to come over here and stay. We already talked about it when I was across the street. In fact, I suggested it."

"Yeah, I assumed Lily would prefer staying home. But we'll let Lily explain it to her sister," Danielle said.

———

"YOU SURE?" Laura asked Lily. She sat on the bed in the downstairs bedroom of Marlow House, talking on her cellphone with the bedroom door closed. "Walt and Danielle said it was okay."

"Yeah, I know. Walt suggested it when he was over here."

"He did?"

"Yeah. But it's a hassle with Connor. It's so much easier if I stick to his schedule and he sleeps in his own bed. And frankly, I don't want to leave my bed. And Sadie is with me, so I'm not really alone." *Plus, I'm sure Marie will stay with me,* Lily said to herself.

TWENTY

Lily didn't bring Sadie over to Marlow House on Thursday morning because she had slept in. When Laura picked Sadie up for her walk, Lily still wore her pajamas and sat in the living room, discussing the upcoming trip to New York with Ian. They all chatted for a few minutes before Laura left with Sadie.

When Laura turned down Frank's street, he was already sitting on the front porch, drinking coffee. The moment he saw her, he stood, waved hello, and gave a second wave, inviting her to join him. By the time she reached his house and walked up the front steps, he had already gone inside, poured her a cup of coffee, and returned outside with it.

"I looked up that pub you told me about," Laura said after she sat down and picked up the coffee Frank had given her.

Frank smiled. "The one I want to take you to when you're in London?"

Laura nodded. "Yes. And people really bring their dogs?"

He laughed. "Yes."

"I'm looking forward to going. What are your plans for the weekend?"

"I had intended to sort through more of my uncle's boxes, but my work contacted me, and it looks like I'll be on the computer most of the weekend, working."

"That doesn't sound like fun," Laura said.

Frank shrugged. "I'm glad they let me work remotely, or my stay in Frederickport would have been much shorter."

"I used to work from home sometimes, at my old job. Which got me to thinking how I might monetize my travels."

"How is that?" he asked.

"My friend Kelly is a blogger. She actually makes money doing that. She told me she would help me set up a blog so I can write about my travels and post pictures. This afternoon we're brainstorming on ways to monetize my blog. Instead of getting a job later, this could be my new career. I'm not really a writer, but how hard can it be?"

Frank smiled. "Sounds interesting. You have that wedding party on Saturday, right?"

"Yeah, it's a coed shower at the Glandon Headquarters. Over the next week, there will be a bachelor and bachelorette party, the rehearsal dinner, and then the wedding."

"And then you start all over again with your friend's wedding?"

"We sorta get a wedding break. My friend's not getting married until the first week in March." Laura told him about Walt and Ian's trip to New York.

"And Danielle and your sister won't be going?"

Laura shook her head and set her half-empty cup of coffee on the side table. "No, both Danielle and my sister are staying home. Being pregnant, they really don't want to take that long a flight. So it will just be me and Danielle at Marlow House for a week. I tried to get Lily to bring my nephew over to Marlow House and we could have a weeklong slumber party."

"She's not going to?" he asked.

"No. She says it's too much of a hassle with Connor, and I get it. It's not like she's alone, she has Sadie."

At the mention of her name, Sadie, who had been lying nearby on the patio, looked up at Laura.

AFTER LAURA AND SADIE LEFT, Frank took the empty coffee mugs back inside the house. He stepped into the kitchen, and his cellphone rang. He set the mugs on the counter and pulled the cellphone out of his coat pocket. Before answering, he glanced at the phone. Hal was calling.

Frank answered the phone. "Hey."

"My brother called. He's in Portland," Hal said.

"Were there any problems?"

"None. He found a van. And I sent him your list."

"We don't want anyone to trace it back to us."

"I understand. I also found the house. But now, you need to set the date," Hal reminded him.

"I'm glad you called, because I have a date."

"You do?"

"Let's just say the window has narrowed. My little friend tells me that right after the first wedding, both Walt Marlow and Ian Bartley are going to New York. Danielle and my friend will be all alone at Marlow House for a week."

"What about the sister?" Hal asked.

"She'll be at her house, across the street. Thankfully, she didn't take Laura's suggestion to stay at Marlow House while their husbands are gone. We don't need to deal with another woman and a kid."

"ARE you sure you don't want to come with me?" Laura asked Lily. She had just brought Sadie home after her walk.

"I've been feeling better, and I don't want to risk feeling nauseous again. And one thing that can trigger me is the smells at Pier Café."

"I don't know why. I don't think it smells bad down there."

"When I'm not pregnant, I don't mind the smell of grilled meat either," Lily said.

Ten minutes later, after Laura left, Lily called Danielle.

"Did Laura come back from her walk?" Danielle asked.

"In a way. She brought Sadie home and then walked down to Pier Café to meet Kelly. They're having a late breakfast—or early lunch—and then going to Kelly's, doing some stuff on the computer. Laura invited me, but I don't want to jinx the fact I'm feeling better."

"I understand!"

"When Laura was here, I tried to get her to talk about her morning walks. But nothing. I don't understand what the big secret is. I'm dying to find out something about this guy. Do you think you could ask Adam, see what he knows?"

"You can ask Adam," Danielle said.

"Come on Dani, you're so much better at this than I am. Seriously. What am I going to say to Adam? How do I ask him? I don't want my sister to know I'm spying on her. I'll have to come up with some story to explain why I want to know about this dude. You are better at this than I am."

"I'm good at making up stories?" Danielle asked.

"It's a gift. Own it."

THURSDAY AFTERNOON, while Danielle ran errands in town, she decided to stop at Adam's office and do what Lily had asked of her. She had to admit she was also curious about Laura's mystery friend. When Danielle entered Adam's office, his assistant, Leslie, was leaving for lunch, while Adam sat at her desk, talking on the phone.

"Hey, Danielle," Leslie greeted. "I was just going to lunch. I assume you came to see Adam?"

"Yeah." Danielle glanced over at Adam, who continued to talk on the phone.

"He should be off the phone in a few minutes. It's about the escrow on the house he and Mel are buying."

Danielle cringed. "I hope there isn't a problem."

"Just the opposite. Sounds like it's closing early." Leslie grinned.

Ten minutes later, Danielle sat in the front office of Frederickport Vacation Properties with Adam.

"It looks like it's closing the day before the wedding," Adam told Danielle.

"That went fast," Danielle said.

Adam shrugged. "Not really. They asked for forty-five days or sooner. If it closes the day before the wedding, that will be thirty days. I feel better about it closing before the wedding. Of course, we won't be able to move in until after we come back from the honeymoon."

"I suppose a thirty-day escrow is typical. But from what Laura told me, she closed on her condo in way less than that."

"Yeah, she told me. But that was a cash deal, and from what she said, they waved all their inspections. So, any special reason for this visit?"

Danielle shrugged. "I thought I'd stop by and say hi. The big day is coming."

Adam grinned. "You know, I'm really looking forward to this wedding."

Danielle returned Adam's grin.

"Before Mel came back to Frederickport, the idea of marrying anyone was not something I remotely wanted to do. I remember Grandma trying to hook me up with different women. Hell, she even tried hooking me up with you."

They both laughed. "And that was all wrong. After all, you're my annoying little brother," Danielle reminded him.

Adam gave a snort. "I'm older than you."

"Only in years."

Adam laughed.

"Hey, are Kelly and Joe still looking for a house?" Danielle asked.

"From what she told me, they're giving it a break. Nothing currently on the market fits what they're looking for. About a week ago, I had her check out a house a couple of blocks from yours. It's not currently on the market, but I figured if she liked it, I could call the guy who owns it. He lives in London, inherited the house from his uncle. I don't think he's ever been here. Last time I talked to him, he wasn't interested in selling, but I figure maybe he changed his mind, wouldn't hurt to ask again. But she wasn't interested."

Danielle frowned. *Did he say London? Inherited the house from his uncle?* "Umm, what was the uncle's name?"

"Sidney Corvin. Did you know him?" Adam asked.

"Umm… I've heard of him. He died a couple of years ago?"

"Yeah."

"He never sold the house?" Danielle asked.

Adam shook his head. "No. I called him after his uncle died. He said he didn't want to sell it now, and that he wasn't interested in putting it in my rental program. I got the idea he has money and didn't need to sell it. He already had someone taking care of the property."

"How did he manage that if he's never been here?"

"Do you know Hal Kent?" Adam asked.

Danielle shook her head. "No. I don't think I've ever heard of him."

"His dad had a handyman service in town. Took care of people's yards, did odd jobs. Hal worked for his dad during high school but moved away after graduation. He was older than me, graduated before I started high school. Although, I knew his brother. Anyway, when Hal moved back to town, he started working for his dad again and took over the business. He took care of Sidney Corvin's house, and he must have had the nephew's phone number, because when I got ahold of the nephew, Hal had already worked out something with him to take care of the property. He has ever since."

"Do you think Hal ever rents the house out for the nephew?" Danielle asked.

Adam shook his head. "No. He doesn't have a property management license. And the last time I talked to Hal, I told him if Corvin wants to list the property or rent, I'd be happy to give him a referral if he uses me."

"Hmm, can you pay someone a referral if they don't have a real estate license?"

Adam grinned. "No law against giving a present to a friend."

FIFTEEN MINUTES LATER, Danielle unlocked her car door and climbed into the driver's seat. She pulled the door shut and then buckled the seatbelt. While putting her key into the ignition, she paused a moment and chuckled. "I can't believe it. I didn't even have to make up a story to get the information from Adam. Dang, I'm good at this."

TWENTY-ONE

"Do you mind if I go into your room and strip the bed," Marlow House's housekeeper, Joanne Johnson, asked Laura on Friday morning. Laura sat in the kitchen with Walt and Danielle, chatting.

Laura stood. "I can do that for you."

"It's my job. But if you don't want me to go into your room right now, I can wait."

Laura suddenly remembered how Lily had mentioned Joanne's possessive nature toward what she saw as her duties at Marlow House. Not wanting to insult the housekeeper, she sat back down. "No, you can go in there. It's fine with me."

When Laura left for her room ten minutes later, to get what she wanted to take on her walk, Joanne had already stripped the bed and left the room. She had to admit, having a housekeeper was rather nice.

"MORNING, LILY," Joanne greeted Lily when she returned to the kitchen later on Friday morning. She found Lily sitting at the kitchen table, where Laura had been earlier, chatting with Walt and Danielle.

"Hi, Joanne," Lily said.

"How are you feeling?" Joanne asked.

"A lot better. In fact, I could even eat another cinnamon roll." Lily looked at Danielle and smiled.

"Sorry, kiddo, we are out of cinnamon rolls. I should have picked some up yesterday," Danielle said.

"Where's Laura?" Joanne asked.

"She just left for her walk," Lily said. "I got here a minute ago; I brought Sadie. Laura's been walking Sadie every morning."

Joanne glanced around the room and looked back at the table. "She took them with her?"

"What are you talking about?" Danielle asked.

"When I was in Laura's room taking the sheets off the bed, there was a sack from Old Salts sitting on the dresser. I'm pretty sure they were cinnamon rolls. I didn't look inside, but I confess, I gave it a sniff. Smelled like cinnamon rolls. Laura's lucky I didn't steal one." Joanne laughed.

Lily frowned. "She had cinnamon rolls, and she didn't share?"

"She had a sack with her when she left," Walt noted. "I didn't notice that it was from Old Salts."

"That is the type of morning walk I could get into." Joanne chuckled. "A pleasant walk along the beach, eating cinnamon rolls."

When Joanne left the kitchen a few minutes later, Lily said, "Well, dang, she's buying her secret pal cinnamon rolls."

"Looks that way." Walt took a sip of his coffee.

"I talked to Adam yesterday," Danielle told Lily. "I was going to call you when I got home, but Laura came back with Kelly, and then they headed over to your house, so I really didn't want to call you while they were over there."

"Did he tell you anything about the guy?" Lily asked.

"Adam said the house isn't being rented, and it hasn't sold. So the person there is probably the nephew who inherited the house."

"Does Adam realize he's in town?" Lily asked.

"No. And I didn't have to make up a story." Danielle then told Lily about her conversation with Adam yesterday.

"That's interesting," Lily murmured. "If the guy Laura is spending all this time with is from London, it explains a lot."

"What do you mean?" Danielle asked.

"Laura's trip to Europe. One place she intends to visit is London. She's obviously interested in this guy. After all, according to Sadie, she stops there every morning and spends most of her time talking with him. At first, I thought it was weird that she didn't tell me about it. After all, she's planning to leave in a couple of months, and if this guy lives in Frederickport, I could see my sister wanting to talk to me about it. Knowing Laura, she would be reluctant to leave a new guy she's interested in. But the fact he lives where she is going in a couple of months, well, that's an entirely different scenario. I'm still annoyed she hasn't told me about him, but it makes more sense now."

"I'm curious about one thing," Walt said.

Danielle looked at Walt. "What?"

"If the owner of the house lives in London and was not interested in selling the property or renting, it might mean he wants to use the house as a vacation home, or he intends to move here someday. Now, if Lily is correct, and he is only visiting, and Laura is planning to see him when she goes to London, I have to wonder, why would he visit Frederickport at this time of year? Why not come in the summer?"

"SHE BROUGHT YOU CINNAMON ROLLS?" Hal asked Frank Friday afternoon. The two men sat in the kitchen, drinking beers.

"Yeah, it almost makes me feel a little guilty having to blow her up," Frank snarked.

Hal laughed. "Damn, you're coldhearted. It won't bother you even a little pulling the switch on that one, will it?"

"She's served her purpose. Meeting her has made this much easier than it would have been."

"Have you decided when?" Hal asked.

"Obviously, during the week Marlow and Bartley are in New York, and when we are fairly confident no one else is going to be around. I don't need one of their nosey neighbors stopping over. I know the two neighbors to the south work during the week, and the house on the other side is empty. Marlow is cozy with Chris Johnson, who lives up the street, but he works during the week too. The only one I'm a little concerned about is Laura's sister. I don't need her stopping over unexpectedly. Yet, according to what Laura told me, Lily usually leaves her kid at home with her husband when she visits Marlow House by herself. But with her husband in New York, maybe she won't be as likely to just drop in."

"What about the husband calling her and she doesn't answer the phone?"

"I'm hoping Laura can find out when the interview is taking place. Because I don't see Marlow calling his wife while he's being interviewed."

"Are you sure we need to go to Marlow House tomorrow night? I don't understand why we need to take that risk. It's not like you've never been in the house before," Hal said.

"It's not just because I want to case the place before I make the final plan—which is one reason I think it's important. But I also want to find a house key. I'm sure they have extra keys someplace in that house, like in a desk drawer. They must have spare keys they give guests."

Hall frowned. "Key? I thought you said you can pick the lock?"

"I can. But it takes time. When we go back to Marlow House to snatch Danielle and Laura, I want to get in and out. I don't want to be screwing with the lock, trying to get in, and then have one of them hear us and call the cops. Having a key instead of picking the lock makes it easier to get in."

"Yeah, with everyone gone tomorrow night, you can take your time picking the lock."

"Exactly."

"SO YOU'RE NOT HAVING a coed bridal shower?" Brian asked Joe on Friday afternoon. The two officers sat in the break room at the police station, drinking coffee before starting their shift.

"The operative word here is bridal." Joe chuckled. "Anyway, I don't think my sister ever considered a coed shower, for which I'm grateful. She already had to cancel once, so even if I wanted a coed shower, I wouldn't mention it now."

"I have to admit, I'm looking forward to tomorrow night. Sounds like there's going to be some good food there."

"Glandon can afford to throw a big party."

"Hey, it's Johnson, remember," Brian chided.

"Wow, you really have changed since you started dating Heather." Joe took a drink of his coffee.

"I thought you considered Chris a friend now?" Brian asked.

"I do. But sometimes it's a little difficult not to feel... well... for example, you know how Kelly and I are trying to buy another house, and even with me selling mine, I'm not sure we can afford what she wants. Chris never worries about any of that stuff. Hell, none of them do. Look at Marlow. He came to Frederickport with nothing, not really. Marries Danielle and all her money, and then writes a damn bestseller and falls into more money."

"I like Walt," Brian said.

"Yeah, I know you do. But I also remember what a jerk he was when he first came to town. And yes, I understand he's a different man now. But I often wonder, what happens if he someday gets his memory back? Will he turn back into the man he used to be? For Danielle's sake, I hope not. Because I know she's happy."

"I don't think we have to worry about that," Brian said.

Joe shrugged. "I suppose. But well, there is still one thing that bugs me about him."

"What's that?"

"The way he dresses."

"The way he dresses?" Brian laughed. "I didn't know you were so fashion conscious."

"You know why," Joe grumbled.

"Kelly still trying to get you to dress like Walt?"

"Not as much. But I hate going clothes shopping with her, because she always finds something that Walt would probably like, and she tries to get me to try it on. Seriously, do you see me in one of those long overcoats? People would think I'm in the Mafia."

"Well, you are——"

"Don't say it," Joe snapped.

"Good, you're both here," the chief said when he entered the break room.

"Are you heading home?" Brian asked.

"Yeah, in a few minutes. I wanted to tell you I just heard from the guy I've been talking to in Canada," the chief said.

"Is this about Charlie?" Joe asked.

"Yes." The chief sat at the table with Joe and Brian. "The DNA on the toothbrush matches Charlie's. They also found his DNA on the dirty clothes from the duffel bag. There was also a shaving razor in the bag with some blood on it. That also matched Charlie's DNA."

"What about the body?" Joe asked.

"I'm not sure they'll be able to get DNA off the remains. Not only were they severely burned, but the chemicals that exploded may have contaminated them. But it was a male who appeared to be the same height as Cramer."

"What about dental records?" Brian asked.

"It would help if they could locate Cramer's dentist. Because of all the traveling he did for work, they haven't been able to track down what dentist he used, assuming he went to the dentist. It doesn't appear he ever had dental insurance, so they can't check that way."

IAN STOOD IN HIS OFFICE, looking through one drawer in his filing cabinet late Friday afternoon.

"Hi," Lily greeted when she walked into the room.

Ian flashed a smile to Lily and then looked back in the file drawer. "Did you finally get Connor down?"

"Yeah, he was so cranky. But he finally fell asleep. I think I'm getting spoiled because he seems more difficult when Marie's not here."

Ian chuckled. After finding what he had been looking for, he set the file on the top of the cabinet and then opened the second drawer.

"Hey, can I use your computer for a minute?"

"Sure." Ian rummaged through the second file drawer.

Lily sat down at Ian's desk. "I'm googling Laura's secret pal. I have his name."

"You know, it might not be him."

Lily looked at Ian. "Why do you say that?"

"Just because Adam told Danielle the guy hadn't rented out the house, it's still possible he loaned it to a friend."

Lily shook her head and turned back to the computer. "No. It makes more sense if it is the guy from London."

A few minutes later, Lily said, "Wow, I think I might have found him on LinkedIn. His bio says he's an American working in London."

"What's he look like?"

Lily shrugged. "He's not a Chris. Boy-cut brown hair, short beard. Wears glasses. Can't tell his eye color. Nothing spectacular."

TWENTY-TWO

Laura had told him the coed wedding shower started at seven p.m. Hal would pick Frank up at six. It would be dark by then, and there wouldn't be much of a moon tonight. He wanted the veil of darkness.

Their first stop was the Barry house. The van Hal's brother had purchased in Portland was already there. Frank hadn't seen it yet, but they intended to use it tonight for the first time.

Dressed all in black, from the knit hat covering his hair down to his pullover sweater, rain jacket, denims, and his boots, Frank stood by the front window and looked out, waiting for Hal. While waiting for him to pull up, he tucked his hands in the pockets of his rain jacket, double-checking to see if the gloves were there. He found them in his right jacket pocket, where he'd put them earlier. The next moment, he spied Hal's car pulling into the driveway.

A few minutes later, he was outside in the driveway, opening the car door on the passenger side of Hal's vehicle. Hal sat in the driver's seat and watched as Frank climbed into the car.

HAL PULLED up into Miss Barry's driveway and stopped. A moment later, the garage door opened. Hal's brother stood inside the garage, next to a white van. Once the door was all the way open, Hal pulled the vehicle into the garage, and the door shut behind them.

When Hal first announced he'd found the perfect property to hold the hostages, he explained, houses on both sides of Miss Barry's were empty, and the one across the street was an Airbnb so if anyone was there, they wouldn't know what cars belong at the old woman's house. There were no security cameras in the area, and they didn't have to worry about Danielle recognizing the interior of Miss Barry's home, thus jeopardizing their plan, because the elderly woman had stopped having visitors long before Danielle Marlow moved to town.

After getting out of the vehicle, Frank walked over to Hal's brother and put out his right hand.

"Do I call you Sid or Sidney?" Stuart asked.

They both laughed.

HAL DROVE the van while Frank sat in the passenger seat, and his brother sat in the back. They drove by Marlow House but didn't stop. Instead, they continued on to the Glandon Foundation Headquarters. As they drove by the property, they looked over the vehicles parked inside the gate.

"That's Marlow's Packard," Hal said. "Lots of cars here."

"Looks like the party's underway," Frank said.

They continued down the street and then turned around, driving one more time by the foundation's headquarters. Down the street, they turned on Beach Drive. When they reached Marlow House again, Hal drove to the next street and turned right and then turned down the alley. Hal stopped the van when they reached Marlow House.

"I'll text you when I want you to pick me up." Frank hopped out of the vehicle. He closed the door, and the van drove off, leaving him standing in the dark behind Marlow House. He pulled the gloves out of his pocket, slipped them on, and headed toward the back gate leading to the rear of the property. When he reached the gate, he found it locked, but that didn't deter him.

He looked at Marlow's neighbor on the south side. The second floor was dark. But downstairs a light came from one side window. According to Laura, the town's new head librarian had purchased that house. Her friend Kelly had wanted to buy the house, but the librarian had outbid her. From what Laura said, the librarian had gotten friendly with the neighbors, and they'd invited her to tonight's party.

Confident no one was around to see him, Frank climbed a nearby tree, going over the fence, and entered the Marlows' backyard. When he reached the side door leading into the kitchen, there was a light inside. He looked in a window and spied a black cat standing by what appeared to be a water or food bowl, either eating or drinking.

STANDING AT HIS FOOD BOWL, Max finished his dinner. The house was quiet. He was alone. Not even Sadie or Hunny was coming to keep him company. Walt had told him they would return later this evening. Wherever they were going, the dogs got to go. Bella stayed home, and while he could have asked Walt if she could come over to keep him company, he didn't mind having the house to himself tonight.

He didn't expect Marie or Eva to drop by either, because they would be with Walt and Danielle. Max felt a brief twinge of jealousy for being left out, but then his ears perked up at the sound of the pet door swinging back and forth.

Max stopped eating and looked at the pet door. It stopped moving. Someone was outside, and they had pushed the pet door. Had Bella gotten out of her house and come over to visit?

Curious, Max strolled over to the door to investigate. As he got closer to the door, there was a jiggling sound. Max glanced up and saw the doorknob moving. He walked closer to the door, pushed his head against the pet door, and peeked outside.

What he believed to be a man was crouched by the door, fiddling with the doorknob. The man said, "Got it," but Max did not know what that meant. The next moment, the man turned the doorknob and opened the door. Max stepped back and looked up, watching the man enter the kitchen.

Once inside, the man closed the door behind him and looked around. Max meowed. The man looked down.

"Hey, cat."

Max meowed again.

The man pulled something from his back pocket. It was that thing humans were always talking into and looking at. The man held it up and stood still for a moment. He then moved the position of the object, still looking at it, and then froze for another moment.

The man headed for the door leading to the hallway. Max followed him. He didn't think the man was supposed to be here. Max trailed behind him as he moved through the first floor while holding the object out and looking at it.

"Maybe I should take a video instead of pictures," the man muttered. Max didn't know what the words meant. The man walked through the entire first floor of Marlow House and then headed down to the basement, all the while holding out the object and looking at it. After he returned to the first floor, he walked upstairs to the second floor and then to the attic office.

While Max didn't believe the man should be in the house—he had damaged nothing—but he did open doors, drawers, and seemed to look for something. After going through the attic and second floor, the man returned to the first floor and headed to the parlor.

Max watched while the man rummaged through Danielle's desk. He took a small box out of one drawer, but Max couldn't see what it held. The man kept the box in his hand and walked out of the parlor and headed toward the kitchen.

The cat wondered if the man intended to leave, and if so, was he planning to keep whatever he had taken out of Danielle's desk with him? Max watched closely. The man walked into the kitchen and headed to the back door. He opened it yet did not step outside. The man took something out of the box and shoved it in the doorknob.

"Bingo!" Max heard the man say. Once again, Max did not know what that meant. Unfortunately, Max knew he would never remember the words he had heard tonight when recounting the events to Walt.

The man shut the back door and then turned and started back toward the parlor. Max wondered if the man would return whatever he had taken from Danielle's desk. Trailing behind the man, Max watched as he returned the box to Danielle's desk. Yet it looked as if he had kept something he had taken from the box.

FRANK LEFT the parlor and headed back to the kitchen. He about tripped over the black cat, who raced into the room as soon as he opened the door. Frank felt tempted to kick the stupid animal, but he didn't want the Marlows to come home to an injured pet and realize someone had been in their house. That would rather defeat the purpose of this visit, so the cat got a pass.

He took the house key he had taken from the box and tossed it on the kitchen table. Before leaving, he wanted to check the photos and videos he had taken of the house to make sure he had everything he needed. After looking through the pictures, he sent Hal a text telling him he was ready to be picked up.

Frank commended himself for asking Hal to order the gloves he wore. Not only did they prevent him from leaving fingerprints all over, but he could still use the touchscreen on his phone. He shoved his cellphone into his denim's back pocket.

He turned around to pick the key up from the kitchen table and discovered the cat had jumped up on the table and now sniffed the key.

"You supposed to be up here? I would never have a cat. Disgusting."

The cat looked up and meowed.

Sidney reached for the key, but before he could pick it up, the cat placed his front right paw over it, holding it in place.

"That's not for you." He shoved the cat to one side and tried to pick the key up again, but this time the cat not only covered it with his paw, but he also hissed.

"What the hell is wrong with you?" Abruptly, Frank pushed the cat off the table, picked up the key, and shoved it in his front pocket. With haste, he rushed to the door, went outside, and locked the door behind him. He ran to the back fence and failed to notice the cat had followed him through the pet door.

The only light came from the kitchen light the Marlows had left on, and one light coming from a downstairs window next door. Darkness blanketed the rear yard of Marlow House, making it difficult to see and impossible to see the black cat stalking him.

Frank intended to leave the yard the same way he had entered by climbing a tree. It wasn't until he was up the tree and inching his way along a branch extending over the fence toward the alley that he realized he was not alone. An animal was in the tree with him.

His intention was to hold on to the branch and lower himself down onto the alley side of the fence. But before he could do that, the animal attacked his face. Sharp claws tore into his skin, making him shriek in pain. He lost his balance and fell from the limb onto the ground below.

The demon from the tree remained perched on the branch. Frank could not see him, but he heard demonic cries. He did not know what type of animal made that sound. Frank scrambled to his feet, relieved he had broken nothing, and raced to the van that had just pulled up.

TWENTY-THREE

W alt drove the Packard up the driveway, stopped, pressed the remote for the automatic garage door opener, and waited for the door to open all the way. Danielle sat next to him in the passenger seat, with Laura in the back seat. While the door opened, the interior garage door light turned on.

"Thanks for letting me ride with you," Laura said as Walt pulled the Packard into the garage.

"Certainly," Danielle said. The garage door closed behind them.

"I didn't want to drive back with Lily, since they were stopping at Ian's parents' to pick up Connor."

"No reason to, since we're all going to the same place." Walt opened his car door.

"I'm surprised they didn't leave Sadie at home, since June wasn't watching Connor there. She's always so weird about dogs around little kids." Laura waited for Danielle and Walt to get out of the car before she exited.

"They often leave Sadie and Hunny over here instead of leaving them home alone," Danielle said. "We have the pet door, and they all get along well. But Chris wanted to take Hunny tonight, and both dogs behave well."

"I can't believe how both dogs stayed away from the food. There were some meatballs sitting on a low table, and Sadie walked right by them. Oh, she looked lovingly at them, but she didn't even try to sniff them," Laura said.

"They both understood if they behaved, they'd be going home with new chew toys and bones," Walt said. They were now out of the Packard and walking toward the door leading to the backyard.

Laura laughed. "And how did they know that?"

"I told them," Walt said without a hint of jest.

"You crack me up. You told them." Still laughing, Laura led the way through the doorway to the backyard while Walt and Danielle followed behind her. The pair exchanged smiles behind Laura's back while Walt flipped off the garage light and closed and locked the door behind him.

The three walked across the dark backyard toward the house. The glow from the kitchen window led the way.

"Good thing I left that light on," Danielle said. "It's dark tonight."

"I have to say, Chris and Heather can throw a party," Laura said. She and Danielle now stood by the back door, waiting for Walt to unlock it.

"I always say the key to a successful party is good food," Danielle said.

"I'll be honest; I had a lot more fun tonight than I expected," Laura said. She followed Walt and Danielle into the house. When they stepped inside, Max greeted them. He sat on one of the kitchen chairs not pushed under the table and meowed at them.

"Well, I'm going to go to my room. Goodnight. And thanks again for driving me! It was fun."

"Goodnight, Laura," Danielle called after her. When Laura exited the kitchen, Danielle looked at Walt, who hadn't told Laura a final goodnight. Instead, he stood silently, staring at Max, who stared back at him.

"What's going on?" Danielle asked.

Walt looked at Danielle and said in a low voice, "Max tells me someone broke into the house tonight."

Danielle's eyes widened. "What?"

Walt nodded. "Max said he looked around and left. But he took something out of the parlor desk with him. Not sure what it was, but by Max's description, I suspect it was a key."

"How did he get in here?" Danielle looked to the back door. "The pet door? We keep putting off doing something about that."

"No, not the pet door. From how Max described it, I suspect he picked the lock."

"He just walked around the house?"

"It sounded like he took pictures of the house. At least, that's what I assume happened by the way Max described it."

"Let's see what he took." Danielle rushed out of the kitchen and headed for the parlor, Walt following behind her. Once in the parlor, Danielle opened the drawer where she kept the box of house keys. Walt silently watched as Danielle counted the keys.

"Yes, one house key is missing," Danielle said.

WALT AND DANIELLE sat in Heather's kitchen late Saturday evening. Before leaving Marlow House, they had knocked on the door of Laura's room and fabricated a story about why they needed to go to Heather's house.

Brian and Heather sat with Walt and Danielle at Heather's kitchen table. Brian was drinking a beer, and before sitting down, Heather offered Walt and Danielle something to drink. They both declined.

"So a guy picks your lock, takes a bunch of pictures inside your house, and all he takes with him is a house key. That's what he steals?" Brian said.

"Why does he need to break in to steal a house key if he knows how to pick the lock?" Heather asked.

Brian looked at Heather. "Exactly what I was wondering."

"Was Max able to describe him?" Heather asked.

Walt shrugged. "As best as a cat can."

Brian groaned, leaned back in the chair, and took a chug of beer.

Danielle leaned over to Brian and patted his arm. "Aren't you glad you're part of the secret club?"

Walt chuckled and said, "According to Max, our burglar was probably a man because of the fur on his face."

"Fur?" Brian asked.

Walt shrugged. "Max is a cat. When a man has a beard, he sees it as fur."

"It obviously wasn't someone Max had seen before," Heather said.

"I'm not sure about that," Walt said.

"What do you mean?" Brian asked.

"Max said he didn't remember seeing him before, but his voice was familiar. He's certain he's heard the voice before."

"That's creepy," Heather grumbled.

"But I know how we might find him."

"How?" Brian asked.

"Max, in his attempt to be a guard cat—"

Brian frowned. "Guard cat?"

"I told Max to keep an eye on things when we're gone. Apparently he took that to heart," Walt said.

"What exactly did he do?" Heather asked. "When you say 'in his attempt,' he obviously did something."

"When leaving, this palooka climbed a tree in the backyard to get over the fence. We've been keeping the back gate locked. Max followed him up the tree. It was dark out, and I don't think he knew Max was following him. When the guy climbed across the limb that goes over the fence, Max attacked."

"Attacked? Attacked how?" Heather asked.

"It sounds like Max vigorously used the guy's face as a scratching post. The palooka was holding onto the branch so he wouldn't fall while trying to get Max away from him. I don't think he was successful in either endeavor. According to Max, he ended up falling out of the tree. I don't think he broke anything because

Max saw him get up and then run toward the alley. Some sort of vehicle stopped, picked him up and drove off."

"Scratched up his face?" Heather cringed. "Cat scratches are nothing to screw with."

"He shouldn't have messed with our guard cat," Danielle said.

"While I can be on the lookout for a guy with a scratched-up face, I can't really arrest him. On what grounds?" Brian asked. "The only witness to the break-in is… a cat."

"We understand that. But we still thought you should know," Danielle said.

"Yeah, I'm glad you told me," Brian said. "I'm not sure what I can do with this."

"Figure out why this guy broke into Marlow House?" Heather suggested.

Brian looked at Walt. "Did Max give you any indication of how old this guy was?"

Walt shook his head. "No. As far as Max knew, he could be a teenager or someone John Bartley's age."

Brian considered Walt's words for a minute and then shook his head. "Considering he didn't really steal anything and—"

"He stole a key," Heather reminded him.

Brian nodded. "Yes, but like you said, why go to all that trouble to steal a key if he can pick the lock? And when he was in the house, he took nothing. Right?"

"My laptop and iPad were both on the parlor desk, and we know he was in that desk, but he didn't touch either of them," Danielle said.

"I suspect he's a teenager," Brian said.

"He had a beard," Heather reminded him.

"Okay, perhaps an older teen or college age. But someone younger. Young enough to climb a tree to go over a fence, old enough to grow a beard. I suspect this was all some sort of prank. Sounds like he took pictures of the interior of Marlow House and then took a trophy—something he didn't think you would miss."

"Or some initiation prank? Take pictures to prove you were there?" Heather suggested.

Brian shrugged. "Perhaps. Or see if those pictures show up on social media. Like on someone's TikTok."

Danielle considered the suggestions for a moment. Finally, she said, "I suppose that might explain why they went to all the trouble to break in but didn't really take anything."

"THAT LOOKS BAD," Hal observed. He and his brother stood in the open bathroom doorway, watching Frank wash his face while inspecting the scratch marks covering his nose and forehead.

"I need you to pick up some antiseptic ointment at the store. This vodka isn't going to be enough." He splashed vodka on his face and cringed when it stung.

"What kind of animal was it?" Stuart asked.

"I don't know. I've never heard a sound like that before. It was demonic. Maybe a racoon. But I don't think they have claws like that."

"Raccoon? Damn, those things get rabies. You getting a rabies shot?" Hal asked.

Turning from the mirror, Frank frowned at Hal. "No, I'm not getting a damn rabies shot. I obviously disturbed some animal that was living in that tree, and it freaked out on me. I've never heard of any animals having rabies around here."

Hal shrugged. "Okay. I was just wondering."

"But I don't want to get infected. You need to get me something now."

"Now? There's nothing open now," Hal grumbled.

"You don't have something at home?"

Hal considered the question for a moment and then let out a sigh. "Yeah, I have some Neosporin. I'll go get it. I hope getting your face torn up and possibly getting rabies was worth going over there tonight."

"I don't have rabies."

HAL and his brother climbed into Hal's vehicle. They had left the van in the garage of the Barry house after leaving Marlow House and before driving back to Sidney's house.

"Do me a favor, google how long it takes symptoms of rabies to show up in humans," Hal told his brother as he turned on the ignition.

"He could have rabies?" Stuart asked as he pulled out his phone and googled.

"If some wild animal scratched me up like that, I wouldn't just be slapping vodka on my face." Hal steered his car from the curb and started driving down the street.

"Here it is. Symptoms. The incubation period for rabies is typically two to three months."

"Good."

"How is that good?"

"I really don't give a crap if he has rabies, but I don't want symptoms to show up before we finish this. We might want to avoid any physical contact with him, just in case."

TWENTY-FOUR

On Sunday morning, Danielle told her friends—the ones who belonged to what she termed the secret club—what Max had conveyed to Walt. She asked them to keep an eye out for a man who had been in a cat fight, who might have a beard. Since Laura was not part of that secret club, she did not receive the memo.

Like she now did every morning, Laura took Sadie for a walk, ending up at Sidney's house.

"Oh my god, what happened to your face?" Laura asked after walking up the steps of the front porch with Sadie.

"I foolishly picked up a stray cat who was on the back porch. It obviously did not want to be picked up," he lied.

Laura cringed, silently noting the inflamed scratches. "I hope you put something on that. You don't want them to get infected."

"Yes, I did. I cleaned them and put some antiseptic on them. Let's talk about something more pleasant. How was the party?"

"HOW DID YOU EXPLAIN YOUR FACE?" Hal asked later that morning.

"I told her I tried picking up a stray cat that didn't want to be picked up."

Hal snorted. "Yeah, you the animal lover."

"The good news, they have no idea I was in Marlow House."

"How do you know? Did you ask her?" Hal laughed.

"Funny. Obviously, I didn't ask her. But as chatty as she's proven to be, if they noticed anything off, or if a neighbor saw anything, she would have told me."

DURING THE NEXT WEEK, Adam and Melony dominated the attention of the Beach Drive friends. Joanne stayed busy, keeping Marlow House clean and ready for entertaining, while also helping Danielle check items off her to-do list. Since Heather had scheduled the coed shower on the weekend before the wedding, the bachelor and bachelorette parties fell on a Thursday. Both were relatively tame affairs, with Chris hosting the bachelor party at his house, while the ladies gathered at Heather's.

On Friday, only members of the wedding party, along with Walt and Danielle, attended the rehearsal at Marlow House, followed by a rehearsal dinner at an Italian restaurant, where Melony picked up the tab. Laura spent the evening across the street, at her sister's house.

Each day, including the wedding day, Laura took her morning walk with Sadie, spending more time visiting with her secret friend than walking. She asked Frank questions about London—he asked her questions about the events on Beach Drive. From Laura's perspective, she found his questions an affirmation that he sincerely cared for her as a person. Men she dated in the past never seemed to be interested in her life. Frank was full of questions, and she enjoyed providing the answers. While their visits remained purely platonic, the vibes he sent told her that when she got to London, their friendship would evolve.

"I CAN'T BELIEVE my son and the woman he married aren't coming to their son's wedding," Marie told Eva before the ceremony on Saturday. The two spirits stood at the top of the staircase in Marlow House, looking down at the first floor, where guests gathered and took seats on the chairs arranged for the occasion. "Who am I kidding? It doesn't surprise me."

Instead of wearing her typical floral sundress and straw hat, Marie wore a dress more appropriate for church—or a wedding. Eva also dressed for the occasion—had the wedding been held in the early 1900s.

"Melony seems like such a lovely young woman. I don't understand why they dislike her," Eva said. "She's a highly respected attorney. One thing they can't accuse her of is being a gold digger. After I eloped with Anthony, my father told me he was a gold digger. Of course, he was correct."

Marie let out a sigh. "Well, dear, I wasn't that wise in my choice either. My husband was a putz. Unfortunately, my son took after his father. But in my day—and yours—one did not get divorced. Fortunately, I got two grandsons out of the marriage. I adore Adam, and while my youngest grandson rarely spent time with me, he isn't a bad boy."

"*Respectable women* did not get divorced," Eva corrected. "Considering my chosen career, the outside world did not see me as respectable. I don't imagine leaving my husband tarnished my image more than it already was. Although, technically speaking, Father had my marriage annulled. But we didn't do it for respectability's sake. It was to keep Anthony's greedy hands off my family's money."

WHILE CONSIDERED A SMALL WEDDING, Adam and Melony's guest list was larger than both Danielle's and Lily's had been at their Marlow House weddings. Danielle had ordered more folding chairs to set up in the foyer, compared to what she'd needed for her and Walt's wedding. It was a tight fit, yet all guests found a seat.

Adam had grown up in Frederickport and never moved away; therefore he knew far more people locally than the grooms at the last two Marlow House weddings. Melony had also grown up in Frederickport, yet she'd lost contact with many of her old high school friends after moving and, since returning to her hometown, had not reconnected with her classmates beyond Adam.

Adam couldn't invite everyone he knew, considering the size limit of Marlow House; however, he'd invited some friends beyond his close social group, such as his assistant, Leslie; Bill Jones, who not only worked for him but had been a high school friend; and Carla the server from Pier Café. To some people's surprise, Bill and Carla came to the wedding together. Danielle wondered if it was a date, or simply two friends attending another friend's wedding.

Marie and Eva moved from their spot on the top of the staircase —where they had been watching the guests arrive—to an upstairs bedroom where the bride and maid-of-honor prepared for the wedding. When the two spirits entered the bedroom, the only other person in the room with Melony and Heather was Lily, who was busy helping Melony with her hair.

Not yet wearing her wedding dress, Melony wore just a full slip. She sat at the vanity, looking into the mirror while Lily arranged her hair. Yet it was Heather who caught both Eva's and Marie's attention when they entered the room. Neither spirit had ever seen Heather look quite like she did at this moment, wearing a feminine light pink dress, with her ebony-colored hair, a wave of curls falling about her shoulders.

"Oh my, you are absolutely lovely," Eva told Heather.

Heather flashed a smile to Eva yet said nothing, as she was the only one in the room who could see or hear the ghosts.

"I agree with Eva," Marie said. "But if I didn't know you, I'd guess you were about twelve."

Heather giggled. She had decided on minimal makeup, abandoning her penchant for the dark and dramatic. Marie had a point. She looked young. Perhaps not twelve, but a sheltered twenty.

Lily and Melony glanced at Heather. "What's so funny?" Mel asked.

"I was thinking how young I look," Heather said.

"You really do," Lily agreed.

When it came time for Melony to slip on her wedding dress, both Heather and Lily helped. The satin ecru gown, with elegant simple lines, fit Melony's trim figure perfectly. While Heather looked young, Melony looked sophisticated. A knock came at the door. The chief had arrived to walk Melony down the aisle, as he had walked Danielle down the aisle at her Marlow House wedding.

DOWNSTAIRS, Walt and Danielle had greeted the guests, directing them to their seats. Adam had arranged for Pastor Chad to officiate, since his grandmother had attended his church. Pastor Chad now stood with Chris and Adam, waiting for the bride to come down the stairs. Lily had come downstairs and now sat between Danielle and Ian, with Walt on Danielle's left. Kelly sat on her brother's right, with Joe between Kelly and Brian.

Melony had arranged for an acoustic guitarist to play for the wedding, including a requested song to replace the traditional wedding march. Joanne stood by the doorway near the kitchen, watching the ceremony about to begin. She had been spending the last hour preparing for the food that had arrived from Pearl Cove.

As the guitarist played, Heather made her way down the staircase, a bouquet of red roses in her hands. Kelly's eyes widened at the sight. She had never seen Heather look so... so... normal... and lovely. On the other side of Joe, Brian stared at his girlfriend as she continued down the staircase.

"Holy crap," Brian muttered under his breath, barely loud enough for Joe to overhear.

"What?" Joe whispered to Brian.

"Heather looks so young." Brian did not sound pleased.

HAD SHE BEEN ALIVE, tears would now stream down her face. Marie had always wanted happiness for her favorite grandson. At one time, she thought that meant him settling down with a woman and having children. She had since come to terms with the fact Adam and Melony did not want children. Heather and Eva had helped her understand. Marie knew it was more important for Adam to find his soulmate, and she believed that soulmate now stood by his side, exchanging wedding vows with him.

THROUGHOUT THE FIRST floor of Marlow House, Joanne had arranged platters of food—in the parlor, living room, and the library. Ian and Walt prepared cocktails while Joanne monitored the food and made sure clean plates and silverware were available.

"I hope you brought your ID," Brian whispered to Heather when they walked into the living room to get a drink from the bar.

"Ha ha. You haven't even said anything about my dress. What do you think?" Heather asked.

"You look… young," Brian grumbled.

Heather stopped walking and looked at Brian. She cocked her head in curiosity as she studied him. "What is wrong? You have been acting weird ever since I walked up to you after the ceremony. What, do weddings make you nervous? Are you worried I'll get wedding fever or something?"

Brian frowned at Heather. "No. It's just that. Well, it's like you're a teenager. I mean, I know you're a lot younger than me. But I'm feeling a little sleazy right now. Like a cradle robber."

Heather arched her brows. "I am not a teenager. Do you think I'm hot dressed like this? Be honest."

Brian let out a sigh. "Honestly?" Heather nodded.

"No. Not to me. Absolutely not. You remind me of a little girl dressed like that. I may have dated my share of younger women since my divorce, but I never saw them as little girls. I never saw you as a little girl."

"Lucky for you, I'm not a little girl. I suppose this means you don't want to role-play where I dress up like a Catholic schoolgirl?"

Brian looked ill. "Absolutely not!"

LAURA HAD JUST EXTENDED her congratulations to the bride and groom when Bill and Carla walked up to the group. They all stood a few feet from the makeshift bar set up in the living room.

While Carla went to tell Ian what she would like to drink, Bill told Adam, "I never thought I'd see the day you'd tie the knot. And I never thought you'd land someone as classy as Mel." The two old friends shook hands and laughed. Bill glanced over at Mel, who stood across the room, talking to a few wedding guests. He looked back at Adam and added, "But then, I remember you two were pretty good together back in high school."

"You and Adam attended high school together?" Laura asked.

"Have you met Lily's sister, Laura?" Adam asked. After brief introductions, Bill looked back at Adam and said, "Speaking of high school, guess who I saw? Stuart Kent is in town. He was with Hal."

"He's alive? I thought he was dead by now," Adam said.

Adam looked at Laura and said, "Stuart Kent is a guy we went to high school with. His older brother, Hal, was in school with Joe. Hal's sort of Bill's competition."

"Hardly," Bill scoffed.

Adam looked at Laura and said, "Back when we were in high school, they made a horror movie in town. Did you see it? It was on TV last week."

Laura shook her head. "No, but I know Walt and Danielle watched it when I was over at my sister's."

"Bill and I, and a bunch of our friends, got hired as extras. It was fun. Stuart actually ended up getting some roles in other films. But I heard he got into drugs, left acting. He ended up in construction, and I heard he about blew himself up on one of his jobs."

Hal? Sidney's Hal? Laura wondered.

TWENTY-FIVE

"Joanne worked her butt off yesterday," Danielle told Walt on Sunday morning. The two sat in the kitchen, having breakfast.

Walt raised his coffee mug to Danielle in salute. "You worked hard yourself."

Danielle grinned. "The bride and groom seemed happy with everything. I imagine Mel and Adam are already at the airport. My instructions to Adam, take lots of photos. I've never been to Jamaica."

"I hope they can relax once they get there. When they get home, they'll be busy moving into their new house," Walt said.

"Too bad you can't help them."

"Marie and I could both help. But I understand why Marie doesn't feel it's in Adam's best interest to learn about everything. Better for him and Mel to start their new life together without adding the complications of an invisible grandmother hanging around."

"She's not exactly invisible."

"She is to Adam and Mel," Walt reminded her.

"True. And I could see Adam getting a little freaked out, not knowing exactly when his grandmother was in the room. It's funny, when our loved ones die and we say they are still looking after us, it doesn't really creep us out. At least, it never did for me. And after what we've learned since meeting Finn Walsh, I understand our parents really are watching over us. But it's a little different from Marie, since we can't see them, and they can't interact like Marie can; it's more abstract. But they are still there."

"Yet Marie, especially if Adam understood we can see her, and if she proved her existence by moving things with her energy, it would seem more intrusive," Walt said.

Danielle nodded. "Exactly. Too real. Maybe one reason people don't get weirded out imagining their loved ones who passed are looking over them is because they don't completely believe it. It is more the possibility than the absolute."

"And when Marie makes her presence known, it's rather absolute." They both chuckled.

"After breakfast, you should probably start packing. In case there's something we need to throw in the wash," Danielle suggested.

"I wish you were going with me."

"I do too. But this is a wonderful opportunity for your career, and you and Ian will have fun. I'm glad you guys can do this. And after the babies are born, you and I can go to New York together. We're lucky. There are several babysitters we trust enough to leave our children with."

Walt laughed.

Danielle frowned. "What's so funny?"

"You say that now. But I wonder, after the babies are born, how willing you will be to leave them with a sitter while we jet off to New York. Even if you trust them."

Danielle let out a sigh. "You have a point."

"I DON'T THINK you need to worry about Adam anymore," Laura told Frank on Sunday morning. She had just told him about the wedding. "They left on their honeymoon, and they'll be gone for a week. So even if he found out you were in town, I don't think he would call you to list your house."

Frank smiled at Laura. "That's nice to know, but Adam is not the only Realtor in town. And I must admit, I've been enjoying my stay in Frederickport. My life is hectic in London. This is the first time in years I've been able to relax and not worry about anything. And I'll be going home soon, so I would rather enjoy the time I have left. Like our morning talks."

Laura blushed. "Umm… when do you have to go back?"

"It's up in the air right now. I'll be talking to the office tomorrow afternoon and discuss when I need to be back."

Laura let out a sigh.

"But tell me, what are your plans for this week?" he asked.

"I imagine it will be a little hectic for the next couple of days. Walt and my brother-in-law drive to the airport tomorrow. So today they're getting ready for the trip. Ian's driving his car and leaving it at the airport."

"What are your plans for Tuesday?"

"It will be just me and Danielle at Marlow House. And Max. That's Danielle's cat. My sister is going to be gone all day Tuesday. They're having this charity thing at the community center, sponsored by the Glandon Foundation. It's where little kids bring their dogs. Oh, so that means I won't be bringing Sadie with me on my walk Tuesday morning." Laura glanced down at Sadie, who sat by her side.

"You're not going with your sister?"

Laura shook her head. "No. After my walk, I'm staying at home with Danielle. Walt made me promise. She doesn't know that he made me promise." Laura chuckled. "He's very protective of Danielle. But Lily had already committed to this thing. She and Ian were planning to take Connor and Sadie before he found out about the New York trip. But Heather and Chris will be there with Lily. And I think Ian's parents are going too. It's an all-day thing."

"So you two will be all alone on Tuesday?" he asked.

"Pretty much. And my friend Kelly, the only person other than my sister or Danielle I might hang out with, she and her fiancé are driving to Astoria on Tuesday to meet with a jeweler. They're having her engagement ring reset."

"IT'S GOING DOWN ON TUESDAY," Frank announced when Hal arrived at his house on Sunday afternoon. He then recounted all that Laura had told him that morning.

"Dang. I have to give you credit. You were right about this Bartley woman. Talk about having someone on the inside." Hal laughed.

"There is one downside."

Hal groaned. "What?"

"It's a full moon. And it'll be up until sunrise."

"Crap."

"Fortunately, the weather report is calling for heavy overcast. Lots of clouds, rain. So if we hit before sunrise, the moon shouldn't be a problem. We need to be there at three a.m. Everyone should be asleep. We get in and out. We get Laura first, she's on the first floor, and then Marlow. I know where her bedroom is. Get them both in the van and then go to the Barry house."

"You still don't think we should get rid of Marlow? After all, we're getting rid of the other one."

Frank shook his head. "No. She's our insurance. If she doesn't follow our instructions and calls her buddy the police chief, they won't grab us when we pick up the loot. They're going to follow us to see if we lead them to Laura. But if we try offing Marlow after she brings us the loot, they'll swarm us before we get away."

Hal let out a sigh. "I guess you're right. If Marlow doesn't follow our instructions, we have a better chance of getting away if she's still alive."

ON MONDAY MORNING, Danielle stood in front of Marlow House, waving goodbye to Walt as he drove off with Ian. Lily stood on the other side of the street with Connor as she waved at the car. After the vehicle drove out of sight, Lily called to Danielle, "Well, it's just you and me again, Dani."

Danielle pointed to Connor, who stood by Lily's side, holding her hand. "And him."

"And my sister." Lily grinned. "Want to go to Pier Café for breakfast?"

"You sure you can handle the smell?" Danielle yelled back.

"I feel pretty good this morning. Let's live dangerously!"

"LILY, it's been ages since you've been in here," Carla said as she filled Danielle's and Lily's water glasses after they sat down in a booth. Connor sat next to Lily in a booster seat. "How are you? I saw you at the wedding, but we really didn't get a chance to talk. Ian told me you haven't been coming into the diner because of the morning sickness."

"I'm a lot better now." Lily handed Connor a cracker.

"Glad to hear it." Carla looked at Danielle. "Adam and Melony's wedding was sure nice. That was really sweet of you to do that for Adam."

"I was close to his grandma. I think she would have liked it," Danielle said.

"I have to admit, I never thought in a million years Adam would settle down. And certainly not with someone like Melony Carmichael. But Mel seems to bring out the best in Adam. To be honest, he used to be a jerk sometimes. Oh, don't get me wrong. I thought of him as a friend. But he could be... well, kinda..." Carla shrugged.

"Yeah, I get it." Danielle grinned.

"I suppose you don't want coffee?" Carla asked.

"Umm... no coffee." Danielle picked up two menus and handed one to Lily.

171

AFTER CARLA PUT in Lily and Danielle's order, she returned to their booth. Without asking permission, she sat next to Danielle, who immediately scooted down on the bench seat to give her more room.

"Where is your sister?" Carla asked Lily.

"Laura? She's been taking Sadie for a walk every morning. She might be back by now, I'm not sure."

Carla grinned. "So she hasn't told you about the guy she's been hanging out with?"

"Guy? What guy?" Lily handed Connor another cracker.

"Do you know Fred Stein? Lives over on the cul-de-sac a few blocks from here."

Lily shook her head. "No, I don't."

"He was telling me about this neighbor of his. Inherited his uncle's house down the street from him. This guy, the nephew who inherited the house, had never been in Frederickport before. He's from London. Well, he showed up a week or so ago and is staying in his house. Doesn't really know anyone in town aside from the guy who takes care of the house when he's gone."

Carla took a breath, and Danielle and Lily exchanged quick glances.

"Despite this guy being new in town and going nowhere—he doesn't even have a car—and not knowing anyone, this attractive young woman has been visiting him every day. She's a little blonde, and she comes every morning, walking her golden retriever. But instead of walking, she sits with this guy on his front porch every morning, drinking coffee." Carla looked at Lily. "The dog sounds like your dog. It's your sister. Isn't it?"

"Umm… well, if it is, she's said nothing to me about it." Momentarily distracted by her son, Lily reached for Connor, who had just climbed out of his booster seat after finishing his cracker. He hugged his mother.

"Really? She hasn't told you?"

Still holding onto Connor, who stood next to her on the bench seat, Lily shook her head.

"Well, I'm kind of annoyed. I mean, really. We have a shortage of available men in Frederickport, and one comes in from London, and your sister barely gets here, and she scoops him up!" Carla laughed. "Dang, I need to start walking in the mornings."

"What do you know about him?" Danielle asked.

"I asked Bill about it the other night. All he knows, Hal Kent takes care of his property. Ironically, the other night, Adam and Bill started talking about Hal's brother. Laura was there, and I could tell by her expression she kind of perked up when they mentioned his name. I have a feeling she's met Hal when she goes over there. According to Fred, Hal stops over there a lot."

"What about the brother?" Lily asked.

"From what Bill told me later, he's sort of schizo. I know Hal, but I've never met the brother. He attended school with Bill and Adam. Hal went to school with Joe. Bill told me the brother was an actor for a while, but then got into drugs. Screwed up his career. He ended up in construction. Not building houses, but the kind that involves blowing up crap. He enjoys blowing stuff up."

TWENTY-SIX

Monday evening, Laura borrowed her sister's car and drove to Old Salts Bakery to pick up turkey sandwiches for dinner. Before coming to Oregon, Laura had sold her car because she wouldn't be taking it to Europe with her when she left next month. When she returned to Lily's house, she found Lily and Danielle in the living room with Connor.

Instead of putting Connor in a highchair, Lily had brought his plastic play table and chair out from his bedroom and let him sit at that while they ate dinner. Sadie lay by Connor's side, waiting for him to drop food on the floor.

Danielle and Lily sat on the sofa, while Laura sat across from them in the recliner. Each had a sandwich. While Lily peeked in her sandwich to make sure they hadn't added an ingredient that might make her gag, she glanced up at her sister and said in a sweet voice, "Umm... Dani and I ate breakfast at Pier Café when you were walking this morning."

Laura looked up from her sandwich. "The smell didn't bother you?"

Lily shook her head. "No. But Carla told us something inter-

174

esting while we were there." Danielle silently glanced over at Lily and smiled.

"Yeah, what?" Laura asked.

"There is this guy who lives a couple of blocks from here on a cul-de-sac. He inherited the house from his uncle. He lives in London, but he's here visiting. He doesn't really know anyone in town, according to Carla. But apparently, he's made friends with an attractive blonde. She walks over to his house every morning. They sit on the porch together. Have coffee. She has a golden retriever." Lily smiled sweetly.

Laura groaned. "What is it about these small towns? Obviously, Carla has rightfully earned her reputation as a gossip."

"Why didn't you tell me? Why the secret?"

Laura set her sandwich on the napkin sitting on her lap.

"He asked me not to."

Lily frowned. "That's a red flag."

Laura sighed. "No. It's not anything like that. And he has been a perfect gentleman. He didn't want Adam Nichols to know he was in town. Of course, now that Adam is on his honeymoon, that's not really an issue anymore."

"I don't understand," Lily said. Laura told Lily Frank's reasoning for wanting to keep his visit a secret.

"Sounds like his neighbor didn't take a vow of silence," Lily snarked.

"Are you mad at me?" Laura asked.

"I'm a little hurt." Lily paused a moment before asking, "Did you tell Kelly?"

Laura flashed her sister a sheepish expression, picked up her sandwich and took a quick bite.

"You did!" Lily burst out.

Fifteen minutes later, when Laura left the room to use the bathroom, Lily looked at Danielle and said, "I suppose this is payback."

Danielle frowned. "What do you mean?"

Lily shrugged. "Laura told me how she gets jealous of you. I know Kelly gets jealous of me because she doesn't feel as close to her brother because of me. So…"

LAURA AND DANIELLE watched a movie with Lily after they put Connor to bed. When the movie ended, Laura and Danielle walked back to Marlow House in the moonlight. Max greeted Danielle when she and Laura walked into the house. After locking the front door, Danielle picked up the cat, gave him a snuggle, and said goodnight to Laura before making sure she had locked the kitchen door. Before reaching the kitchen, Danielle set Max on the floor. Max followed Danielle into the kitchen, back into the hall, and up the stairs to her bedroom. Meanwhile, Laura was already in her room, preparing to go to bed.

After taking a shower, Danielle climbed into bed. Max curled up beside her, and they both fell asleep. Several hours later, Max woke up and decided it was time to patrol the house. For several hours, he wandered the first and second floors of Marlow House. Eventually he made it up to the office attic, where he jumped up on the windowsill and gazed out at the moonlit night. Eventually, he fell asleep.

TUESDAY, at three a.m. silence blanketed Beach Drive, as did the cloud covering overhead, obscuring the full moon. The white van pulled up the alley and parked behind Marlow House. There would be no tree climbing. They had brought bolt cutters to open the back gate. Three dark figures emerged from the van. Dressed in black, they each wore a ski mask covering their faces. One carried a cloth bag holding their supplies, while another carried a large, wheeled briefcase.

Moving swiftly and silently, they made their way to the gate, quickly opening it with the tool they had brought. Once inside Marlow House's backyard, they ran to the back door. Moments later, they were inside, closing the door behind them, careful not to make a sound.

LAURA HAD JUST RETURNED to her bed after waking up and visiting the bathroom. She snuggled down into the blankets, her back to the door, and closed her eyes and prepared to fall back to sleep. Laura's eyes flew open at the sound of her doorknob turning, followed by the door slowly opening. Had Danielle come downstairs to check on her?

The sound of footsteps entered her room. They weren't loud, but she strained to listen. Had someone broken into the house? If she feigned sleep, perhaps they would take what they wanted and leave without hurting her. Whoever it was, they came closer.

No longer able to stay still, Laura turned quickly, preparing to battle whoever had breached her sanctuary, when she found three enormous figures looming over her. Before she could release her scream, hands grabbed her while other hands covered her mouth with duct tape, preventing the scream from leaving her body.

Hands moved over her, yet not in any prurient manner, but more like an efficient cowboy roping a calf. Before she knew what happened, she found her ankles tied together and her wrists plastered against her body, held in place by tightly bound ropes. The intruders lifted her off the bed for a moment and then set her back on the mattress. She didn't see them remove the bedspread from the bed when they had lifted her up, nor when they laid it out on the floor after they had set her back down. Hands effortlessly lifted her wiggling body from the bed a second time, but instead of putting her back on the mattress, they placed her on the edge of the bedspread they had placed on the floor. Once on the bedspread, they rolled her up like a human burrito.

Laura thought she might suffocate. Not only did the duct tape cover her mouth, the bedspread covered her nose. Jerking her head back, she rolled her head around, attempting to push back on the bedspread, giving her room to breathe.

Through it all, the intruders had not uttered a single word. She felt them securing more ropes around her, this time to keep the bedspread in place. When they finished, they lifted her and carried her into the entry hall, where they deposited her on the floor. She heard their footsteps moving away from her and then up the stairs. *They are going for Danielle*, she thought.

WHEN THEY REACHED Danielle's bedroom, they found her door slightly ajar. With great care, they eased the door open. They could hear gentle snoring coming from the bed. They already had the duct tape ready when they reached her side. Unlike Laura, Danielle slept on her back, her mouth in full view, making their task easier.

Two men prepared to secure her while the third applied the duct tape. They were grateful for the night-lights strategically positioned around Marlow House, making it unnecessary to use the flashlight they had brought. While moonlight might have helped illuminate the interior, the cloud cover and window shades prevented most of the moonlight from making its way into the house. They were also grateful neither bedroom door was locked, which would have required them to pick the locks, giving one of their victims a chance to wake up and use their cellphone to call for help.

Since Danielle had been in a deep sleep when duct tape covered her mouth as hands grabbed her, she jerked frantically in confusion. Yet her efforts could not prevent the inevitable, and like they had done to Laura, they did to her.

After carrying Danielle downstairs, one man slung her over his shoulder, while the other two men picked up Laura. The three intruders left the house with one carrying the cloth bag with their remaining supplies, and the other two men each carrying a hostage over a shoulder. The man with the cloth bag opened the doors for his accomplices.

Had Olivia next door been awake—which she wasn't—and had she looked out her bedroom window—she hadn't—she would have seen three shadowy figures making their way across Marlow House's side yard, from the kitchen door to the back gate. Two of the figures looked as if they each carried a roll of carpet.

MAX WOKE ABRUPTLY. He looked out the attic window at the dark night. Hints of moonlight broke through the cloud cover. He leapt down from the windowsill and ran across the wood floor toward the open doorway and then made his way down the stairs to Danielle's room. Once in the bedroom, he jumped up onto the mattress. Danielle was not there. He noticed the bedding seemed to be in odd disarray.

Leaping from the bed, Max raced to find Danielle. But she wasn't in the bathroom or in any room on the second floor. He went downstairs and found Laura's door wide open. After investigating Laura's room, he found her missing, too.

Max explored every room on the first floor. When he could not find either Danielle or Laura, he checked outside. As he exited out the pet door to the side yard, he heard the back gate closing.

Max raced toward the gate. By the time he reached the fence, the gate had closed all the way. Without thought, he climbed the closest tree along the fence, making his way up to a branch beyond the top of the fence. Max sat on the branch and looked toward the alley. He saw a vehicle parked next to the garage. Three dark figures moved toward it. Two of them each carried a long cylinder-shaped object. Max watched as one figure opened the back door of the vehicle and then helped one of the other humans load whatever he had been carrying into the back. Those two humans then helped the third load whatever he was holding into the back of the vehicle. Just as they did, Max noticed the long object move.

Was someone inside there? Just as that thought came to Max, one human climbed into the back of the vehicle while another slammed the door shut. The remaining two figures ran to the front of the vehicle, each opening a door on either side and climbing in.

The moment Max realized the someones wrapped inside those objects could be Danielle and Laura, he let out an unholy cry and leapt off the fence. The vehicle drove off, with Max running behind it.

Max tried to keep up, but after three blocks, he lost sight of the vehicle. Max sat down on the side of the road, lifted his face to the moon, and wailed an eerily high-pitched call.

TWENTY-SEVEN

While Danielle did not know where she was, she was fairly confident she hadn't left Frederickport, considering she didn't think they had been in the vehicle for over fifteen minutes. After her abductors unrolled her from the bedspread, she found herself on the floor of a room she had never been in before. The desire to breathe took precedence over a demand for answers. With duct tape covering her mouth, she could only breathe through her nostrils, yet that had been almost impossible rolled in the bedspread. She breathed deeply and looked around at her surroundings.

Three ominous figures stood in the room with her. Dressed all in black, and their faces covered by knit ski masks, she guessed they were men, judging by their body types. Two were much taller than the third figure, with football-player physiques. She guessed one of them had carried her, not the smaller one.

The three moved to the far wall and huddled there, whispering. She could barely hear their voices and couldn't understand what they said. Still lying on the floor, she looked up. Overhead, vintage ceiling tiles covered the ceiling with a gaudy crystal chandelier hanging from its center. It was the type of lamp she imagined someone wanting to convey the impression of class might purchase yet was perceived by those who society deemed classy as a tacky fixture.

Movement from another corner of the room caught her attention. Danielle turned her head and saw Laura tied to a chair, struggling to get free. She knew it was Laura even though she couldn't see her face. She wore the same pajamas Danielle had seen Laura wear, but duct tape covered her mouth, and a red scarf served as a blindfold, covering the top half of her face.

Trying to process the terrifying situation, Danielle studied her surroundings, trying to make sense of what was happening to them. She wasn't only worried about her and Laura's safety; she worried about her unborn son and daughter.

The shorter man pointed at her and then at a nearby chair. The two larger men moved to Danielle. She held her breath, not knowing what to expect. The next moment, they grabbed her, jerked her to her feet, and roughly sat her in the chair. She sat frozen as they tied her as they had Laura. After securing her to the chair, one slowly peeled off the duct tape.

Danielle silently licked her lips and was grateful they hadn't ripped the duct tape from her face. What she didn't know, the gentle removal had nothing to do with minimizing her pain. They simply did not want to leave marks on her face and raise questions when they sent her off to do their bidding.

"Why are we here?" Danielle asked.

The shorter man walked to her chair and stopped three feet from her. He reached into his pocket, pulled out a small recording device, and turned it on.

"Danielle Marlow," the voice on the recording device said. Someone had obviously altered it to conceal the person's identity. Which made her wonder, did she know her abductors?

"Listen carefully to what I have to say if you and your friend wish to return home unharmed."

Danielle quietly listened to the words while her gaze darted around the room, eyeing each one of her abductors who focused their attention on her. "In a few hours, we will return you to Marlow House, and you will be put in the garage. You will be blindfolded.

When we leave you, count to one hundred before you remove the blindfold. If you want your friend to be returned safely, you will do exactly what we say."

Danielle silently listened while Laura, on the other side of the room, shifted in her chair.

"You will go into your house, get dressed. Answer your landline if it rings. But remember, we are listening. Don't bother looking for your cellphone. You won't find it. In your bedroom, you will find a large briefcase on wheels. You're to take it to the bank. Remove the Missing Thorndike and gold coins from your safe-deposit box. Put them in the briefcase. It will make it easier for you to carry them out of the bank."

Gee, thanks, Danielle thought to herself. *How considerate of you.*

"Do not tell anyone at the bank what you're removing from your safe-deposit box."

You don't think they'll notice I have a freaking briefcase with me? Danielle silently asked.

"Drive to the north exit out of Frederickport, pull into the gas station. Park by the trees on the north side of the parking lot. Do not lock your trunk. Go to the bathroom and stay there for fifteen minutes. When you come back, go home."

I assume someone is taking the briefcase out of my car at the gas station, Danielle thought.

"When you get home, wait for our call. We will call you within forty-eight hours, after we have safely left the country. We will tell you then where you can find your friend. If we don't call, that means they have captured us. In that case, your friend is screwed. There is a bomb in this house, and it will go off in forty-eight hours after we leave. And you need to know there are more than three of us. The others will be watching you." The recording stopped.

"A bomb?" Danielle squeaked.

In response, the shorter man pointed to the two men and then to a table on the other side of the room. The two men walked over to Danielle and picked her up—chair and all—and carried her to the table. Still tied to the chair, Danielle found herself lifted, allowing her a view into a box sitting on the table. Her eyes widened. It looked like a bomb.

THE SUN WAS COMING UP. Max had wandered the streets for hours. But he hadn't been able to find the vehicle he had seen leaving Marlow House. He headed home. When he finally reached the back alley behind Marlow House, he saw Heather walking to her car. He wanted to ask her for help, but he knew she wouldn't be able to understand him. Then he remembered someone who could help him, Marie.

Before leaving on this trip, Walt had sat down with Max and told him he and Ian were leaving for a week on business. Danielle and Laura would be home alone. He told Max that Marie would stay with Lily to help with Connor since Lily had been getting sick on and off now that she was having another baby.

Max checked the house one more time before going across the street to find Marie. Maybe Danielle and Laura had returned while he had been off looking for them. Twenty minutes later, after going through all the rooms in Marlow House, Max once again exited through the pet door, and this time headed across the street.

MARIE SAT in the rocking chair, watching Connor run around in his diaper while trying to catch the plastic pterodactyl currently circling his bedroom. Chuckling to herself, Marie thought how young mothers would have it so much easier if they had her and Walt's powers to move things without ever having to get up.

Connor had already eaten breakfast, and Lily had brought him back to the bedroom to play with Marie while she showered and got dressed for the day. If Marie knew what Lily wanted Connor to wear, she would dress him, but Lily had failed to mention what she planned to dress her son in for the charity event.

The sound of tapping from the window broke her train of

thought. She looked to the window and saw little black paws repeatedly beating on the glass. Marie frowned. "Max? What is wrong?"

With her attention diverted to the window, the pterodactyl made a crash landing, falling to the floor. Connor picked up the toy dinosaur and handed it toward Marie.

"Just a minute, dear," Marie said before disappearing and moving from inside the room to outside, standing on the other side of the window with Max. Curious, Connor toddled to the window, dinosaur toy still in hand. Now standing at the window, looking outside, Connor dropped the toy and cupped his hands around his eyes as if they were makeshift binoculars, and pressed his face against the glass.

"What are you doing over there?" Lily asked her son when she came into the room a moment later. She walked to the window and looked outside. "Oh, it's Max." She waved at the cat and then turned back to Connor.

"We need to get you dressed. Your grandma is picking us up soon. Remember, we're having fun today with Sadie and Hunny and lots of other doggies and kids." She glanced around the room. "Marie, are you here?" Silence. Lily looked back at the window. Max was gone.

Lily walked over to Connor's dresser to pick out his clothes. Just as she was about to call Connor over to her, the dry-erase pen from the nearby board lifted into the air. The next moment it wrote on the dry-erase board: *I have to leave. M.*

Lily read the words and shrugged. "I guess Marie doesn't want to go with us today."

MARIE HAD TOLD Max to go back to Marlow House and wait for her there while she went to find Eva. When the two spirits arrived at Marlow House, they found Max sitting in the middle of the entry hall.

Eva looked down at the black cat. "Max, dear, Marie has told me everything."

185

Max meowed pitifully.

"Yes, Max, we are getting help, but first we need to check out the house, see what we can find," Marie told him.

"Are you sure you don't want to go directly to Chris and Heather?" Eva asked Marie. "Heather can call Brian, get the police immediately involved."

Marie shook her head. "Before we go to them, let's look around and see if there are any clues. My fear of going to them right now is the chaos that might ensue. For one thing, I don't want the police to swarm Marlow House. What happens if the kidnappers have someone watching and then they get spooked and decide to cut their losses and hurt Danielle and Laura? And Lily is with Heather and Chris. I don't want her to panic about her sister and Danielle, not in her condition."

"Let's start in their bedrooms," Eva suggested.

The next moment, the two ghosts stood in Laura's bedroom. As they looked around the room, Max joined them. He meowed.

Eva looked at the bed. "It looks like someone was sleeping there."

"It's missing its bedspread," Marie noted.

Eva frowned at the bed. "Hmm, you're right."

"Max, we're going upstairs. You can meet us in Danielle's bedroom," Marie told the cat.

The next moment, the ghosts vanished, and Max ran from the bedroom and headed upstairs.

"I know Danielle always makes her bed," Marie said when she saw the unmade bed.

"Danielle obviously went to bed last night," Eva said.

Marie glanced around the room. "Her bedspread is also missing."

Eva pointed to the large briefcase sitting in the middle of the room. "Why do you think that's there?"

Marie looked at the briefcase and shrugged. "I've never seen that before. Perhaps Walt bought it and planned to take it on his trip but decided not to take it."

"But why would he leave it in the middle of the room like that?" Eva asked.

The sound of footsteps running up the staircase made them all freeze.

"Someone's here!" Marie whispered.

They all turned to the open doorway, preparing to move to the hallway, when the person doing the running suddenly burst into the room.

"Danielle!" Eva and Marie called out at the same time.

Danielle, wearing her pajamas and no shoes, stopped abruptly and looked at the two spirits.

Max let out a meow, ran to Danielle, and began rubbing against her ankles.

Danielle burst into tears.

TWENTY-EIGHT

D anielle sat on her bed, with Marie and Eva sitting on either side of her, and Max curled up on her lap. She had just told them all that had happened since the strangers had woken her up during the night.

"You can't imagine how relieved I am that you're both here," Danielle said. "I wasn't sure how I could get you to come over here."

"You knew I was across the street," Marie reminded her.

"I assumed you would be with Lily at the community center," Danielle said. "And even if Lily hadn't left yet, I couldn't risk going over there to get you. They said people would be watching me. They could be bluffing, but I can't risk it. I'm supposed to go to the bank and then return to Marlow House and not leave."

"And you have no idea who they might be?" Eva asked.

Danielle shook her head. "No. Like I said, they wore ski masks. I never even heard them talk. Just that creepy recording they played." Danielle glanced at the clock on her nightstand. "The bank is going to open soon, and I have to get dressed and get down there. If they think I'm not following their instructions, they'll hurt Laura."

"We'll go with you, of course," Marie said. "Do you want to call Edward?"

Danielle shook her head. "They claimed—sort of—that they bugged my phone. Anyway, it might be safer right now if the three of us handle this."

The landline rang. Danielle froze momentarily and looked at the phone. "They told me to answer the phone." She took a deep breath, stood, and walked to the nightstand.

Danielle picked up the receiver. "Hello?"

"Danielle! I've been calling your cellphone for the last thirty minutes. I was getting worried. You didn't even answer my text."

"Hi, Walt." Danielle glanced at Marie and Eva and cringed. "I'm sorry. But I've been looking all over for my cellphone," Danielle lied. "I forgot to plug it in, so it's dead, and I can't find it."

"As long as you're okay. I wish you could have come with me."

"I do too." *You have no idea how much I wish I were with you right now,* Danielle thought to herself.

"I just wanted to tell you I love you before we go to our first meeting. I won't be able to call you until tonight."

"I love you, Walt."

"I love you too. But I have to go."

"What's the plan?" Marie asked when Danielle got off the phone with Walt.

"First, I'm getting dressed." Danielle walked to her closet.

"They didn't give you a specific time when they want you to be at the gas station?" Marie asked.

Danielle shook her head. "No. I assume someone's watching—following me."

"After you deliver the ransom, I should stay with it, watch it," Eva said. "Marie will need to stay with you and keep you safe."

"We need to find out where they're holding Laura." Danielle pulled clothes from her closet and tossed them on her bed.

"You don't have any idea where they kept you?" Marie asked.

"They wrapped me in that damn bedspread, and I couldn't see anything. Before we left to come back here, they blindfolded me. I don't even know what kind of vehicle I was in, but I suspect it was something like a van, station wagon, or maybe even the back of a truck with a camper shell."

"Hopefully, after they take the ransom, they'll go to wherever they have Laura," Eva said.

About to change out of her pajamas, Danielle paused a moment and looked at Eva. "Maybe we do need to let someone know what's going on. Eva, can you go to the community center and find Chris or Heather? Tell them everything I've told you and have them contact the chief so he can be prepared. But tell them, do nothing until they hear from us. I don't want to do anything to jeopardize Laura. And whatever they do, don't let Lily know what's going on. She doesn't need that stress right now, not while she's pregnant."

"Honey, you are pregnant, too," Marie gently reminded her.

Danielle shrugged. "Yeah. But no reason to put Lily through this stress. I want Lily to find out what's going on after we have Laura safely with us."

DANIELLE SAT at the kitchen table with Marie, watching the clock. The bank didn't open until ten on Tuesdays. She had already dressed and only ate something because Marie had insisted.

"It's going to be alright. We will find Laura," Marie promised.

"I wish I knew where they took me."

Snowflakes fell from the ceiling. Marie and Danielle looked up. The next moment, the snowflakes vanished, and Eva materialized.

"I've talked to Chris, but Heather hasn't been told what happened," Eva told them. "Chris and I agreed it would be best if Heather spend the day with Lily without the burden of knowing. There really is no reason for her to get involved right now. Chris made an excuse that he had to make a quick business call, and he called the chief."

"Thank you, Eva." Danielle stood.

WHILE DANIELLE WAS WORRIED about Laura, she also felt grateful Marie and Eva were with her. She drove to the bank with Marie in the passenger seat and Eva in the back seat, who leaned forward between the two front seats while she talked to Danielle and Marie.

"Even if they don't return to wherever they took you, I'm sure they will say something that will lead us to where they have Laura," Eva said.

"The fact they kept Laura blindfolded makes me feel a little better," Danielle said. "If they were planning to kill her, why bother blindfolding her?"

What Danielle didn't expect to see when she pulled up to the bank was the police car parked in front of it. No one was in the vehicle. Danielle parked her car and sat there for a moment.

"The police are here," Danielle grumbled.

"It's okay," Marie cooed. "Police go to the bank, too."

Danielle took a deep breath and unfastened her seatbelt.

A few minutes later, Danielle walked into the bank. She paused a moment inside the doorway and glanced around. It was busy, with lines at all the tellers. She took a few more steps into the bank and then halted when she spied Brian Henderson standing at one teller. It looked like he was cashing a check. She could hear him thank the teller before turning around. A few moments later, as he walked away from the teller while shoving bills into his wallet, he looked up and smiled at Danielle.

"Morning, Danielle."

Danielle smiled weakly. "Umm… morning, Brian."

"Hey, I ran into an old friend of yours, Eva. I can't remember her last name. She told me to tell you hi when I see you."

Danielle's eyes widened. "Really?"

Brian gave Danielle a smile and a nod. "Yeah. She told me to tell you everything was good with her."

"Oh…"

"Have a wonderful day, Danielle."

Eva chuckled. "I see the chief has sent someone to monitor the situation."

DANIELLE STOOD at the desk of Susan Mitchell, preparing to go back to her safe-deposit box. Susan eyed the large, rolling briefcase at Danielle's side.

"I have some papers I need to get out of my safe-deposit box," Danielle said, speaking a little louder than normal. She nodded to the briefcase and added, "I didn't want to leave this in my car."

Danielle wasn't sure if Susan believed her response to the unspoken inquiry.

DANIELLE'S KIDNAPPERS obviously did not consider—nor care —how difficult it would be for a pregnant woman to lift the brief-case into the back of her car after filling it with the gold coins. While it had been relatively easy to push it along after leaving the bank, lifting it would be far more difficult. Fortunately, she had Marie with her. If anyone watching her saw her lifting the briefcase into the back of the Ford Flex, they would assume it wasn't heavy. Yet it was actually Marie's energy doing the heavy lifting.

As Danielle opened the driver's side door of her car, she glanced around. Brian's police car was no longer parked in front of the bank but was now parked across the street at Lucy's Diner. Glancing up to the diner, she spied Brian sitting inside at a window side booth, looking out while drinking coffee.

Turning back to her car, Danielle climbed into her vehicle and prepared for the drop-off.

"A WHITE VAN has been following us for a while," Eva announced. "I saw it parked by the museum, and it pulled out into the street after we drove by. It let a car pass, and when that car turned down another street, it let another car pass and stays two cars behind us."

"I think you should check it out," Marie said.

"Be right back." Eva vanished.

"KEEP an eye out for any cop cars," the driver of the white van told the man in the passenger seat. "So far she's doing exactly what we told her to do."

"I about died when Henderson walked into the bank," the passenger said.

Eva took a closer look at the passenger and realized she had seen him in the bank when they had first walked in.

"But then I realized he was cashing a check, so I took a deep breath and made my withdrawal."

"Did they wonder why you were practically cleaning out your account?" the driver asked.

The passenger shrugged. "If they did, they said nothing."

"Henderson went across the street to the diner. I didn't know they had donuts at Lucy's."

Both men laughed.

Eva returned to Danielle's car.

"It's them. One of them was in the bank when we were there," Eva said. "I recognized him. He said he was concerned when he first saw Brian in the bank, but then wrote it off as a coincidence after he realized he was cashing a check."

"We'll be at the gas station in a few minutes. Marie, can you quickly check the van's license plate and get that information to Brian and then come back?"

"Yes, dear." Marie vanished.

"CHRIS, WHAT IS GOING ON?" Heather asked when she cornered him alone late Tuesday morning. "What did Eva tell you? You've been acting weird ever since she was here."

"I'll explain later. I can't now. But please, let's get through this day without you asking me again. There are too many people around."

"What are you talking about?" Heather asked.

The next moment, Marie appeared. "Chris, I can only stay for a moment. Do you have something to write with?"

"Hi to you too, Marie," Heather grumbled. "What is going on?"

Chris pulled out his phone and ignored Heather.

Marie quickly recited the license plate and then asked, "Please read it back to me."

"That sounds like a license plate number," Heather muttered, looking from Marie to Chris.

"Call Edward," Marie told Chris. "It's a white van, two men. That's the license plate number. We'll be at the drop-off in a few minutes." Marie vanished.

"What is going on?" Heather demanded.

Ignoring Heather, Chris called the police chief and quickly conveyed the message. When he got off the phone, Heather stood in front of him, arms folded across her chest, as she waited for his answer. Chris glanced around the room and saw everyone seemed to be having a good time and no one was looking in their direction. He grabbed Heather by the hand. "Come on, let's go outside, and I'll tell you."

TWENTY-NINE

"Here we are," Danielle said when she parked by the trees on the north side of the gas station parking lot.

"The white van pulled up over by the market," Marie noted.

Danielle let out a sigh. "Okay, I'd better go to the restroom." Danielle and Marie got out of the car. Before heading to the restroom, Danielle double-checked to make sure she had unlocked the back hatch.

"Don't worry, I'll keep a close eye on the necklace and gold. You'll get them back," Eva said.

"I'm more concerned about getting Laura back," Danielle said.

"I understand. But we'll get all of them back safely," Eva promised.

Danielle flashed Eva a smile before turning and heading for the bathroom, with Marie by her side.

"Eva has a special interest in that necklace," Marie reminded her as they approached the public restrooms. "She hopes it will one day pass to your daughter."

Danielle glanced at Marie but said nothing because the woman who had just exited the bathroom was walking by, and she didn't want the woman to think she was talking to herself. But when they entered the bathroom and were alone, Danielle asked in a whisper, "Did she really say that?"

Marie nodded. "You know, that necklace was supposed to stay in the Thorndike family, but the line ended with Eva. The fact her parents left the necklace to Walt, she sees it as a sign that it now be passed down in the Marlow family."

"Did Eva really tell you she hopes we'd someday give the necklace to our daughter?"

"She did. She said she understood if you sold it someday, but she also admitted her secret hope is that someday Walt's eldest daughter will wear her necklace."

"Umm… eldest daughter? I have a feeling this will be our only daughter."

Marie chuckled and then said, "You stay here. I'm going to see how Eva is doing."

EVA STOOD by the Ford Flex and watched as the white van backed out of the parking space in front of the store and then drove toward Danielle's car. The man was no longer sitting in the passenger seat, and Eva assumed he had moved to the back of the van.

A moment later, the van drove by the rear of the Ford Flex and stopped. Its back door opened. The passenger jumped out of the van, opened the back hatch of Danielle's car, and grabbed the briefcase. Eva noted he wore gloves.

He slammed the hatch shut and then quickly jumped back into the van with the briefcase, struggling a bit as he did. The back door slammed shut, and the van drove off. Marie, who had been watching the scene from afar, saw Eva disappear as the van drove off.

EVA SAT in the back of the van, watching as the passenger fumbled to open the briefcase.

"Is it all there?" the driver called out.

"Hold on, I'm trying to get it open. But damn, this sucker was heavy."

"Of course, all those gold coins." The driver laughed.

"I don't know how that Marlow woman lifted this thing up and got it in the back of her car. You saw her. It was like no big deal."

"Would you just open the damn thing?"

The briefcase lid flipped open.

"Yes! It's here!" The passenger dug his fingers into the pile of gold coins, lifting them out while some slipped through his fingers. He opened his hands and let them fall back into the briefcase and then scooped up more. He laughed in glee as the gold coins scattered over the van's floor.

"What are you doing back there?" The driver glanced over his shoulder.

"We did it!" The passenger picked up the velvet case that he found sitting atop the coins. He gently opened the case and then let out an audible gasp. "Oh, it's amazing!"

"What are you doing?" The driver unhooked his seatbelt to enable him to turn in the seat, providing him a better view of the passenger.

"The Missing Thorndike. Damn, this is even more beautiful than the pictures. Shame we have to take it apart."

"You are not taking that necklace apart," Eva told deaf ears. She wished she had Marie's gift and could give the idiot a good smack.

"You need to put that all back," the driver demanded.

"I will in a minute."

"No, I mean it. Now. If we get pulled over, we don't need some nosey cop looking in the back and seeing a bunch of gold coins."

The two men started arguing, with the driver demanding his partner return the stolen items to the briefcase, while his partner told him to turn around and pay attention to the road; he would put it all back in a minute.

Annoyed at the bickering, Eva moved to the passenger seat, up front. She looked out the windshield and noted they headed toward Pilgrim's Point. As they neared the dangerous curve, she glanced over to the driver, who seemed more focused on what was going on in the back of the van than on the road ahead.

The bickering accelerated, as did the speed of the van.

"You'd better pay attention to what you're doing," Eva warned. "You're going much too fast."

But they couldn't hear Eva's warning, nor her scream the next moment when she realized they would not make the turn.

WHEN EAVESDROPPING on a conversation at Pier Café, Eva had once overheard a teenage boy trying to talk his father into letting him buy a van. The father had been against the purchase and said, "You drive a van and get in an accident, you're nothing but a pea in a whistle."

Considering how these two men bounced against the interior walls of the van, along with the loose coins, Eva had to admit the father wasn't wrong. She cringed when the velvet box, which had been closed moments before the van missed the turn, hit one van wall and flew open, sending the Missing Thorndike flying. Unwilling to witness the carnage—the potential damage to the necklace, not the men—Eva moved to the beach below the cliff, waiting for the van to arrive at its final destination.

She watched as the white van plummeted down the face of the hillside, hitting protruding rocks along the way, sending those tumbling down with the vehicle. When it finally landed on the beach, some twenty feet from the water's edge, it rocked back and forth on the sand for several minutes before growing still.

Eva hesitantly approached the van, curious to see how the men and Danielle's property had fared. The van, now settled on its side, had its windshield broken out and the back door missing. During the tumble down the hillside, the back doors had flown open before being torn off the vehicle. Standing by the rear of the van, Eva peeked inside.

She smiled when she spied the Missing Thorndike lying on a pile of gold coins, unharmed. Eva looked at the two men, wondering if they had fared as well as the necklace. When they sat up abruptly the next moment, leaving their lifeless bodies, she knew they hadn't.

"You could have gotten us killed!" the passenger yelled at the driver.

"We need to get everything back in the briefcase before the cops show up!" the driver yelled.

Still arguing, the men tried picking up the coins, yet the gold simply moved through their hands. Cursing, the driver turned and stared at his lifeless face. He reached for his partner, trying to get his attention, but just as he could not pick up the coins, he could not grab hold of the other man's arm. He screamed.

"What?" the passenger snapped.

The driver pointed at the two dead bodies.

The two new spirits bolted from the back of the van, and a moment later stood on the beach next to where their vehicle had landed.

"Who are those guys?" the passenger asked. "And how did they get in our van? They look dead."

"Hello," Eva said.

The two spirits turned abruptly, coming face-to-face with Eva.

"Who are you?" the driver asked. The two men looked around nervously.

"We need to talk," Eva said. "About Laura Miller and where you have her."

The two men exchanged quick glances before the driver blurted, "We need to get out of here!" The next moment, they both vanished, leaving Eva alone on the beach.

JOE AND KELLY had been on their way to Astoria to meet with the jeweler about a new setting for Kelly's engagement ring when they spied a white van driving erratically on the road heading to Pilgrim's Point. The erratic driver's speed accelerated, and to Joe and Kelly's horror, he missed the turn, sending the van hurling over the cliff.

Joe turned off on the overlook. After stopping, both he and Kelly rushed to the edge of the cliff and looked down. On the beach below, they saw the van had landed on its side, with pieces of the vehicle scattered along the beach, and no sign of life.

"Oh, my god, how could someone survive that?" Kelly muttered. Joe immediately got on his cellphone and called in the accident. When he got off the phone, he informed Kelly that he needed to go down to check on whoever was in the vehicle.

"Of course," Kelly said. "We can go to Astoria another day. I'll call the jeweler and tell him what happened."

JOE DROVE down to the beach, going as far as his vehicle would take them. He asked Kelly to stay with his car and wait for the police and paramedics to arrive. If necessary, he needed to administer CPR before the responders showed up. He gave Kelly a quick kiss, turned, and ran toward the wreckage. From where Kelly stood, large boulders blocked the accident scene from her view.

When Joe reached the van, its engine was still running. With the front of the van wedged between two boulders, there was no way for him to access the cab. He raced to the back of the van, its rear door missing, and looked inside. He saw the two bodies yet did not know if they were dead or alive. Without hesitation, he climbed inside the vehicle.

Eva stood nearby, watching. She intended to follow Joe inside the van but froze when something caught her attention. Fuel was leaking from the gas tank. And then she saw smoke. The engine had ignited a small fire. Eva disappeared.

Inside the van, Joe immediately recognized the two men. He

took the pulse of the first one he reached. Joe crawled to the second man and took his pulse. Inching toward the front of the van, he found both the passenger and driver seats empty.

The engine was still running, but he couldn't safely reach the key to turn it off. Knowing there was nothing he could do for the men, he started crawling back toward the rear of the van and then noticed it—a pile of gold coins. And on top of the pile, a necklace.

Joe picked up the necklace and looked at it. "The Missing Thorndike," he muttered.

IN EVA'S panic to get Joe out of the van before the fire ignited the gasoline, she traveled to Marlow House, where she found Marie and Danielle sitting at the kitchen table after having just returned from the gas station. Without explanation to Danielle, Eva insisted Marie come with her.

When Eva and Marie returned to the site, they found Joe still inside the van, unaware of the growing fire inching its way to the leaking gasoline. Without saying a word, Marie jerked Joe from the van, sending him flying from the vehicle. He landed on the beach and hit his head, knocking him out.

Eva moved to Joe's side and leaned close. "He's alive." She noticed something clutched in his right hand, the Missing Thorndike. Eva smiled.

They heard sirens.

The next moment, the dead bodies flew from the van, followed by the briefcase and the gold coins, landing a distance from the wreckage.

Down the beach, where Joe had parked his car, Kelly heard the approaching sirens. Moments after the responders pulled up beside Joe's car, an explosion shook the beach, sending flames high into the air. Kelly called out Joe's name and started running toward the wreckage, only to be held back by Brian Henderson.

THIRTY

The firetruck headed toward the flames, followed by the other responders, while Kelly reluctantly agreed to wait by Joe's car after Brian promised he would call her as soon as they arrived on the scene. He reminded her a civilian's presence could jeopardize lives.

Moments later, when the responders arrived at the wreckage, they found two dead bodies sprawled some distance from the burning vehicle. The van's back door had ripped off during its fall down the cliff. Because of this, the responders initially assumed both men had flown from the van before they and the vehicle landed on the beach.

They found Joe Morelli some twenty feet from the two dead bodies. He lay next to a pile of gold coins. Paramedics resisted the temptation to investigate the gold coins and turned their full attention to the unconscious off-duty police officer.

Brian reached Joe moments after the paramedics arrived.

"Is he alive?" Brian asked.

Before a paramedic responded, Joe opened his eyes. Dazed, Joe looked at Brian and asked, "What happened?"

The paramedics started asking Joe questions, assessing his condition while checking for vitals.

"Thank God," Brian muttered. He immediately pulled out his cellphone to call Kelly.

While talking to Kelly, Brian overheard a paramedic asking Joe, "What are you holding?" The next moment, the paramedic pried the Missing Thorndike from Joe's grasp.

Chief MacDonald showed up on the scene fifteen minutes later. By that time, they had loaded Joe into an ambulance and had left for the hospital. Kelly followed them in Joe's car.

After Joe had regained consciousness, he remembered going into the van and finding the two dead bodies but had no recollection of how he or they had ended up on the beach. Speculation among the responders was that Joe had removed the two bodies from the van, along with the gold coins, before the explosion. While they assumed Joe had used the briefcase to move the gold coins from the vehicle, they wondered why the briefcase was open, and the gold piled on the sand instead of in the briefcase.

They suspected Joe had escaped the vehicle while carrying the Missing Thorndike moments before the explosion, and in the panic to get away, he fell and hit his head, rendering him unconscious. Because of the lack of specific surface injuries, they didn't feel the explosion had thrown Joe or the other men from the vehicle.

Police Chief MacDonald and Brian Henderson did not share those opinions. The two men stood some distance from the group as the fire department dealt with the vehicle fire and others processed the scene. Brian had already handed over the Missing Thorndike to the chief, and they had secured the area around the coins.

"It had to have been Marie," Brian told the chief.

MacDonald nodded. "That's what I'm thinking. So what do we have on our kidnappers?"

"At the moment, we're the only ones here who know they're kidnappers," Brian reminded him. "Although, the fact they were in the possession of the Missing Thorndike and Marlow's gold coins, the general assumption is we have two thieves trying to escape."

"Did they have any identification on them? One looks familiar, but the other one doesn't."

"Yes, but Joe had already told me who they were before he left in the ambulance. He recognized them both. They're brothers, Hal and Stuart Kent. Hal went to school with Joe. He's a local handyman. The brother recently returned to town."

"There were only two of them in the van?" the chief asked.

"According to Joe. He claimed the brothers were the only ones in there."

"We have at least one kidnapper still on the loose. One who won't be happy because his blundering accomplices drove off the cliff with the ransom," the chief grumbled.

"You told me Eva intended to stay with whoever was picking up the ransom. If she did, that means she was there when they died."

"Which means she might get them to tell her where Laura is, and identify their accomplice," the chief said.

"Now what?" Brian asked.

"The only thing we can do, go to Marlow House, and talk to Danielle. After all, that's what we'd do if we had just come across this accident without prior knowledge of a kidnapping. Something we're only aware of because of a ghost. We'd be wondering how the Missing Thorndike and gold coins ended up with these guys."

DEJECTED, Danielle leaned forward on the living room sofa, burying her face in her palms. After a moment, she lifted her head and said, "If only they would have stuck around and told you where Laura is." *They* were the two men killed in the van. Eva and Marie had just updated Danielle on all that had happened since Eva had come for Marie to save Joe.

"Perhaps they'll show up at the morgue," Marie suggested.

Danielle sat up straight. "They told me the bomb would go off automatically in forty-eight hours. It could be a bluff about how many accomplices they have. But there is at least one more out there. I saw him. He's going to find out what happened to the ransom. Will he just blow up Laura and disappear?"

"I would assume the accomplice would simply realize he needs to cut his losses and leave Frederickport. After all, once they investigate his now dead partners, it will only be a matter of time before they connect those men to him," Marie said.

"But he might simply leave Laura tied up with a ticking bomb while he makes his escape," Danielle said.

"Are you sure the place they took you was in Frederickport?" Eva asked.

"I'm pretty sure. We weren't in the car that long. My guess, fifteen minutes from here."

"Then the police can check every house in Frederickport," Eva suggested. "Or, better yet, Marie and I can simply go through them!"

"Perhaps we can do this a little faster. Was it a house? Maybe a warehouse, an office?" Marie asked.

Danielle shook her head. "No. It was a house. I was only in one room, but I'm pretty sure it was someone's living room."

"What do you remember about it?" Eva asked. "After all, I've been in most of the houses in Frederickport; I might recognize it."

"That might be a possibility." Danielle closed her eyes and visualized the room. After a moment, she said, "It looked like the living room in an older house. It had hardwood floors. Old hardwood floors. But there were a couple of dingy big throw rugs under some of the furniture. And some really ugly fabric curtains with big red roses. It looked like someplace a little old lady would live."

Marie frowned. "I think I'm insulted. What does that mean, exactly? I was a little old lady when I died. And the way you said that, it doesn't sound like a compliment."

Danielle blushed. "I'm sorry. I didn't mean it that way. It's just that, now that I think about it, it didn't seem like a room in a house any of those men would live in. While I didn't see their faces, I'm pretty sure they were all men."

"At least two of them were," Eva said.

"And considering their chosen life of crime, I don't see them as living in a house with rose-pattern drapes and a hideous glass chandelier, antique ceiling tile, and a cherrywood curio cabinet filled with cut glass and old china."

"Hideous glass chandelier and antique ceiling tile?" Marie asked.

Danielle nodded. "Yeah. When they unrolled me from my bedspread, I was on the floor. One of the first things I noticed was the ceiling. It was vintage ceiling tile. And by the looks of it, I think it has been there a long time. In the middle of the room there was this gaudy crystal chandelier."

"I think that's Gerty Barry's house!" Marie declared.

"You know it?" Danielle asked.

"I haven't been in her house in years, but knowing Gerty, I doubt she's changed anything. She was very proud of that chandelier." Marie cringed.

"Who would use her house? Her sons?" Danielle asked.

Marie shook her head. "No. Gerty was never married. She became something of a recluse years ago. But I ran into a friend of mine at the cemetery who was getting ready to move on. She'd been living at Seaside Village." Marie shivered at the thought. Seaside Village was where Marie had been murdered. "My friend mentioned Gerty had gotten her room after she passed. Gerty broke her hip. This wasn't long ago. So, my guess, someone found out she was at the care home for rehab and borrowed her house."

"Sounds like someone intends to blow up Gerty's house," Danielle said.

"Not if I can do something about it," Marie said before disappearing.

While it might have taken Danielle fifteen minutes to travel from Marlow House to Gerty Barry's, it took Marie less than a minute. She immediately knew she had come to the right place, because Laura Miller sat tied to a chair, her eyes blindfolded as Marie heard muffled sobs coming from the young woman. Laura looked miserable, the duct tape making it impossible for her to cry out, her hands and feet bound tightly to the chair. Marie understood she had been sitting in that chair for hours.

Marie glanced around the room, looking for the bomb. On the far table, she spied the box Danielle had described. Moving to the table, Marie peered into the lidless box and saw what looked like a bomb, its steady ticking an ominous reminder of what was to come.

"CHIEF... BRIAN," a frazzled-looking Danielle said when she answered the front door, her hair barely combed; she didn't look happy to see them.

"Can we come in?" the chief asked.

Peeking outside, Danielle glanced around, looking to see if anyone was in the street. Reluctantly, she stepped back, opened the door wider and let the two officers inside.

She closed the front door and turned to Brian and the chief. "I wish you guys wouldn't have come here. What if the kidnappers are watching?"

"Danielle, the men you gave the ransom to got in a car accident and are dead," the chief explained.

"Yes, I know. Eva told me." Danielle turned and headed for the living room, motioning for them to follow her. "But only two of them. There is at least one more still out there."

"We understand, but considering the entire town is probably going to know about the accident within the next hour, along with what we found," the chief began. "Think about it, Danielle. If we knew nothing about all this and then found the Missing Thorndike —not to mention the gold coins—at an accident scene, wouldn't we immediately contact the known owner of those items?"

"He has a good point," Eva, who had been silently observing, told Danielle.

Before Danielle could respond, Marie appeared.

"Oh no, she wasn't there?" Danielle blurted upon seeing Marie.

"Who are you talking to?" the chief asked.

"Oh good, Edward and Brian are here. That will save some

time," Marie said before turning to Danielle. "She is there. She's fine. I need to go back and take care of the bomb. Have Brian and Edward meet me at Gerty's house. But tell them not to come into the house until they know I've taken care of the bomb. I don't want anyone to get hurt." Marie vanished.

THIRTY-ONE

Laura wondered what was more painful, death by blood clot or being blown up? She knew the threat of a blood clot was real, considering they'd tied her to this damn chair hours ago. She could not move with her hands and feet tightly restricted. The men who had secured her to this chair were freaking sadists. She knew there were at least two of them, because after the garbled robotic voice gave Danielle instructions, she'd heard footsteps and rustling, followed by the sound of a door opening and closing. Laura was certain she was alone. Sometime later, someone entered the room. She heard them talking. Not the garbled voice that had given Danielle instructions earlier, but the voices of what sounded like two men.

Since they'd left, she had been saying one prayer after another, asking the Good Lord to send angels to rescue her, and then asking for the least painful death. If she had to die, did it have to hurt? She was already hurting.

Unlike Danielle, she knew the men didn't intend to let her go. When they had returned after taking Danielle to Marlow House, they had not been shy about talking in front of her. What did they care? She was going to die anyway.

They talked of the bomb going off in forty-eight hours. Their promise to Danielle to reveal Laura's location after getting away with the ransom was nothing but an empty promise. She'd overheard the men say they needed to blow the house up to destroy the evidence—to destroy anything that could link this crime to them.

She was going to die.

As she was about to say another prayer, the sound of the door opening made her freeze. Laura held her breath, waiting for the sound of footsteps or voices. Had the men returned, or had there been a miracle?

But there was no sound of footsteps. Instead, someone lifted the chair—with her in it—up off the floor. She wiggled her feet, the floor beneath them gone. The chair moved again—flying across the room. Had she already died? Laura wondered.

The sensation of flying continued. The surrounding air changed. She was suddenly cold, no longer warm. Had they moved her outside? If so, why no footsteps? No hands touched her. How could they lift the chair without touching her?

Abruptly, the chair stopped moving. It lowered, and once again, her feet touched the ground. She wanted to ask what was happening, but duct tape still covered her mouth. And then, as if someone had read her mind, she felt the duct tape being pulled away from her mouth. Slowly, gently, as if whoever was removing it did not want to hurt her.

"Hello? Is someone there?" Laura hesitantly called out after they finished removing the duct tape. She twitched her lips, stretching and puckering a lip-like exercise before licking them, trying to make them feel normal again. She waited for a response. Nothing. Afraid to call out, she asked, "Please? Talk to me."

AFTER REMOVING THE DUCT TAPE, Marie realized it was probably a mistake. It would have been wiser for Edward or Brian to remove it. What if Laura started shouting and a neighbor came outside in time to witness her removing the bomb? But it was too late now.

Marie also wanted to untie Laura from the chair; the bindings looked painful. But she would leave it to Edward or Brian. It was not only because it would confuse Laura to remove her blindfold and find herself alone, wondering how someone had untied her and then vanished, Marie also wanted to keep her a safe distance from the bomb.

So far, Laura hadn't started screaming for help, but Marie had placed her on the sidewalk across the street from Gerty's, and no one seemed to be home in the nearby houses. Leaving Laura in the chair and hoping Brian or Edward would be here soon, Marie reentered Gerty's house and moved to the table.

Marie looked down at the bomb. It continued to tick. She didn't want to blow up Gerty's house, and she did not know how powerful this thing was. Would it just destroy the living room if it exploded, or an entire neighborhood?

Marie paused and looked upwards. "Please guide me. I really don't want to blow anyone up."

Marie looked back down at the box holding the explosives and focused her energy. The box lifted from the table. Slowly, Marie moved from Gerty's house, the box holding the bomb floating before her. Marie told herself she needed to ignore everything but the bomb; the last thing she wanted to do was get distracted and drop this thing like she'd occasionally dropped one of Connor's toy airplanes or plastic dinosaurs after making them fly around the room.

Once she and the bomb made it outside, she was grateful there didn't seem to be any neighbors milling around or cars driving by. Yet she understood that could change any moment, and the last thing she needed was for someone to walk out of their house, see a box floating down the sidewalk and run over and grab at it to see what kind of trick someone was playing.

To prevent that from happening, once Marie and the box were in Gerty's yard, both she and it floated high into the air.

EN ROUTE to Gerty Barry's house, Brian Henderson and Edward MacDonald discussed the alternate story they would need to tell the others involving this case.

"My life was less complicated when I still believed Danielle was a sociopath," Brian told the chief. He drove the police car while the chief sat in the passenger seat.

Edward chuckled. "You actually thought Danielle was a sociopath?"

Brian shrugged. "That or a narcissist. Or both. I was certain she killed her cousin. Even later, when we knew Danielle hadn't killed her, I still believed Danielle was the one who dumped all Cheryl's things in the suitcase and ruined them. I mean, who does that?"

"Walt?" MacDonald asked.

"Yeah." Brian laughed and then in a serious voice said, "I'm grateful for certain ghosts right now. Joe was foolish going into that van. If Marie hadn't intervened when she did, we'd be looking forward to his funeral instead of his wedding."

"We turn left up there," MacDonald interrupted.

Brian flipped on his turn signal. "We're not supposed to go into the house until Marie takes care of the bomb."

"I hope she knows what she's doing," Edward muttered.

A few moments later, they turned down Gerty's street. Brian slammed on the brakes and pointed up to the sky. "Look."

"What's that?"

Brian shook his head. "Umm… at first glance, I thought it was a drone."

"Looks like a box."

Still stopped in the middle of the street, Brian looked around for any cars, but the street was still empty. He glanced down the road, speculating on which house belonged to Gerty Barry. When he did, he spied a woman tied to a chair, sitting on the sidewalk.

"We found Laura," Brian announced before taking his foot off the brake and starting down the street.

The chief moved his hand toward Brian in a stopping motion.

"Wait a minute. Remember what Marie said, wait until she takes care of the bomb, and I think that's what she's doing now." He pointed up into the sky. The object Brian had seen a moment ago inched toward the ocean.

NOW FLOATING over the sea with the bomb, Marie looked down into the box.

"I can't just drop it here. What if this thing washes to shore and then goes off?"

Frowning, Marie studied the bomb while she and the box that held it hovered above the surf some twenty feet in the air.

"I wonder what I have to do to detonate this thing?"

After considering her options, Marie smiled. The next moment, the box began rocking in midair, sending its contents sliding from side to side, hitting one interior wall in the box and then another. Just as Marie was about to try another tactic to detonate the device, it exploded, sending its parts flying through the illusion of her body.

"HOLY CRAP. DID YOU SEE THAT?" Brian asked.

"Looks like she did it. Let's go get Laura," the chief said.

A few moments later, Brian pulled the police car along the sidewalk near Laura and parked. The two policemen got out of the car.

"Hello?" Laura called out tentatively.

"Laura, it's okay. It's Police Chief MacDonald."

"Oh my God!" Laura sobbed. "But be careful, there is a bomb!"

"It's okay, that's been handled," MacDonald promised.

Brian crouched down by Laura and said in a soothing voice, "Laura, it's Brian Henderson. I'm going to remove your blindfold. Close your eyes; it'll be bright. You've had that thing on for a long time."

Laura nodded and then held perfectly still. The next moment, Brian removed the blindfold. Laura froze, her eyes closed. Brian inspected the bindings. "I need to get something from the car to cut these off."

Laura nodded again and then slowly opened her eyes. Squinting, she looked around. "I'm outside?"

"It's going to be okay," the chief told her as he got out his phone to make a call. "We're taking you to the hospital and have you checked out."

WHILE WAITING for the ambulance and more police officers to arrive, Laura told Brian and the chief all that she knew. They told her what had happened to the kidnappers who had picked up the ransom, and that Danielle was safe at Marlow House. They also informed her that as soon as the other officers arrived, they would do a thorough search of the house across the street.

When Laura asked how they'd found her and why they'd thought the house across the street was where the kidnappers had taken her, the chief made up a story about how after he and Brian had gone to Marlow House after finding the Missing Thorndike and gold coins at the accident scene, Danielle had told them about the kidnapping, and the chief said he had asked Danielle to describe what she remembered about the location the kidnappers had taken her and Laura to. Brian claimed to have recognized Gerty's house by Danielle's description, as he had once taken a call at her residence. While it was true, he had made the call, he had never actually been in Gerty's house.

EDWARD MACDONALD STOOD outside Gerty's house, talking on his cellphone as his officers searched her house. The chair they'd found Laura tied to matched Gerty's dining room set, and while that didn't surprise the chief or Brian, it helped verify for the other officers that Gerty's house was where the kidnappers had taken Laura and Danielle.

Just as the chief ended the phone call, Brian came outside from Gerty's and walked up to him. "Um, Chief, we found something in Gerty's bedroom."

Edward frowned. "What?"

"I think you should see for yourself."

POLICE CHIEF MACDONALD stood in Gerty's bedroom with Brian and several other officers, looking at a dead body lying face-down on the carpet. The chief didn't have to check the body's vitals to determine if he was alive, considering the three obvious gunshot wounds in the man's back, along with the massive amount of blood soaking into the carpet, outlining the body. MacDonald assumed it was a man, yet he told himself he could be wrong.

MacDonald silently watched as one officer turned the body over. When they did, MacDonald and Brian stared at the dead man's face in disbelief.

"If I didn't know better, I would say this is…" Instead of finishing his sentence, Brian shook his head and said, "But it can't be."

"It sure looks like him," the chief said.

THIRTY-TWO

Heather pulled Lily away from the group, leaving Connor with his grandmother and Sadie with Chris.

"First, Laura is fine. So is Danielle. They are both okay," Heather began.

"What's wrong?" Lily asked.

Heather told Lily all that had happened to Danielle and Laura, beginning with the kidnapping. Unlike the version that would be told to the wider community, Heather gave Lily the complete story.

LILY RUSHED into the hospital room. She found her sister sitting up in the hospital bed hooked up to an IV, a nurse standing by her side, clipboard in hand.

"Oh, Laura!" Lily hurried to her bedside. Before hugging her sister, Lily paused, wondering if it was okay to hug her.

Laura smiled up at her sister. "You can hug me. I'm okay."

Lily threw her arms around Laura.

Still embraced by her sobbing sister, Laura peeked up to the nurse and said, "This is my sister, Lily. I think she's a little emotional because she's pregnant."

Lily pulled away from Laura and sniffled. "I'm emotional because I could have lost you!"

The nurse smiled down at the pair. "Your sister is going to be fine. But she was a little dehydrated, so we have her on some fluids."

A few minutes later, after the nurse left the two women alone, Lily sat in a chair next to Laura's bed. After grabbing a tissue, Lily blew her nose and then said, "I can't believe everything that happened to you and Dani today, and I had no idea. No one told me anything until they found you."

"I'm glad they didn't tell you. You didn't need to deal with that. I was worried enough about Danielle. How is she?"

"She's fine," Lily said. "I talked to her on the way over here. Heather brought me. She took Sadie with her, and June took Connor back to her house. Heather is dropping Sadie off at Marlow House."

Laura, who had been sitting up in the bed, flopped back on the pile of pillows and let out a sigh. "There is just so much I'm still confused about. Like, who moved me outside and took the duct tape off my mouth? None of it makes sense. Brian told me the guys Danielle gave the ransom to drove off a damn cliff and got themselves killed. Talk about karma coming quick."

"Yeah, Heather told me. Joe and Kelly saw the van go over the cliff. They were on their way to Astoria to see the jeweler. Joe immediately called in the accident. They obviously didn't go to Astoria. He was the first one on the scene. He must have fallen or something. Hit his head. Not sure what happened, but he's in the hospital too. A few doors down. I think Kelly is with him."

Laura sat up. "Oh no! Is Joe okay?"

"I think, like you, he's here more for observation. So tell me, what happened? Heather told me what they told her."

Laura leaned back on the pillows again and proceeded to tell Lily all that had happened from her perspective. When she was done, she looked at Lily and added in a whisper, "I peed myself. Soaked my pajama bottoms."

Lily smiled. "They had you tied up a long time."

"I thought I was going to die. So I figured, why try to make myself even more uncomfortable and hold it in? I confess, I got a little embarrassed when Brian helped me out of the chair. But he and the chief were super sweet about it. And I was just so grateful to be alive. But I would like to find out who moved me. I'm sure Danielle and I were inside some sort of room. My feet were bare, and I could feel the carpet on the bottom of my feet. It was warm. I can't figure out how someone moved my chair without ever touching me. It's like the chair floated out of that house on its own. Who moved me? Brian and the chief had no answers. They didn't even seem to think it was that important."

Lily reached out and took Laura's hand. "I know who moved you."

Laura frowned. "You do? Who?"

"An angel."

HEATHER WAS at Marlow House with Danielle when Brian arrived late Tuesday afternoon. Eva and Marie were also with them, sitting at the kitchen table.

"Would you like anything to eat or drink?" Danielle asked when Heather led Brian into the kitchen, Sadie trailing behind them with her tail wagging.

"I can make you something," Heather offered.

"Actually, a sandwich would be great, but first I need to tell you what they found at Gerty Barry's house."

Marie moved from the chair she had been sitting on and said, "Tell Brian he can sit here." The chair moved out from the table, and Marie took a seat in an imaginary chair.

"Sit down and tell us." Heather nudged Brian toward the chair Marie had pushed out. "You look exhausted."

Brian smiled weakly at Heather. "Thanks." He sat down.

"So what did you find? Another bomb?" Danielle asked.

Brian shook his head. "No. Charlie Cramer."

"Charlie Cramer?" Heather and Danielle chorused.

Brian nodded.

"I thought he was dead?" Heather asked.

"He is. At least he is now," Brian said.

"I don't understand. He didn't die in Canada? What happened? Was he hiding at the Barry house and one of your guys shot him?" Heather asked.

"Someone shot him, but it wasn't anyone from the Frederickport police force. We found his body in a bedroom in the Barry house. Someone shot him three times in the back. Coroner believes time of death was early this morning," Brian explained.

"Are you sure it was him?" Danielle asked.

"I recognized him immediately, but he looked a little different from the last time I saw him. Much thinner, for example. Initially, I wondered if it was an uncanny likeness, considering everything. But the fingerprints verified it. It was him," Brian said.

"Who died in Canada?" Danielle asked.

Brian shrugged. "We don't know."

"This is weird," Danielle muttered.

"Another thing, we've been getting reports about the explosion over the coast near the Barry house. No one but the chief and I know it's connected to the kidnapping. But unfortunately, when Laura warned us about the bomb, we said we handled it, and now we're backpedaling on that comment." Brian groaned.

"Does everyone on the case know there was supposed to be a bomb?" Danielle asked.

"Since Laura heard the kidnappers telling you about a bomb, we couldn't very well pretend there was no mention of one. When the responders arrived, they swept for explosives immediately. Of course, they found nothing," Brian said.

"Except for Charlie," Heather grumbled. "That jerk had better not show up here."

"Actually, I hope he does. Maybe he can tell us what's going on," Brian said.

"Back to the bomb. Aren't they worried about a missing bomb?" Danielle asked.

"The chief and I thought we should go with the story that what they showed you probably wasn't really a bomb, just something they made to scare you. And we assume they took it with them because they didn't want to leave any evidence behind that could trace back to them. The chief and I came up with a description we could say you gave him, and by that description, he's convinced it wasn't really a bomb."

"What about the dead body?" Heather asked. "They left that behind."

"Yeah, well, we came up with the bomb story before we found Cramer," Brian grumbled.

"I'd like to find out what the connection is between Cramer and the guys killed in the van. The chief told us who they were, and while Marie knew them, she didn't recognize them when she pulled them out of the van," Danielle said.

"I hadn't seen the younger brother for years. But he was always trouble," Marie said.

"According to Joe, the older brother was a high school classmate of his. Which means he was also one of Cramer's classmates," Brian said.

"Has Joe been told about Cramer?" Danielle asked.

Brian shook his head. "No. But after I leave here, I'm going to the hospital to see Joe and talk to him. And the chief went over to talk to Gerty Barry."

WHEN EDWARD MACDONALD walked into the front lobby of Seaside Village, he only recognized one staff member at the front nurses' station. Since Marie's murder at the facility, the care home had changed owners. Yet he understood much about Seaside Village remained the same. Long-term residents of the facility, primarily Alzheimer's and dementia patients, lived in rooms in the front portion of the building, while rehab patients, such as Gerty Barry, had rooms along the rear of the building. There was a second nurses' station for those rehab patients, yet they rarely staffed it.

Visitors of the short-term patients could enter through the rear entrance and bypass the front nurses' station, yet that required knowing the password to unlock the back entrance. The chief walked up to the front nurses' station, said hello to the one familiar face, and asked to see Gerty Barry.

———

"WHEN THEY TOLD me I had a visitor, I didn't expect the police chief," Gerty told MacDonald after a nurse wheeled her out from her room. The nurse left Gerty alone with the chief and returned to her other duties. They sat in a private corner of the open lounge, with Gerty in her wheelchair and the chief on a sofa. "Although I couldn't imagine who was here to see me. The bossy nurse expected me to walk out here. Use your walker, she said. But I just finished physical therapy, and if she wanted me to talk to you, I told her she had to bring me out here in a wheelchair. I'm done walking for the day."

"I could have come to your room," the chief offered.

Gerty frowned. "I don't let strange men come to my room."

The chief smiled weakly and then said, "Ms. Barry—"

"It is Miss Barry. Miss," she corrected.

"Sorry. Miss Barry, I just have a few questions."

"I can't imagine what you would have to ask me. But go ahead."

"Do you know Hal or Stuart Kent?" he asked.

She shrugged. "It doesn't sound familiar. What were their names again?"

"Hal Kent and—"

"Yes. That one," she interrupted.

"So you do know Hal Kent?"

"No. I didn't say that. I never met him before. But I'm pretty sure that's the name of the man my neighbor recommended."

"Recommended for what?" the chief asked.

"My neighbor next door. He and his wife came to visit me before they left. They go to Palm Desert this time each year for a couple of months. He suggested I call this Hal person to watch my house while I'm in this place."

"Did you?" the chief asked.

"No. There was no reason. This time of year, it's not like plants need to be watered. I had my mail forwarded. No reason to spend money on something like that."

"I assume Hal watches your neighbor's house when he goes away?" the chief asked.

She shook her head. "No. But he takes care of another neighbor's house. Why are you asking?"

"First, your house is fine. But I'm afraid someone broke into it."

THIRTY-THREE

K elly sat on the edge of Joe's hospital bed, holding his hand. Before leaving the room, the nurse had adjusted Joe's bed, so he sat up, leaning against a pillow instead of lying flat. The doctor had just left the room, and other than medical staff, no one had been to visit Joe since they had admitted him to the hospital.

"I don't want to spend the night here," Joe grumbled.

"Hey, you got knocked out, and you can't even remember how you got out of the van, much less how you got the other people out of there, along with all the gold."

"I didn't."

"You keep saying that, but you heard what they said back at the beach. There was no way an explosion threw them from the van, and you yourself said they were in the van when you arrived on the scene before it exploded."

"I understand what you're saying. But I checked their pulses, and they were both dead. There was no reason I'd risk my life dragging them out of there. The engine was running, and I was aware of the risks. I was getting ready to get out, and then saw the gold coins and the Missing Thorndike. I picked up the necklace, and well, that's all I remember."

"Which is why you need to spend the night here," Kelly insisted. Joe groaned.

"I'd like to find out how they got their hands on Danielle's gold coins and necklace. Are you sure it was the Missing Thorndike?" Kelly asked. "The coins could obviously belong to someone else."

"It looked just like the Missing Thorndike. I've seen the necklace up close enough times to recognize it. But it could also be a good fake."

Kelly's cellphone rang. She stood, walked over to a nearby chair, picked up her purse, and fished her cellphone from it. Before answering, she glanced at the phone. "It's Mom. She's probably going to ask me about my ring."

When Kelly got off the phone a few minutes later, she looked at Joe and said, "Laura's in the hospital, too."

"Why?"

"Mom didn't know. Lily got a call that they took Laura to the hospital. Mom took Connor home with her, and Heather dropped Lily off at the hospital and took Sadie over to Marlow House."

"She didn't say why Laura was in the hospital?"

Kelly shook her head. "Wow. This has been a really weird day. Both you and Laura end up in the hospital."

"I hope she's okay," Joe said.

"Yeah, me too. I'm going to see if I can find out what room she's in and check on her."

IT DIDN'T TAKE LONG for Kelly to find where they had Laura. She stepped out of Joe's hospital room and came face-to-face with Lily in the hallway.

"Hey, Kelly. How's Joe? I was just going to his room to see how he was doing," Lily greeted.

"I just got off the phone with Mom, and she said Laura is here," Kelly said.

"Yeah. She's two rooms down from Joe's." Lily pointed to the open doorway down the hall. "How is Joe doing?"

"Umm… okay. How did you find out about Joe? Mom didn't even know until a few minutes ago."

"Heather told me," Lily explained.

Kelly frowned. "Oh. I imagine Brian told her?"

"Umm… something like that."

"Why is Laura here? Is she okay?"

"She's going to be fine. I'll let her explain. She'll be happy to see you. And I'll go say hi to Joe while you visit Laura."

LAURA HAD JUST FINISHED TELLING Kelly about her harrowing morning and afternoon, beginning with her abduction before daybreak and eventually being admitted to the hospital. Kelly sat in a chair she had pulled next to the hospital bed, hanging on Laura's every word.

"So that really was the Missing Thorndike and Danielle's coins at the accident?" Kelly asked after Laura finished her telling.

"Yes. Danielle went to the bank this morning and took the necklace and gold out of her safe-deposit box. She took them to the designated drop-off. Did everything they told her to do."

"She didn't call the police? The FBI?" Kelly asked.

"No. They told her if she didn't do exactly what they said, they were going to blow me up."

"You must have been utterly terrified!"

"That is a freaking understatement. I thought I was going to die. I really did."

"Hey, I can remember that feeling," Kelly said.

"You mean when that crazy sister of your old roommate held you hostage?" Laura asked.

Kelly nodded.

"I really need to work on my feelings about Danielle."

"How do you mean?" Kelly asked.

Laura glanced at the open door and then looked back at Kelly. "Can you shut the door? I really don't want my sister to come back and overhear this."

With a nod, Kelly stood, walked to the door, closed it, returned to the chair, and sat down.

"First, don't get me wrong, I've always liked Danielle. But just like you get a little annoyed about that thing Joe used to have with her, sometimes her friendship with Lily kinda bugs me."

Kelly smiled. "Yeah. I get that."

"I understand it's super petty of me. Hell, Danielle graciously let me stay at Marlow House and practically refuses to let me pay rent."

"And?"

"I feel like a major jerk. Danielle, without hesitation, turned over a fortune to save my life. I need to work on my pettiness."

Kelly let out a sigh. "I can relate to that."

They sat in silence, each reflecting on their own private thoughts. After a few moments, Laura resumed the conversation. "Anyway, after karma came for those jerks, Brian and the chief headed over to Marlow House to talk to Danielle."

"I imagine they wanted to find out why those men had the Missing Thorndike and gold coins," Kelly said.

"Something like that. That's when Danielle told the police about the kidnapping. Fortunately, after Danielle described the place they took us, Brian recognized the house. And they rescued me. Crazy thing, there ended up not being a bomb."

"You've met one of the kidnappers," Kelly said.

Laura frowned. "I have?"

"Hal Kent. The caretaker for your secret friend."

"No? You're kidding?"

Kelly nodded. "Joe recognized them. It was Hal and his brother. Remember, Joe went to school with Hal."

"Oh, my god. I remember Frank telling me how when Hal first contacted him to watch his house, he really wasn't sure about it. But when he got here, he said he was happy how he found the house, that Hal obviously did a good job."

"A great job when he's not busy kidnapping women."

"I wonder if Frank missed me when I didn't stop by there this morning," Laura mused. "I wonder if he knows why I didn't come over."

Kelly shrugged. "Not sure how much information is out there to the public. Heck, I didn't hear about the kidnapping until you told me. And even though Joe found the ransom, we didn't know it was a ransom."

"Considering Frank doesn't really know anyone in town, and he doesn't go anywhere, unless one of his neighbors stops by and tells him, I doubt he knows."

"What I want to find out, who took you out of the house and left you on the sidewalk?"

"Lily said it was an angel."

"Perhaps the same angel who got Joe out of that van before it exploded," Kelly suggested.

BEFORE ENTERING Joe's hospital room, Brian looked inside the open doorway. He saw Lily sitting by Joe's bedside. Kelly was nowhere in sight. Brian knocked on the doorjamb, called out a hello, and walked in.

"Hey, Brian," Joe greeted. "Lily was just telling me about the kidnapping. Hal and Stuart, I can't believe they were kidnappers."

"Yep, looks that way." Brian walked all the way into the room. He glanced down at Lily and asked, "How's your sister?"

"She's doing much better. Kelly's in with her."

Brian gave Lily a nod and turned his attention to Joe. "How are you doing, buddy?"

"I want to go home, but the doctor wants me to stay overnight for observation, and Kelly agrees."

"I agree with Kelly," Brian said.

"While I can't remember everything, I feel fine. My head is a little sore, that's about it."

"Just relax, and take care of yourself, because after you get out of here, we're going to need your help to figure this thing out," Brian said.

"From what Lily was telling me, there were at least three kidnappers. Hal and Stuart were obviously two of them. So one of them is still out there," Joe said. "Any usable fingerprints where you found Laura?"

"In a way," Brian said.

"Dani told me they all wore gloves," Lily said.

"Umm… I'm not sure this set of fingerprints was another kidnapper. And we didn't exactly lift them from any doorknobs or furniture in the house," Brian said.

"What fingerprints are you talking about?" Joe asked.

"We found a body in the house where they took Laura and Danielle. It was in one of the bedrooms. He had been shot three times in the back. I recognized him, but I assumed I had to be mistaken. It couldn't be who I thought it was. But he was. His fingerprints verified it," Brian explained.

"Who was it?" Lily asked.

Brian took a deep breath, exhaled, and said, "It was Charlie Cramer."

"Charlie?" Lily muttered.

Joe sat upright in the bed. "Charlie died in Canada."

"Apparently not," Brian said. "It was him. Like I said, someone shot him three times, and the coroner estimates the time of death was early this morning."

"Was he one of the kidnappers?" Lily asked.

"We're not sure at this point. The chief is trying to get a hold of his contact in Canada. We have to inform them their dead body is not who they think it is."

"But the DNA?" Lily asked.

"The DNA on the toothbrush and clothes belonged to Charlie, but they never got DNA from the body. At least the results weren't in the last time the chief talked to them," Brian explained.

"Didn't they say someone up there saw him?" Lily asked.

"From what the chief's contact in Vancouver said, Cramer called a woman he once dated to bring him money. He tried to convince her he was innocent. She believed him at first, but once she looked up the case online, she started having doubts, so she told her uncle. And they called the police. The calls he made to her came from Vancouver. So while he was there, he obviously didn't die in Canada. Someone else did, and he returned to the States."

"Do you think he faked his death?" Lily asked.

Brian shrugged. "Possible. Or after the place caught fire, he just took off. It's also possible he didn't even realize anyone else was in the warehouse. And after he heard on the news that the world thought he was dead, he felt it safe to return."

"What do you know about the place where the kidnappers took Danielle and Laura?" Joe asked.

Brian told him all he knew. Joe considered the various scenarios and then said, "Maybe after Charlie returned, he found out the Barry house was empty and figured that would be a good place to hide out."

"And he walked in on the kidnappers, or they walked in on him?" Brian asked.

Joe shrugged. "It's possible."

"If that's the case, it's some twisted karma," Lily said.

THIRTY-FOUR

F rank began to think Hal and Stuart had double-crossed him. Since they had left to pick up the ransom from Danielle Marlow, he hadn't heard a word from either brother. Standing at the kitchen window, looking out at the street, he spied the neighbor Fred Stein walking up the road with his schnauzer. Glancing at the wall clock, he remembered this was about the time for Laura to be showing up for her morning coffee. But he knew Laura would not be showing up today, just like he knew he had no intention of showing her around London.

It wasn't that he didn't find her attractive. After all, she was built just like her sister, Lily: well endowed in an otherwise petite package. Unlike Lily, she wasn't a redhead, but he always preferred blondes, anyway.

Of course, none of that mattered, because in a few hours Laura would be dead, and he would be a very rich man, providing the Kent brothers hadn't double-crossed him.

LILY WALKED into Laura's hospital room carrying a plastic bag. She held it up and said, "Hello, ready to go home?"

"You brought me some clean clothes?" Laura asked. She sat on the side of the bed, dressed in a hospital gown.

"I did. When do you get to leave?"

Laura took the bag from Lily after she climbed out of bed. "They said I should be out of here within the hour. Let me get dressed. Be right back."

As Laura turned from Lily and headed to her hospital room's private bathroom, Lily called out, "Okay, but then I need to talk to you about something."

Five minutes later, Laura returned from the bathroom, dressed in the clothes her sister had brought her, and asked, "Do you have a brush?"

Lily pulled a brush from her purse and handed it to Laura.

"Thanks. Who has Connor?" Laura started brushing her hair.

"I left him with Dani when I picked up your clothes."

Still brushing her hair, Laura nodded and then said, "Last night I should have asked you to get someone to bring me my purse, or at least my cellphone." Laura paused a moment. "Oh, crap."

Lily frowned. "What is it?"

"Something the kidnappers said to Danielle in that recording they played. They told her not to look for her cellphone."

"Oh, that. Yeah, Danielle can't find her cellphone. She didn't say anything about yours. But I suspect if they got rid of hers, they got rid of yours, too."

"Crap," Laura grumbled.

"Don't worry, we can replace a cellphone."

Laura let out a sigh. "You're right."

"I wanted to let you know I called Mom and Dad and told them what happened."

Laura cringed. "I was going to do that when I got home, but I'm sorta glad you already did it. I didn't want to go through it all again."

"You have to call them, anyway. Mom made me promise to have you call after you get out of the hospital. I told her you didn't have your cellphone with you, and she wanted to call here last night, but I told her you were sleeping and needed your rest."

"Thanks. I really did crash after you left yesterday." Laura handed the brush back to Lily.

"There is another thing I need to talk to you about."

Laura frowned. "Sounds serious."

"Not really. But I'd like you to stay with me until Ian and Walt come home."

"But I promised Walt I'd stay with Danielle. Although I wasn't really much help, was I?"

Lily smiled. "I don't think Walt expected you to fight off kidnappers. Anyway, she won't be alone. Someone else will stay with her. And I got to thinking, it would be nice if you and I had some sister time. You can sleep with me. I don't kick anymore."

Laura laughed. "Promise?"

"Also, full disclosure, it would also get June off my back."

"June?" Laura frowned.

"Yeah. I didn't go home last night. When I went to pick up Connor after leaving here, June insisted I stay with them. She even had a bed already made for me. But I don't want to spend the rest of the week over there, and I think it would be fun having some sister time, just you and me."

"Okay. As long as Danielle won't be alone."

"She won't be. Chris and Hunny are staying with her."

"Chris?" Laura fairly whined. "You rat. You mean if I stayed over with Danielle this week, I'd also be sleeping under the same roof as Chris?"

"You're not planning to renege on me, are you?" Lily asked.

Laura let out another sigh. "No. I'll stay with you. But sheesh…"

BRIAN HAD STAYED with Heather on Tuesday night. With at least one kidnapper still on the loose, he thought it best to stay close to Marlow House. Both Eva and Marie had agreed to stay with

Danielle, and with him just one door down, if they needed to summon the police, he wouldn't have far to travel, plus he would have his ghost translator with him.

He sat with Heather at her kitchen table on Wednesday morning, eating a poached egg and toast breakfast she had prepared, and drinking coffee, while she sipped green tea.

"And Walt is good with Chris staying with Danielle this week?" Brian asked Heather after she explained the new arrangements.

"It was Walt's suggestion," Heather said.

Brian raised his brow. "Really?"

"Yeah. Chris is staying in the room Laura was using, while Laura stays with Lily. Eva promised to hang out at Marlow House until you guys wrap up this case."

"I don't know how long that's going to take," Brian grumbled.

"Joanne is coming in this morning to get the room ready for Chris," Heather explained.

"Where is Marie planning to be?"

"She'll sort of bounce from Marlow House to Lily's. With Laura staying over there, she can't really help that much with Connor, not without Laura freaking out."

Brian chuckled.

"What's your plan today?" Heather asked.

"Joe's being released from the hospital this morning. And we plan to go over to Hal's house, see what we can find and talk to the neighbors."

"I thought they searched his house yesterday?" Heather asked.

"They did. But we want to go through it again. And we want to talk to the neighbors. Joe knows some of them."

"I KIND OF FEEL STUPID," Danielle told the chief. She sat with him in the police car in front of the Frederickport Bank on Wednesday morning. In the back seat was the briefcase, again filled with the gold coins and the Missing Thorndike.

MacDonald eyed Danielle inquisitively. "Why would you say

that?"

"I'm going to walk in there, and everyone will know how I took this all out yesterday to give to a blackmailer."

"Everyone?"

Danielle shrugged. "Susan Mitchell, at least. I understand I really didn't have a choice. And it all worked out. Well, not for two of the kidnappers, but for me and Laura. But there is just something about letting someone bully me and basically forcing me to give them something that doesn't belong to them. It's hard to explain. But it makes me feel… stupid."

"Like you say, it all worked out. And remember, for now, these are still evidence. I just would rather have them here instead of locked up at the station."

"Yeah, me too." Danielle flashed the chief a smile.

"You should feel sorry for me," the chief said.

"Why is that?"

"Because I have to listen to all of my officers trying to come up with a theory about how Joe moved the gold coins from the van to a neat pile on the beach. Had Joe never told them the coins were in the van when he first got there, they would think someone had left them on the beach, and the van just landed nearby after it drove off the cliff."

Dannielle chuckled.

"It's not funny. Seriously. There are some major conspiracy theories going around the station, and I understand over at the fire station, too."

"Have they figured out how our dead kidnappers made it out of the van?" Danielle asked.

"They're convinced Joe dragged them out before he fell and hit his head. They just figure he can't remember because of the head injury. And again, had Joe not told them he found the Kent brothers in the van when he first arrived at the scene, they would probably assume they flew from the van when it came down the cliff."

"According to what Lily told me, Laura has her own mystery to unravel. She's trying to figure out who moved her outside and removed the duct tape before you arrived."

"Some of my people have also been discussing that and have already come up with a theory."

"What is it?" Danielle asked.

"The theory includes two more kidnappers instead of just the one you saw. Not wanting to face a murder rap, they move her outside so someone would find her. Because, had Laura stayed alone in that house, tied up, she would have died with or without a bomb going off. Gerty Barry won't be coming home for a few months."

"That makes sense. I can see two people being able to move Laura outside. And how does a dead Charlie Cramer fit into all this?"

"One theory, he was hiding in the house, and they walked in on him. But why didn't they hide his body if they didn't want a homicide rap?" the chief said.

"We know the reason for that. The bomb was supposed to get rid of the evidence," Danielle reminded him.

"While I appreciate Marie's help, it sometimes gives me a headache." He nodded to the briefcase sitting on the rear seat. "Let's get your valuables back in your safe-deposit box, and remember, I need to keep the briefcase for evidence."

BRIAN DROVE up in front of Hal's house and parked. Joe sat in the passenger seat. The two officers did not immediately get out of the vehicle but studied the house. Police tape blocked off its entrance.

"From what I understand, the Kent brothers inherited the house from their parents," Joe said. "But only Hal lived in it after the parents died. As far as I know, Stuart left Frederickport years ago and never returned."

"I understand he was in acting for a while?" Brian asked.

Joe nodded. "A few years after I graduated from high school, they made that horror movie in Frederickport. They hired high school students as extras. Stuart impressed one director. He ended up dropping out of high school right after that and left town to pursue his acting career. He actually got a few good parts, but then I heard he was spending more time partying and tanked whatever career he had. But I suspect he was already into drugs, considering who his brother was."

ONLY ONE OF Hal's next-door neighbors was home, an elderly woman who had lived next door to the Kent family for over thirty years. They stood with her on her front porch, asking questions.

"They were wild boys when they were younger," the woman said. "Gave their parents fits. The youngest one was a character. Always into mischief. Set his father's shed on fire once, playing with fireworks. He was a natural mimic and could be quite entertaining. It didn't surprise me he got into acting, but it was probably the worst thing for him. He didn't last. Never saw him again after he quit school and left home. But his mother would tell me about him. He worked for some construction crew where they made roads, and his job was to blow up mountains or something."

"You didn't see Stuart over at Hal's this past week?" Brian asked.

"I just meant I never saw him again until recently. On Saturday morning when I went outside to look for my cat, I saw Hal drive away, and he had someone in his car with him. I realize now it must have been Stuart. He looks a lot like his brother. But his brother was driving."

"What do you know about Hal?" Brian asked.

"Like I said, both he and his brother were wild boys. But when Hal came home to take care of his parents, he seemed to have grown up. Took over his father's business, was always polite. Kept to himself. Never had any wild parties or anything."

"And his brother never visited him?" Brian asked.

"No. But I got the impression that they got together a few times each year. Not here in Frederickport. Once I asked Hal how his brother was doing, and he mentioned he had just seen him. That's when he had just gotten back from vacation."

THIRTY-FIVE

L aura lounged on her sister's living room sofa Thursday morning, talking on her cellphone, when Lily walked into the room. Laura glanced at Lily. "I'll talk to you later. Lily just walked in, and I want to talk to her for a minute."

"You didn't have to get off the phone." Now standing by the recliner, Lily faced Laura.

"That was Kelly. We were done with our conversation anyway." Laura tossed her cellphone on the sofa next to her. Like Danielle, she hadn't found her old cellphone, but Chris had picked up two cellphones the night before, one for Danielle and the other for Laura. He explained that even if the police found their phones, the police would probably keep them for evidence. He helped them both set up service, and when Laura tried to pay him, he refused her money.

"Anything new in the case?" Lily asked.

"They purchased the van they were driving last week in Portland. Stuart bought it, paid cash. They can't figure out where he got that much money," Laura said. "They checked his bank account, and he had little in it and no withdrawals or deposits since December. He lost his job a couple of months ago."

Laura sat down on the recliner. "Any word on the third kidnapper?"

"No. Unless he's that Cramer guy. But Kelly and I think Cramer was hiding out at that house, and the kidnappers walked in on him. There were no gunshots when I was there, so either the coroner was wrong about the time of death, or they used a silencer. That's assuming the kidnappers killed him."

"So if it isn't Charlie, I wonder who the other guy was and what happened to him," Lily mused.

"I have a theory."

Lily arched her brows. "Which is?"

"If this Stuart didn't have the money to pay for the van, his partner must have paid for it. And for whatever reason, they put the van in Stuart's name. We know Stuart arrived in Frederickport sometime last week. He probably showed up at his brother's house with whoever this third person was. And they told Hal their brilliant plan to extort Danielle. I bet when they broke in, they thought they were planning to take Walt and Danielle but got me instead."

Lily shrugged. "It's possible."

"It's just a theory. They looked into Hal's finances too, and it didn't look like the money for the van came from him either. But he did practically clean out his bank account at the same time Danielle was at the bank getting into her safe-deposit box. Kelly said they found that money on Hal's body."

Lily stood up. "I need to get Connor dressed. You going with us?" Lily was taking Sadie across the street to play with Hunny.

Laura shook her head. "No. I'm just going to hang out here if that's okay with you."

ABOUT TEN MINUTES after Lily walked across the street to Marlow House with Sadie and Connor, Laura picked up her cellphone and checked the time. On previous mornings, this was about when she would walk up Frank's street. She wondered if he knew what had happened to her. She hadn't seen him since Monday morning.

It was entirely possible he was unaware of the kidnapping or that his caretaker was dead. He didn't go anywhere or know anyone in town aside from her and a few of his neighbors. It was possible a neighbor had told him about Hal.

Frank didn't have a car. When she had asked him why he hadn't rented a car, he said it was a waste of money because he could simply walk where he wanted to go. He had hired an Uber to bring him to Frederickport from the airport, and he would hire another when it was time to go home.

"I bet I could walk over to Frank's house faster without Sadie," Laura said aloud. She glanced at the time again.

FRANK STILL HADN'T HEARD from Hal or Stuart. Had something gone wrong, or did they take off with the ransom and leave him to rot? He pulled his cellphone from his back pocket and tried calling Hal again. But like before, nothing. He returned the phone to his pocket and wondered, had something gone wrong? Had they arrested Hal?

Restless, Frank walked through the house, trying to decide what to do. He felt isolated from the outside world and frustrated being unable to get any information. His cellphone was nothing more than a burner phone Hal had picked up, with prepaid minutes and no internet. Stopping at the television, he shook his head. "Useless thing," he muttered. When first arriving, he'd discovered it wasn't hooked up to an antenna, and he certainly wasn't about to sign up for cable.

He wondered if there might be a radio somewhere in the house. Frank walked back into the kitchen and heard barking. He walked to the window and looked outside. It was the neighbor's yappy schnauzer taking his morning walk. But what was the mutt barking at? It was then he saw her—Laura Miller.

"No! It can't be!"

He watched as Laura stopped in the street, talking to his neighbor with the yapping dog.

"GOOD MORNING," Fred Stein greeted Laura while Fritz strained at his leash. "He won't bite; he's just nosey."

Laura smiled at Hal's neighbor, then knelt and put her right hand out to the schnauzer. "Hi there."

Fritz wagged his tail, and Fred let him get closer to her.

"Don't you usually walk a golden retriever?" Fred asked. Laura petted Fritz, who had stopped barking and demanded more of her attention with wet kisses and a wiggling butt.

"Yeah, it's my sister's dog," Laura said. "But Sadie—that's the dog, not my sister—is off playing with one of her dog buddies, so I thought I'd take a quick walk by myself." She glanced up at Frank's house.

"You're friends with Sidney, aren't you?" Fred said. "I've seen you over talking to him."

Laura gave Fritz a last pat and stood back up, turning to Fred. "I met him during my walks, but I haven't been by in the last few days. Umm, have you talked to him?"

Fred shook his head. "No, and now that you mention it, I haven't seen him around in the last couple of days."

"Did you hear what happened to the guy who was taking care of his house?" she asked.

Fred groaned. "Oh, you're talking about Hal Kent. Yeah, that was really something. I never imagined he would do something like that. Not that I knew him very well. I imagine Sidney is going to have to find someone else to take care of his place when he goes back to London."

"You think he knows yet?"

Fred shrugged. "I don't know. I haven't seen him since I read about it in the paper. And to be honest, I don't think he really talks to any of the other neighbors. He has been spending all his time inside, going through his uncle's things. I have a feeling he's getting ready to put that place up for sale, but he wanted to first go through old Sid's things rather than have someone else do it. Heck, you never know what you might find. I remember the old guy was into stamp collecting."

"If he intends to sell the house, then he won't need a caretaker. He'll need a Realtor."

FRANK WATCHED as Laura talked to Fred. After a few minutes, Fred continued on his walk, and Laura looked Frank's way. She walked up the patio steps and headed toward the front door. She glanced toward the window he looked from. He immediately ducked out of sight and held his breath. A few minutes later, the doorbell rang.

His back flattened against the wall in an effort not to be seen from the window. Frank held his breath and listened. A few minutes later, someone knocked on the door.

"Hello, Frank. It's Laura. Are you there?"

Silence. After a few minutes, Frank peeked out the window and saw Laura looking into the living room window. She moved from the window back to the front door and rang the bell again. He held his breath, waiting for her to leave. But instead of leaving, he watched as she reached for the doorknob and turned it. The door was not locked. She pushed it open.

Frank looked around for a weapon. He spied the knife rack sitting nearby on the kitchen counter. Careful not to make a sound, he moved toward the knife rack. He didn't know how she'd managed to get out of the Barry house, but she wouldn't be leaving this one.

LAURA STOOD at the open doorway, her hand still on the doorknob as she peeked inside. She had never been inside Frank's house before. She could see beer cans on one table, along with what looked like crumpled-up fast-food bags.

"Hello?" she called out. "Frank? It's Laura."

WHEN LILY, Connor, and Sadie returned from visiting Danielle, she found her house empty. But there was a note waiting for her on the kitchen table. It read: *I went for a walk. Laura.* Tossing the note aside, Lily took Connor into his bedroom and changed his diaper.

Thirty minutes later, Lily tried calling Laura. Voicemail answered. When Lily couldn't reach her sister, she called Danielle.

"Laura didn't stop over there, did she?" Lily asked Danielle.

"No. What's wrong?" Danielle asked.

"Not saying anything is wrong. But when I got back from your house, Laura wasn't here, and she left a note saying she took a walk."

"She's probably still on her walk," Danielle suggested.

"I tried calling her. I wanted to see when she was going to be back, but she's not answering her phone."

"I wonder if she charged her new phone. After Chris set it up, he told her she needed to charge it."

"I'm sure she did. But considering what happened to you guys the other day, and the fact all the kidnappers haven't been arrested, this makes me nervous. I just want to know where she is."

"She's probably over there talking to her secret friend," Danielle suggested.

"Yeah. I just wish she would answer her phone."

"Would it make you feel better if I had Marie or Eva go check on her for you?" Danielle asked.

"Would you? I'd appreciate that. And if she is over there on his porch, I just might get in my car and go get her," Lily grumbled.

DANIELLE ASSUMED Laura had simply lost track of time and was visiting with her secret friend. Yet she understood Lily's concern, considering what she and Laura had been through. When she explained the situation to Eva and Marie, Eva volunteered to go, and Marie remained with Danielle. While Chris was staying with Danielle until Walt returned, he had gone to work that morning, but had left Hunny behind at Marlow House.

Danielle told Eva about Laura's secret friend and where Eva would probably find her.

Once outside, Eva rose into the sky, enabling her to look down at the neighborhood. She didn't see Laura walking on any of the nearby streets, so she moved to the cul-de-sac where Laura's friend lived. Eva understood that if Laura was there, sitting on his porch, visiting, she would not be able the see her at her current elevation because of the patio's roof.

A few moments later, Eva stood on the street in front of the house where Laura's secret friend supposedly lived. A pair of weathered Adirondack chairs sat on its front porch, yet both were empty. She noticed movement from one window upstairs. Glancing up to the window, she spied a man looking outside. A moment later, he turned and disappeared.

"EVA'S BACK," Danielle told Lily when she called her after Eva returned. "But Laura wasn't at his house. She looked all around the neighborhoods but didn't see her anywhere."

When Lily got off the phone with Danielle, she immediately called the chief.

"Morning, Lily," the chief answered his cellphone.

"Laura's missing," Lily blurted.

THIRTY-SIX

B rian and Joe walked into Pier Café late Thursday morning and
glanced around. Brian saw her first and gave Joe a little elbow
nudge. When Joe turned to Brian, Brian nodded toward the
woman.

"Just what I thought," Joe said before he and Brian started
walking toward the booth where the woman sat alone. When they
reached her, she looked up and smiled.

"Hey, Joe, Brian," Laura greeted. "You having breakfast too?"

"No. We're looking for a missing person," Joe said.

Laura's eyes widened. "Really? Who's missing?"

"You," Brian said.

Laura frowned. "What are you talking about?"

"You guys having breakfast?" Carla's voice came from behind
Joe and Brian.

Brian turned to Carla and said, "Why don't you bring us some
coffee?" He turned back to Laura.

"What do you mean I'm missing?" Laura asked as Carla left to
get the coffee.

"Your sister called the chief. She said you were missing," Joe
explained as he sat down across from her in the booth.

"I'm calling Lily and telling her we found you." Brian walked a few feet from the booth to make his call.

"I'm not missing," Laura told Joe. "I left Lily a note, told her I was taking a walk."

"She's been trying to call you. She's understandably worried, considering what happened."

With a frown, Laura picked up her cellphone from the table and looked at it. She groaned and glanced up to Joe. "I… uh… put it on silent mode last night. This morning when I called Kelly, I forgot to change it back."

"You don't keep it on vibrate when you put it on silent?" Joe asked.

"No. And let it shake on the nightstand? Sort of defeats the purpose. I slept with Lily last night, and I didn't want my phone to go off and wake her up."

"Your sister has been worried about you."

Brian returned to the booth at the same time as Carla arrived with the coffee. Laura scooted down in the bench seat, making room for Brian to sit down. She then picked up her phone, turned off silent mode, and called Lily. The two officers sipped their coffee while listening to Laura's side of the conversation.

"I'm sorry, I left a note… no, I charged my phone, but it was on silent… Yeah… Okay. Yeah. I ordered some breakfast. You want to come down and join me? I can order you something too. Okay."

When Laura said goodbye and hung up a few minutes later, Joe asked, "Is Lily coming down?"

"No. She said she's a little nauseous. Not full-blown morning sickness, but she's afraid the smells down here might make it worse."

"I thought she was over morning sickness," Joe said.

"It's been kinda off and on. She has good days and not-so-good days. And I really feel bad I made her worry. Have you guys been looking for me for a long time?"

Laura glanced at Brian when he chuckled at her question.

"When the chief called us, both Joe and I immediately said you probably stopped here. So this was the first place we came," Brian explained.

"Actually, I'm glad you guys are here. I'm kind of worried about someone."

"Who's that?" Joe asked.

Laura took a deep breath, exhaled, and then leaned back in the booth. "I've been taking walks every morning with Sadie. On one walk, I met a guy. He lives a couple of streets over on Sand Dollar. We sorta became friends, and on my walks, I would stop and have coffee with him. This is his first time in Frederickport, he's from London, but he inherited his house from his uncle a while back. Hal Kent worked for his uncle, doing maintenance on the house, and when my friend inherited the property, Hal contacted him, and well, he hired Hal to watch his house. I'm worried Hal did something to him."

"Why do you think that?" Brian asked.

"Because I walked over there this morning, and according to one of his neighbors, he hasn't seen Frank for a couple of days."

"I assume Frank is your friend?" Brian asked.

"Actually, his real name is Sidney, but he goes by Frank, but that is another story. So this morning, when I stopped over there, I knocked on the door, and no one answered. I... uh... tried the doorknob, and the house was unlocked. I looked inside, and I didn't see anything out of place. But I called for him, and he didn't answer. I didn't go inside. I left. But I keep wondering if Hal did something to him. After all, Hal kidnapped me."

"Perhaps he went to the store or took a walk and forgot to lock the door?" Brian suggested.

"He doesn't have a car, and I think I would have run into him had he been on a walk. Considering what we've learned about Hal, it has me worried. The neighbor hasn't seen Frank for a couple of days, and the neighbor always walks his dog around the same time I would go over there. I just have this gut feeling that something is wrong."

"I know who you're talking about," Joe said. "Considering what happened, it might be a good idea if Brian and I go over there and look around."

Laura smiled hopefully. "Would you?"

"We should question him, anyway," Brian said. "We've been interviewing anyone who had contact with Hal, trying to piece together the last few weeks in Hal's life, which might lead us to his accomplices."

BRIAN PULLED the police car up in front of the Corvin house and parked. Joe sat in the passenger seat. The two officers looked up at the house.

"Maybe he's back," Brian said. "Laura said he doesn't have a car, but he could have taken a walk without her running into him."

A few moments later, the two officers got out of the vehicle and made their way to the front door. Brian rang the doorbell. There was no answer. Brian rang the doorbell again while Joe walked around the patio, peeking into the various windows.

Brian reached for the doorknob and tested it when Joe returned to his side. "It's still unlocked."

"Let's talk to the neighbors," Joe suggested.

With a nod, Brian released hold of the doorknob. The two officers spent the next thirty minutes interviewing the neighbors on the cul-de-sac. The neighbors they spoke to had either never seen Mr. Corvin or had not seen him after Monday. Several neighbors said the only people they ever saw over at the Corvin house was a young blonde woman with a golden retriever, and Hal Kent. Some neighbors, who did not know Hal, described a vehicle occasionally parked in the Corvin driveway. That car matched the one owned by Hal Kent.

After speaking to all the neighbors who were home, Joe and Brian felt justified entering the Corvin house, on the premise of a wellness check. Before doing so, they called the chief, letting him know what they intended to do. The chief agreed.

Before entering the house, Brian rang the doorbell one more time. A moment later, he grabbed hold of the front doorknob, turned it, and then gently pushed the front door open.

"Hello? Mr. Corvin? It's the police," Brian called out. There was no answer.

Brian stepped into the house, followed by Joe. "Hello? Mr. Corvin? It's the police." Silence.

The two officers looked around. They spied the crumpled-up bags from take-out food that Laura had seen earlier, along with several empty beer cans. They proceeded to check out the other rooms in the house while calling out for Mr. Corvin.

HEATHER DIDN'T FEEL like going out to lunch on Thursday. She kept thinking of the leftover homemade enchiladas sitting in her refrigerator at home. She had intended to bring them to work with her but had forgotten. But now it was almost lunchtime, and she craved enchiladas. So instead of going to a restaurant to pick up something to eat, she headed home.

After parking in her driveway behind her house, off the alley-way, Heather got out of her car and headed up the back walk to her side door. She glanced next door to Olivia's house, where Pearl Huckabee had once lived. All was quiet, and she assumed Olivia was at work. Next door to Olivia was Marlow House. Heather wondered how Danielle was doing after her recent ordeal.

Once at the side of her house, Heather used her key to unlock her door. Instead of going straight to the kitchen, she shoved her keys into her purse, dumped the purse on an end table, and headed to the bathroom. But the moment she stepped into the living room, en route to the bathroom, she froze. There, standing in the middle of the living room, stood Charlie Cramer.

"Oh crap," Heather grumbled.

Charlie glared at Heather. He looked just as she remembered, clean-shaven with black horn-rimmed glasses, a husky physique, and in his hand, he held a gun, aiming it at her.

"What are you doing here?"

Charlie frowned at Heather's question. He expected her to sound afraid, not annoyed.

"Sit down," he demanded, pointing to the sofa with the gun.

"Oh, you sit down. I have to use the bathroom." Heather flashed Charlie a scowl and stomped across the room to the bathroom.

"Stop right there!" he shouted angrily as Heather turned her back to him and continued walking.

Heather was afraid he would follow her into the bathroom. She knew locking the door would not keep him out, but she really had to pee. Fortunately, he didn't come into the bathroom, yet it did not surprise her to find him standing in the hallway, pointing the gun at the bathroom door after she opened it.

"You're going to have to come into the kitchen with me," Heather demanded as she headed that way, walking past Charlie.

"Do you want me to shoot you?" Charlie screeched.

"I don't really care, but I'm hungry, and my lunch hour is ticking away."

"Do you have a mental problem?" Charlie asked Heather after he followed her into the kitchen. He stood in the dining area of her kitchen, the hand holding the gun now by his right side as he watched her take something from the refrigerator, remove it from foil, and set it on a plate.

"Some people say I do." Heather grabbed a fork and carried the plate to the dining area.

Charlie frowned at the plate of food as she set it on the table. "What is that?"

"Enchiladas. And I'm not sharing. Not that you could eat them, anyway." Heather walked back into the kitchen area, made herself a glass of iced tea, and returned to the table and sat down.

As she started to take a bite, he asked, "Are you eating that cold?"

"What's it to you?" Heather leaned over and shoved a chair away from the table. "Sit down. We need to talk."

Reluctantly, Charlie sat down. "Why aren't you acting like you're supposed to?"

"You aren't the first person who has asked me that." Heather took a bite of the enchilada.

"I can't believe you didn't warm that up," he grumbled.

"So tell me, Charlie, why are you here?"

"I needed a place to hide out, and I figured I could use a hostage."

"I think you're too late."

Charlie looked nervously toward the doorway leading outside.

"Don't worry, Brian is at work. He doesn't know you're here. Nobody does. Just me." Heather took another bite.

"This makes little sense." Charlie shook his head. "You should be afraid."

"Charlie, I need to ask you a question."

"What? If I'm going to kill you?"

"Nah. I already know the answer to that one."

"You don't know anything. Just stay there." A cellphone suddenly appeared in Charlie's free hand while his other hand continued to point the gun at Heather.

Seeing the cellphone, Heather arched her brows. "Hey, you get good reception on that thing?"

"Shut up!" The gun disappeared, and Charlie's right index finger poked at the phone for a moment, and then he placed it by his ear.

Continuing to eat her enchilada, Heather muttered, "I wonder if they're now handing out cellphones in the hereafter."

"This thing is dead!" Charlie yelled, tossing the cellphone to the floor. It disappeared.

"That's not the only thing that's dead," Heather said before taking another bite of enchilada.

"What did you say?" Charlie demanded. Once again, his right hand held a gun, pointing it at her.

Heather set her fork on the table, took a drink of her tea, and then looked at Charlie. "Who killed you?"

Charlie vanished.

THIRTY-SEVEN

Chief MacDonald was just getting off the phone when Brian and Joe walked into his office on Thursday afternoon. "Did you find Laura's friend?" he asked.

"He wasn't in his house, and there were no signs of foul play," Joe said as he took a seat in one chair facing the chief's desk.

"But there was something kind of odd." Brian sat in the chair next to Joe.

"What was that?"

"Corvin told Laura he came here to go through his uncle's things," Brian began.

"I thought the uncle died a few years ago," the chief said.

"He did. But this is the first time the nephew has been to Frederickport, and his first opportunity to go through his uncle's belongings. But there wasn't anything there, not really. Furniture, but the closets were basically empty. Nothing in the attic or garage. The house reminded me of a rental with bare essentials. Towels, linens, dishes in the kitchen. But no personal belongings aside from a few clothes and toiletries in the master bedroom. There was some food in the refrigerator and one cupboard. It looked like someone was staying there and had just stepped out. But I can't imagine what belongings of his uncle he could possibly be going through," Brian explained.

"Perhaps he finished going through everything and took it somewhere," the chief suggested.

"One neighbor told us the only cars that have been at that house were Hal Kent's and the Uber that dropped Corvin off when he first arrived. An elderly man who lives a few doors down, who seems to be the self-designated neighborhood watch, claims Corvin never left the house and only came outside in the mornings to sit on the patio and visit with an attractive young woman," Joe said.

"Laura," the chief said.

Joe nodded. "That neighbor talked to Corvin when he first arrived. He was curious to find out who was at the house. Corvin told him pretty much the same thing as he told Laura."

"He did mention he was a little surprised at first, because he thought the house had already been gone through. He remembered some people had been there after the uncle died, cleaning things up," Brian added.

"Doesn't mean they didn't box up belongings for the nephew to go through," the chief said.

"That's pretty much what Corvin told the neighbor. But like I said, there was no sign of any boxes that he might have been going through. I have to wonder, what's he been doing over there?" Brian asked.

"Maybe he just made up an excuse to appease nosey neighbors, and he simply came to Frederickport to relax," the chief suggested.

"Perhaps. But he told the same story to Laura, and from what she said, he not only welcomed their morning talks, but talked of showing her around London when she goes over there. I have to wonder, where is he?" Brian asked.

"He could be anywhere. And we really don't know how long he's been missing. If he is actually missing. You found nothing suspicious in the house aside from the fact he obviously lied to neighbors and Laura about how he spent his time? If he doesn't show up tomorrow, I think we need to take a deeper dive into him, considering Hal Kent seemed a little overly attentive to this client if he really stopped by the house so frequently over the last week. Hal and his brother were obviously planning a kidnapping during this time, so why get so chummy with a client you just met?" the chief asked.

"I'll stop by again tonight and in the morning," Brian said.

"By the way, when you walked in, I had just gotten off the phone with my contact in Canada. Their DNA report is back from the remains," the chief announced. He had talked to his contact after they had found Cramer's dead body, so authorities in Canada were already aware the remains found in the warehouse fire weren't Cramer.

"Have they identified who he is?" Joe asked.

"Yes. It was a career criminal, and his DNA was in the system. They don't have a cause of death, but he had a known substance abuse problem, so it is entirely possible he passed out in the ware-house before the fire started," the chief explained.

"Any connection to Charlie?" Joe asked.

The chief shook his head. "Not that they know of."

The chief's office phone rang. He excused himself to answer it, and Joe and Brian left his office.

Twenty minutes later, Brian returned and peeked into the office. The chief was no longer on the phone, so he walked in.

The chief looked up at Brian. "Good, I need to talk to you. Where's Joe?"

"He's in the bathroom, and I want to tell you something before he comes back," Brian explained.

The chief waved him all the way into the office.

Brian stepped up to the chief's desk and spoke in a low voice. "Heather called me. She had a visit from Charlie."

"And? Did he tell her anything?"

Brian shook his head. "According to Heather, he's at that stage where he doesn't realize he's dead. He pulled a gun on her, planned to take her hostage."

The chief arched his brow. "Really?"

Brian shrugged. "But when she asked him who killed him, he disappeared."

"Sounds like she might have scared him off."

"I mentioned that to Heather. She told me she was hungry."

The chief frowned. "Hungry?"

Brian shrugged. "She had gone home to grab lunch. Heather doesn't have a lot of patience when she's hungry."

"If he doesn't understand he's dead, I doubt he can identify a killer," the chief said.

"Heather said that too. Since they shot him in the back, he probably didn't see it coming."

"I'm heading home," a voice called out from the open doorway. Brian turned around and saw Joe.

The chief waved Joe into the office. "I want to tell you both something before you leave for the day."

A few moments later, Joe and Brian sat in the chairs they had been occupying thirty minutes earlier, while the chief sat at his desk.

"That call I received when you were leaving earlier," the chief began, "It was from the police investigating Cramer's escape from jail. They know where he was hiding out before he got to Canada."

"Where?" Joe asked.

"Sounds like the woman in Canada wasn't the only woman Charlie hit up for money," the chief said. "A woman from Washington has come forward and confessed she let Charlie stay with her for a while and then loaned him some money. She believed him when he said he was innocent. He told her his plan was to go to Canada until he straightened everything out and proved his innocence. She gave him forty thousand dollars."

"Holy crap! She just handed over forty thousand bucks to him?" Brian asked.

"She claimed they were in a relationship. They had been planning to get married. And from what they told me, forty thousand was pocket money to this woman."

"Sounds like Charlie," Joe said with a snort.

Brian looked at Joe. "What do you mean?"

"Charlie's job involved a lot of traveling. One of the few times I saw him after they closed the bike shop, he made a comment about a perk with traveling: you could have a woman in every city. When we were in high school, dating a girl didn't mean he stopped looking or wouldn't take an opportunity when one came up." Joe gave a shrug.

"Ahh, he was a player," Brian said.

"He liked to think so. And it sounds like as he got older, he gravitated toward women with money," Joe said.

"This woman, the one who gave him the forty thousand, she hadn't heard about him supposedly dying in Canada, but she heard how they found his dead body in Oregon. She thought he had gone to Canada, and then started worrying he had been lying to her, and I suspect, worried about her role in helping him after he broke out of jail. So she contacted her attorney and, with her attorney, went to the police and told them everything she knew."

"Did Cramer have a connection in Canada?" Brian asked.

"As far as she knew, he was working alone," the chief said.

"Wonder what happened to all that money," Joe said.

"It could be stashed in the Barry house," Brian suggested.

The chief considered Brian's suggestion for a moment before saying, "That's entirely possible. One theory is that Cramer was hiding out at the Barry house when he encountered the kidnappers, and they killed him. If the money had been on Cramer, they would have taken it. But the only money found on the Kent brothers was the money Hal had taken out of his account that morning, and about five hundred on his brother."

"They were obviously heading out of town," Brian said. "After all, Hal practically cleaned out his bank account, and I can't imagine him leaving Cramer's money behind if they found it."

"It's possible someone other than the kidnappers killed Charlie, and they took his money. Perhaps the kidnappers didn't even realize Charlie's body was in that bedroom?" Joe wondered.

"And then we have the other theory some have suggested that Cramer was the third kidnapper, and the Kent brothers double-crossed him," the chief said.

"Which would make Charlie a really busy guy," Joe said. "Breaks out of prison. Hooks up with a woman he's been seeing, convinces her to give him forty thousand. Then books it up to Canada, tries to hit up a second woman, barely escapes without getting blown up—considering his things they found in the warehouse. And makes it back to his hometown in time to hook up with an old classmate to kidnap two women but ends up getting double-crossed. No. I think it's more plausible Charlie came back here for some reason and simply chose the wrong place to hide out."

THIRTY-EIGHT

D anielle woke up on Friday morning to a surprise when Walt walked into the kitchen at Marlow House.

"Look who's here," Eva said. She sat at the kitchen table with Danielle, Chris, and Marie.

"Walt? You're home!" Danielle jumped up from her chair and threw her arms around her husband. She gave him a hug, a kiss, and then pulled back slightly and looked into his eyes. "Why are you home early?"

Chris, who sat at the table, drinking his coffee, watched the couple embrace as Hunny happily nosed Walt, her butt and tail wagging. Before taking another sip of coffee, Chris said, "It's because I'm here, right?"

Walt flashed Chris a grin and said, "Thanks for staying over here."

Chris shrugged and set his cup on the table. "Marie and Eva have been here most of the time, so not sure how much good I was."

"People watching the house can't see Eva and Marie, but they can see Hunny and you," Walt said. No longer embracing Danielle, he went to pour himself a cup of coffee while Danielle sat back down at the table.

"I'm glad you're home, but I'm so sorry this messed things up for your promotion," Danielle said.

"We explained what was going on here, so we filmed two interviews yesterday," Walt said. "But honestly, I couldn't focus, not knowing what was going on back here. And neither could Ian."

"I imagine Laura will need her room back," Chris said.

"I'll change the sheets for you," Marie offered. "I never cared for changing sheets when I used to have to do it with my hands. But it's rather challenging to manipulate a sheet with energy. Good practice."

"Thanks, Marie. But Joanne is working this afternoon, anyway," Danielle said.

Marie let out a sigh. "Okay."

"Now that Walt is home, do you want to cancel the plans for tonight?" Chris asked Danielle.

"What plans did you have for tonight?" Walt asked.

"I was buying Chinese takeout for dinner. Everyone was coming over."

"And you're buying?" Walt asked.

Chris shrugged. "Yeah. I just said that."

"I like Chinese," Walt said.

WHEN CHRIS SAID everyone was coming for dinner, he wasn't kidding. Dinner guests included the chief, the chief's two sons, Heather, Brian, Joe, Kelly, and the Bartley household. They invited their new neighbor, Olivia, but she had prior plans. Lily hadn't suggested inviting her in-laws, not just because she didn't expect Ian to be home, but she knew Ian's parents already had plans to go bowling with a neighbor.

Heather was the first to arrive. Since Laura was still across the street at Lily's, Heather told Walt about seeing Cramer's ghost.

They sat in the living room, Heather, Walt, Danielle, Eva, and Marie.

"And no one else has seen him again?" Walt asked.

"No, and considering his situation, Eva doesn't feel he has moved on yet, so we might see him," Heather said.

Walt looked at Eva. "Why do you think that?"

"Considering Charlie Cramer's sins, I don't imagine he is eager to move on. Of course, souls like him are typically not given the opportunity to stick around indefinitely," Eva explained. "And when Heather saw him, he still didn't understand his new reality."

"Reminds me of Tagg and Felicia. So creepy. The powers that be did not wait around to snatch up their souls when they died. I doubt they realized they were dead, either." Danielle gave a shiver at the memory of two evil spirits the Universe had sucked up not long after their death.

"And I'm sure Charlie Cramer will eventually have to face a similar reality," Eva said.

"Too bad he didn't tell you something about how he died," Walt said.

"When I first saw him standing in my living room, for an instant, I thought he was alive. He looked so real. But then I told myself he was dead. And after he left, I kept thinking, what if he had broken into my house before someone shot him? If I'd walked in on him, I would have assumed it was a ghost, because we all thought he died in Canada, and I would have gotten myself shot." Heather shivered at the thought.

"Fortunately, that didn't happen, because if it had, we would now be having a conversation with your ghost," Danielle said.

Heather looked at Danielle, considering her words for a moment. Finally, she smiled. "True. Not that I want to become a ghost anytime soon, but it makes the possibility of some homicidal maniac killing me less scary."

"I wonder how much help he will be in solving all this if he shows up," Walt asked.

"Oh, and another thing. When I told Brian that Charlie looked just like the last time I saw him, he said that while he immediately recognized his body, he didn't look the same. For one thing, he had lost a lot of weight," Heather said.

"A spirit has the ability to present an image they believe represents them. And I suspect when one does not realize he's dead, the image presented might be one closest to their preferred reality," Eva said.

"What about the spirits of the men killed in the van?" Walt asked.

"No one has seen them. Eva and Marie have even stopped by the morgue a few times where their bodies are being held, and they weren't there," Danielle explained.

A discussion of Charlie Cramer's ghost ended when the other guests began arriving.

NOT LONG AFTER Police Chief MacDonald showed up at Marlow House with his two sons, he approached Laura in the living room. "Laura, I was hoping you could stop by the police station tomorrow."

"Is this about Frank?" Laura asked. "I know he still hasn't shown up at his house. I'm so worried that Hal did something to him."

"Yes, this is about Frank. I want you to meet with a friend of mine tomorrow, Elizabeth Sparks."

Laura frowned. "Who is that?"

"She's a local artist who at one time studied to be a police artist. I use her services sometimes, and I'd like you to sit down with her so she can do a drawing of your friend."

"Why?"

"So we'll know what he looks like."

"Why not just use a photograph?" Laura asked.

"Do you have a photograph of him?" the chief asked.

"No. But when I googled him, I found a picture of him online."

The chief arched his brows. "Really? You sure it was him?"

"It looked like him. Wasn't a great likeness, but it was him. It was on his LinkedIn page."

"The thing is, the man you met is not Sidney Corvin. His real name may be Frank, but he is not the Sidney Corvin who owns that property."

"I can't believe that."

"You told Kelly your friend didn't want Adam to know he was in town because he kept contacting him to list the house," the chief began. "We couldn't ask Adam because he's on his honeymoon. But we talked to Adam's assistant, Leslie. She had Sidney Corvin's contact information, his phone number, along with the company he works for. We couldn't reach him on his phone, but we reached someone in his company. Sidney Corvin is currently on a business trip in South Africa. He is not in the US. In fact, the person I spoke to saw him personally the day before he left for Africa. And that was after you had already met this person who claimed to be Sidney Corvin in Frederickport."

"He's an imposter?" Laura asked dully.

THEY SAT around the living room, each with a plate of Chinese food. Instead of eating in the dining room, they decided on something more informal. Danielle and Chris had set up the food Chris brought on the dining room buffet, along with beverages, plates, utensils, and napkins. After helping themselves to the food, they retired to the living room. The only ones who did not eat in the living room were Evan and Eddy Junior, who ate dinner in the parlor while watching a movie on the television.

Laura quietly ate her food, silently mulling over the fact she had been flirting with someone who had broken into the Corvin house and had lied to her. The other people in the room had overheard her conversation with the chief involving Frank, and soon they began discussing the imposter. Laura felt like a fool.

While the chief did not come out and say it, Laura knew he—along with everyone else—believed the man she knew as Frank was probably in some way involved in her kidnapping. Her stomach churned as she silently recalled their morning conversations, including all the intimate details she had readily handed the stranger, including their plans, discussions on where Danielle kept the Missing Thorndike, the gold coins, and how she and Danielle would be alone at Marlow House on Tuesday. She felt like an utter fool and could not bring herself to disclose all that she had shared with this man. She wondered, where had he gone? Had he left Frederickport?

"I was telling Joe how being a fugitive had played a toll on Cramer," Laura heard Brian tell everyone. She hadn't been paying attention to the conversation. She glanced at Brian.

"What do you mean?" Kelly asked.

"For example, he lost a lot of weight," Brian said.

"Par for the course, I imagine," Chris said.

"Looked like he hadn't shaved since he broke out of jail," Brian said.

"If I were a guy on the run, the first thing I would do is start growing my beard out," Heather said.

"And then there were the scratches," Brian said.

"Scratches?" Danielle asked.

"Yeah, his forehead was all scratched up. Asked the coroner about it, and he said it looked like a cat attacked him."

Walt and Danielle exchanged quick glances and then looked over to the fireplace, where Max napped on the hearth. They each wondered the same thing. Had Charlie Cramer been the one who had broken into Marlow House? Had he been the one Max attacked?

"Did he wear glasses?" Laura blurted out.

"Charlie? Yeah. He wore black horn-rimmed glasses," Heather said.

"Actually, he wasn't wearing those when we found him," Brian said. "He was wearing glasses, but they were wire rimmed."

"Oh god!" Laura stood abruptly, the plate of food dropping off her lap onto the floor.

"Laura, you just spilled your food all over Dani's throw rug," Lily scolded.

Making no attempt to pick up her plate, Laura shook her head in disbelief. "I think Frank is Charlie Cramer."

"WHEN DID you first meet this Frank?" the chief asked Laura.

After she told him, he pulled out his cellphone and looked at his calendar. Shaking his head, he returned the cellphone to his pocket and said, "He was in Canada the day you met him. So it couldn't have been him."

"Are you sure he was in Canada? After all, they thought he died up there, and he obviously didn't," Chris asked.

The chief considered the question a moment and then said, "No one actually saw Cramer in Canada."

"The fastest way to find out if the man Laura knew as Frank was Charlie Cramer, take her down to the morgue and look at his body," Heather suggested.

"His dead body?" Laura squeaked.

"Oh, it's not that big a deal. I've seen lots of dead bodies," Heather said.

"You mean you've tripped over lots of dead bodies," Chris snarked.

Heather shrugged. "Same thing." She looked at Laura and said, "I'll go with you for moral support if you want."

"If Laura is right and Cramer was masquerading as Sidney Corvin, this could mean we can stop looking for the third kidnapper," the chief said. "I know they implied there were more than the three men Danielle saw at the Barry house, but we haven't come across any information to suggest anyone else was involved. I suspect that was simply a scare tactic to get Danielle to follow their instructions."

"What about their cellphones?" Ian asked.

"You mean the Kent brothers' cellphones?" the chief asked.

Ian nodded. "I'm just curious about what you found on their cellphones. I would expect that's where you'd find leads to potential accomplices."

"We checked out their cellphones," the chief said. "The only cellphone on Stuart was a recently purchased one with prepaid minutes. The only calls on that phone were to his brother. And the only calls on Hal's phone were to Stuart, a number that appears to be a burner phone, and a couple of his clients. Clients who all have alibis and were not in Oregon at the time of the kidnapping."

"Could that burner phone be the one Cramer was using? If he is Frank?" Chris asked.

"Possible." The chief shrugged.

"I'll take Laura down there tonight," Brian said. "The chief really can't. He has his boys. And Heather can come with us."

THIRTY-NINE

The security guard unlocked the door for Brian. The chief had called down to inform him that Officer Henderson would be there with two women to view a body in the morgue.

"This is so creepy," Laura muttered as she held Heather's hand after entering the building.

"Just remember, dead people can't hurt you. Only living people," Heather said.

"I guess," Laura muttered. Her gaze darted around her surroundings as Brian led them down a hallway. When they reached the door leading to the room with Charlie Cramer's body, Laura froze for a moment and squeezed Heather's hand.

"Ouch," Heather yipped. She used her free hand to loosen Laura's grip. "It will be okay, but don't squeeze my hand off."

"Sorry," Laura squeaked. Brian opened the door and turned on the light.

When Heather stepped into the room with Laura, the first thing she noticed was the sudden drop in temperature and chemical smells. The second thing she noticed, they were not alone. Sitting together on the otherwise empty stainless steel exam table were the

Kent brothers. She recognized them from the recent newspaper article.

"Dang, it's cold in here," Laura said.

"What's Brian Henderson doing here?" Hal grumbled.

"That's kinky. He brings women down to the morgue on Friday nights?" Stuart quipped. Both brothers laughed.

Unaware of the ghosts sitting on the nearby table, Brian walked past them, heading to the drawer where they held Cramer's body. After reading the drawer's label to make sure he had the right one, Brian paused a moment and looked back at Laura. "Are you okay?"

Laura nodded.

Brian turned back to the drawer and started pulling it out.

"Dang, he's going to show her a body. I wish we could jump out of that drawer, scare the crap out of that cop," Stuart said.

"That would be hilarious," Hal agreed.

"They don't know we're here. They think they're so brave; if I could whisper boo in his ear, that joker would wet his pants," Stuart said.

"This being dead isn't so bad. I figured when you died, you just went to sleep. I have to admit, I'm glad that's all I was wrong about. It would have really sucked if that hell thing turned out to be real," Hal snarked.

"No kidding. One reason I stayed in the Pacific Northwest, I hate the heat," Stuart said.

Laura stepped up to the drawer and looked inside. She let out a gasp and nodded. "Yes. That is the man I knew as Frank."

"Oh, whoopee, they figured out one piece of the puzzle," Stuart snorted.

Heather, who had followed Laura to the drawer, turned abruptly while Laura focused all her attention on Charlie's body. Now facing the two ghosts, her back to Laura and Brian, Heather grinned and then stuck her left thumb in her left ear, her right thumb in her right ear, waved her fingers like little flags, and stuck her tongue out at the two ghosts.

The next moment she wished she had a camera capable of capturing the images of ghosts, because she found the shocked expressions of the Kent brothers priceless as they attempted to grab each other as a frightened person might take hold of someone when seeking support, yet only moved through each other, causing them to fall off the table. That surprised Heather. She never imagined a ghost could fall like that.

"Wow, that was interesting," Heather muttered.

"You can see us!" Hal accused, now standing next to his brother by the table.

Thinking Heather's comment was regarding her identification of Cramer, Laura shrugged in response. She stepped back from the drawer as Brian closed it.

"Are you okay?" Brian asked Laura.

"I think so. Can we go now?" Laura asked.

Brian nodded and took Laura by the elbow, leading her from where they stored the bodies and by the two ghosts, who stood speechless in the corner.

"Can I meet you outside?" Heather told Brian. "I'll just be a minute."

"You're staying in here? Alone? Why?" Laura asked.

Heather smiled. "I would like a few private words with Charlie Cramer. After all, he tried to kill me. I would like closure."

Brian glanced around the room and then looked at Heather and said, "We'll be outside."

"But, Brian," Laura protested, unable to fathom why Heather would want to stay alone in the morgue for even a minute, but Brian ushered her outside.

THE MOMENT BRIAN closed the door, leaving Heather alone with the two ghosts, Heather turned to the Kent brothers and folded her arms across her chest. "I've been looking for you."

"You can really see us," Hal stammered.

"Of course, it's my job," Heather said.

"Your job?" Hal frowned.

267

"I'll be filing my report on you two and sending it up to my supervisor."

"What are you talking about?" Stuart asked.

"As you both realize, you're dead, and any minute now my supervisor will call you up." Heather pointed to the ceiling. "Or down." She pointed to the floor and shrugged.

"We understand we're dead, but what's all this about a supervisor and a report?" Stuart asked.

"You didn't think when you died, you'd wander around for eternity like an invisible Peeping Tom, watching the living. Did you?"

Stuart shrugged. "Well, yeah. It is kinda cool."

Hal frowned. "You mean there is more than this?"

"Of course. Full disclosure, it's better for you—unless you really like severe heat—to complete your exit interview and let me submit my report. Obviously, the big boss will know if you answer the questions truthfully. If you fudge on your answers, that will ultimately be held against you. You have free will to submit truthful answers or make up whatever you want, or simply refuse to answer my questions. It's all up to you. It doesn't matter to me one way or another. You're the ones who have to face the consequences if you fail to truthfully complete your exit report. Not me." Heather shrugged. "But if I were you, I'd go with the total transparency thing. The big guy loves that. And it is never a good idea to piss him off."

Heather grinned at the Kent brothers, rather pleased with her outrageous story.

"Are you talking about God?" Hal asked.

"He… or she… goes by many names. It's the power who has the ultimate say on how you spend your eternity. And considering some choices you made during your lifetime, I have a feeling you're going to have a rough time when you get to the next level. So doing whatever you can to get some extra points might be in your best interest."

"What do we have to do?" Hal asked.

Heather pulled her cellphone from her back pocket and opened her dictation app and then looked at Hal. "It's simple. I ask questions, you answer them, and then I record the answers and send them to my boss."

Stuart's eyes widened as he stared at the cellphone in Heather's hand. "Wow, you can talk to God with an iPhone?"

HEATHER LOOKED smug as she practically bounced out of the morgue, leaving two confused and frightened ghosts sitting in the now dark building, waiting for someone to beam them up—or down.

"I can't believe you stayed in there alone for so long," Laura said when Heather got into the car with her and Brian. "I wanted Brian to go in and get you."

"Everything okay?" Brian asked Heather, sounding bemused.

"Yes. Everything is perfect," Heather chirped.

ON FRIDAY NIGHT, after leaving Marlow House, MacDonald listened to the audio recording Heather had airdropped to his cellphone. Heather had recorded the questions she had asked of the ghosts and then their answers. Obviously, their voices would not record, so Heather had recorded their answers by repeating them. He could never enter it into evidence, yet it answered many of his questions. Heather explained she couldn't repeat everything they told her. It would have taken too long, so she just made notes of the most important points. The chief wanted to sit down and discuss the recording with her before he wrapped up the case. Before going to bed, he sent her a text message, asking if he could come over to her house the next morning. He knew Brian would already be there.

THE CHIEF ARRIVED at Heather's house on Saturday morning with fresh cinnamon rolls from Old Salts Bakery. Heather led him

269

into her kitchen, where she poured them all coffee. The three sat around her kitchen table, discussing her interview with the spirits while drinking coffee and eating cinnamon rolls.

"So basically, the kidnapping was all Cramer's idea, bankrolled by the money he took from the woman in Washington, and the Kent brothers cut him out at the last minute," the chief summarized.

"Pretty much." Heather tore off a piece of cinnamon roll and popped it into her mouth.

"And Cramer was never in Canada?" the chief asked.

"Nope. He was in Washington State for a while, but he was never in Canada. Stuart went up there, impersonated Cramer, using his old acting skills. He was obviously pretty good at imitating voices."

"It made me think of Darlene," Brian interjected. Like Stuart, Brian's ex and now deceased lover Darlene Gusarov had once been an actor, and she had used her skills to impersonate Danielle's voice.

"Meanwhile, Charlie was hiding in plain sight in his hometown, taking on the identity of Sidney Corvin. With a beard, he already looked a little like the guy. Although, his beard was not as long as Laura thought. Did you know he put mascara on it to make it thicker?" Heather asked.

"Yes, which didn't surprise me," the chief said. "After all, he didn't have a beard when he escaped."

"Charlie didn't want to be a fugitive on the run for the rest of his life, living on the streets. Once he escaped, he started thinking of ways to make a big score, and then he figured he would disappear," Heather explained. "He needed to fake his death so the police would stop looking for him."

"Forty thousand wasn't enough for him?" Brian asked.

Heather shook her head. "No, that was just seed money to pay for things like the van, the burner phones, whatever they needed to pull off the kidnapping. That woman in Washington who gave him the money, Cramer met her several years ago, when he was visiting Stuart."

"We didn't realize Stuart and Cramer were friends. Joe certainly didn't know," the chief said.

"I wouldn't call them friends, exactly, considering Stuart is the one who killed Cramer. Didn't want to share the ransom. But those two had been involved in shady deals for several years, including smuggling Cramer did while traveling as a salesman. So when Charlie was hiding out with the woman in Washington and he cooked up this idea, he called up Stuart. He had forty thousand to bankroll his scheme, and once Stuart got his brother on board, they moved ahead with the plan."

"I wonder when they decided to cut Charlie out of the deal," the chief asked.

"They never really trusted Charlie," Heather said. "After all, he had already killed one business partner. I think that was the plan all along. Oh, and I know who took the suitcase out of Charlie's house."

"Who?" the chief asked.

"It was Hal. Inside the suitcase was an extra pair of glasses. They were wire rimmed. An older pair Charlie kept as a backup in case he lost his glasses. The prescription was a little outdated, but he could use them. Without glasses, he was practically blind."

"Joe mentioned that," Brian said.

"He didn't want to wear the horned-rimmed glasses, afraid one of Sidney's neighbors might recognize him. His photo had been all over the evening news. He also wanted Hal to send his glasses up to Stuart, who was already in Canada. They also sent some other stuff to Stuart with his DNA on it," Heather explained.

"In the recording, you mentioned the man killed in Canada. It wasn't clear; did Stuart murder him?" the chief asked. "Or was he already dead?"

"Stuart befriended this guy when he got to Canada. They did drugs together. After the guy passed out, Stuart arranged the explosion. So yeah, he killed the guy, but fortunately for the victim, he passed out before the explosion."

"I assume the glasses Stuart wore when impersonating Charlie were plain glass, a pair he bought and not the pair they sent him," the chief asked.

Heather shrugged. "We really didn't talk about that, but probably. They told me they had burner phones, so when Hal talked to his brother when he was in Canada, they didn't do it from his regular cellphone. They didn't want anyone to trace calls made to Canada to his phone."

"Do you think the Kent brothers are still over at the morgue… waiting?" the chief asked.

Heather shook her head. "No. Before you got here this morning, Eva stopped by. She says from the vibrations she's picked up, the Kent boys have moved on, now facing whatever consequences the Universe—or God—has in store for them."

"And Charlie Cramer?" the chief asked.

"I'm afraid he hasn't moved on yet, and we may see more of him." Heather let out a sigh and added, "When I say we, I mean the mediums."

———

AFTER THE CHIEF and Brian left, Heather headed to Marlow House to talk to Walt and Danielle. She first went to the back door, but after peeking in the window and finding the kitchen empty, she walked around to the front door and rang the bell. Walt answered the door and then led Heather to the dining room.

There, Heather found Lily and Ian sitting at the dining room table with Danielle. By the dirty dishes on the table, it was obvious they had recently finished brunch, and by the number of place settings, Heather guessed Laura had joined them.

"Where's the kid?" Heather asked as she took a seat at the table.

"Laura took him," Lily explained. "Kelly picked them up. They went over to Ian's parents'."

Walt took a seat at the table and focused his energy on the dirty dishes. One by one the dishes lifted from the tablecloth before floating to the end of the table and stacking themselves. Walt telepathically arranged the dirty dishes while the rest of the people ignored Walt's efforts, as if it were quite natural, while Heather recounted her recent discussion with the chief and Brian.

"I keep thinking how we might have avoided this nightmare if we hadn't dismissed the break-in as a prank," Danielle said. "We should have at the very least replaced our locks once we knew he had a key."

"But the guy would have just picked the lock, like he did when he broke in the first time," Heather reminded her.

"There should be locks out there that aren't easy to pick," Danielle said. "Or maybe we should have installed a security system."

"I've been thinking of that myself," Walt said.

"There is one thing that I keep wondering about this case," Lily said.

"What's that?" Heather asked.

"If Cramer was never in Canada, and that woman who was supposed to give him money showed up at his room, was that Stuart dude planning to kill her after she brought him the money?"

"I wondered that, too," Ian said.

"From what they told me, they never expected her to show up with the money. Cramer knew the moment she hung up, she would be on the computer, looking up his case. She was too impatient. And he was certain that after she read the articles, she'd run to her uncle. They were just using her to set up his fake death. But if Cramer had been wrong, and she did show up with the money, yes, Stuart intended to kill her and keep the money."

FORTY

There was a time Danielle vehemently avoided cemeteries. During that period, none of her friends had been aware of her gift. While she had told her first husband, Lucas, he never truly believed her. As a small child, she'd naively shared with several close family members her paranormal experiences. Their reactions had taught her to guard her secret.

A cemetery, where she was more likely to encounter an earthbound spirit, was an uncomfortable place for her. Because even if she tried concealing her gifts, they always seemed to sense her ability and would seek her out, pestering her until they had her attention and her promise to contact some loved one.

But the Universe had realigned Danielle's world since moving to Frederickport. She not only had other mediums in her life, but nonmediums aware of her gifts and accepting of them. While Danielle never imagined she would attend a funeral at Frederickport Cemetery on a March afternoon, just days before Kelly and Joe's wedding, the prospect didn't terrify her.

The deceased wasn't a friend, nor someone whose death she would mourn. Danielle would shed no tears. The gathering was small, with some attending out of respect for Charlie's mother, some out of curiosity, and for others, like Joe Morelli, for closure. Danielle and some of her closest friends wondered if the guest of honor might drop by.

There was no church service, just a few words said at the graveside by Pastor Chad. Danielle stood with Walt, Chris, and Heather, away from the others attending. Minutes earlier, Pastor Chad had finished saying his few words and was now talking to several elderly members of his congregation who had known Charlie's mother.

Danielle watched as Charlie's casket lowered into the ground. "I figured he'd be cremated. But according to the chief, Charlie's mother made her own funeral arrangements a few years before she died. And when she did, she bought two funeral plots, side by side. One for her, and one for her son."

"That's a little creepy," Heather said.

"Not only that, didn't his mother ever consider her son might someday marry?" Danielle asked.

"Or maybe she was clairvoyant," Heather suggested.

Learning Charlie already owned a funeral plot and had given his attorney instructions regarding his final arrangements was not the only thing Danielle and her friends learned that week. It turned out Charlie had left his entire estate to Shannon Langdon—his second victim. Of course, he had made that will not long after he sold the bike shop and years before he murdered Shannon. They all assumed the estate would now go to Shannon's cousin, Eden.

Danielle glanced over at Joe, who stood a short distance away, out of earshot. Kelly stood next to his right, and next to Kelly stood Laura, Lily, and Ian. Danielle couldn't help but wonder what thoughts went through Laura's and Joe's minds. In their own ways, they each grieved for a person they once cared for—yet that person was not Charlie Cramer. That person never existed.

Like Danielle, Chris eyed Joe. "I wonder how Joe is processing all this. It was bad enough when they first arrested Cramer. And now Joe knows Charlie was behind the kidnapping," Chris said.

Because of what Heather already told him, the chief understood Charlie had masterminded the kidnapping. Yet it wasn't until the subsequent investigation that information proving Charlie's involvement made it into an official report. Police had located a bag the Kent brothers had tossed in a dumpster before picking up the ransom. It held the burner phones used by Charlie, Hal, and Stuart during the planning of the kidnapping. In a hurry to get rid of the bag after killing Charlie, the Kent brothers had not bothered wiping down the phones to remove prints, nor did they remove the memory cards.

They found the firearm used to kill Charlie hidden in the van after they had towed away the vehicle and had it thoroughly searched. And like the phones, fingerprints remained. The police also went through the Corvin house, where they not only found Charlie's fingerprints throughout the home, but the suitcase taken from Charlie's house. He had shoved it in the back of a closet. Brian and Joe had overlooked the suitcase the first time they walked through the Corvin house. They found Hal's fingerprints on the suitcase, along with Charlie's.

In Canada, the police searched through security camera footage taken near the home of the man killed in the warehouse fire. The day before the fire, the video captured the man leaving his home with Stuart Kent.

DANIELLE WAS ABOUT to suggest they walk over to their other friends when an apparition appeared, standing a few feet in front of them, his back to her.

"I can't believe this is how it all ends!" the apparition complained. Danielle recognized the voice: Charlie Cramer.

"Why are you still here?" Heather asked.

Charlie turned abruptly, coming face-to-face with the mediums. He frowned when he noticed not just Heather staring at him, but so were her three friends.

"I wondered if you would show up," Danielle said.

"You can see me too?" Charlie asked.

"Be glad you're dead, or you'd be sitting on the top of that tree right now." Walt nodded toward a nearby towering pine. To prove it wasn't an empty threat, a small branch broke from the tree, flew toward Charlie, taking a swing at him before falling to the ground.

Charlie jumped back in response and stared dumbly at Walt, trying to process what had just happened. Danielle glanced around to see if anyone had witnessed Walt's outburst. Yet she assumed if anyone had, they would assume a gust of wind had broken the branch from the tree.

"You can't stay forever," Chris told Charlie. "Eventually they'll make you move on."

Before Charlie responded, Chris and the others shifted their attention to something behind Charlie. Turning to see what they looked at, Charlie found himself staring into the face of an old friend, Joe Morelli. Joe wasn't alone.

"You really didn't have to come today," Joe said.

Danielle smiled at Joe. "I think we all needed closure."

Joe nodded. "You're probably right."

"I'm glad you came, Joe," Charlie said to deaf ears.

"I find this very surreal," Laura said as she looked toward Charlie's last resting place.

Charlie frowned at Laura. "Why is she even here?"

"I can't believe it. I liked him. I really did," Laura said.

"Does she realize who I am?" Charlie looked at the mediums for answers. They all ignored him. He looked back at Laura.

"Yeah, I get how that feels," Joe said.

Laura reached out and touched his hand. "I'm sorry, Joe. It's way worse for you. You knew this guy for years. Thought he was your friend. I can't even imagine how you're dealing with this. I only knew him for a few days. Or should I say, I thought I knew him."

"Joe was my friend," Charlie argued.

Joe shrugged. "He conned all of us."

"I never conned you," Charlie insisted. "My problem was with Rusty, not you. And I had no choice with Shannon."

"I'd like to know where he came up with the name Frank," Lily said.

"Charlie's middle name was James. So it wasn't that. It was probably just some name that popped into his head," Joe said.

Charlie shook his head. "No, it wasn't."

"He said he was going to tell me in London. But he knew that was never happening," Laura said.

Heather looked at Charlie. "Joe's probably right. It was just something he randomly made up."

Charlie twirled around and faced Heather. Scowling, he said, "You don't know what you're talking about. I didn't just make up a name. Frank Morris was one of the men who broke out of Alcatraz. They never captured him. He died over forty years later under an alias. They never caught him!"

Heather smiled sweetly. "Or perhaps he imagined he was another Frank Morris."

Laura frowned. "Who's that?"

"He's a man who escaped Alcatraz and was never captured. I bet Charlie fancied himself a Frank," Heather said.

"Nah." Chris shook his head. "The dude wasn't that deep. I doubt he ever heard of Frank Morris. And if he imagined himself a Frank Morris, he was delusional. He would never have gotten away with his cockamamie scheme. The guy couldn't even embezzle from his own business without getting caught."

Charlie vanished.

"WOW, THAT WAS HARSH," Heather teased Chris when she got into the passenger side of Chris's car after the funeral. She had come to the cemetery with Chris, as Brian was working, and Danielle and Walt had driven to the cemetery in the Packard.

"The guy tried to kill one of my best friends, and then he tried kidnapping another close friend." Chris climbed into the driver's seat and slammed the door shut. "He pisses me off."

Heather's eyes widened at Chris. "Did you just call me one of your best friends? Or were you talking about Laura?"

Chris rolled his eyes at Heather as he shoved the key in his ignition. "Don't be goofy. Laura's a casual friend at best."

THERE WAS ONLY one thing that could ruin the wedding for some attending—the wedding crasher. Charlie had showed up right before the ceremony, dressed in a tux identical to the one Brian wore. And when Brian took his place as best man, standing beside Joe, Charlie tried pushing Brian aside. Of course, none of the guests noticed; only the mediums sitting among the guests could see.

"What is he doing?" Heather whispered to Danielle.

"It looks like he wants to be best man." Danielle cringed when Charlie stubbornly stood in the same spot as Brian.

"Ew… that is icky." Heather grimaced. "Someone needs to get him off Brian!"

Chris, who sat next to Heather, leaned toward her and whispered, "That is gross. Wonder if Brian can feel him."

"What is he doing?" Heather asked.

Walt, who sat on the other side of Danielle, said nothing, but just shook his head.

"He's regretting his life choices," came a familiar voice. The mediums looked to the left and saw Eva standing next to Chris.

Eva glanced at Heather and smiled. "Charlie is regretting the choices that brought him to where he is today. He knows if he had taken a different path, he would probably be standing where Brian is now. A best man for one of his closest friends."

"The dude murdered one of his closest friends," Heather grumbled.

Eva moved toward Charlie. She didn't walk—she floated—and when she reached him, he looked at her, confused. Eva put out a hand and said, "Time for you to go now, Charlie. They are waiting."

The next moment, Charlie disappeared.

IT WASN'T EXACTLY the beach wedding Kelly—or Laura—had initially envisioned, yet no one was disappointed. Danielle always said good food can make the event, and in that respect, Pearl Cove did not disappoint. When they served the food after the ceremony, Lily's morning sickness had finally subsided, and she took full advantage of taste testing the wide variety of appetizers.

Holding the wedding on an evening the restaurant was normally closed was the only way they could reserve the entire dining room, which was why the wedding fell on a Thursday evening. June had tried to talk her daughter into considering a day wedding, to take advantage of the ocean view, yet that would also be on a Thursday, and Kelly felt it would be too hard for some guests to attend because of work.

Brian and Heather stood with Walt and Danielle, discussing the wedding ceremony.

"Here I was thinking this place was really drafty," Brian said.

"Nope. No draft. Just Charlie grasping at straws, thinking a do-over might be possible," Heather said.

"I wonder where he is now," Brian asked.

"Probably at a much warmer place than that chilly spot you were standing in during the ceremony," Walt snarked.

Danielle glanced around the dining room and spied the bride and groom talking to the groom's grandmother. Danielle couldn't help but smile. Kelly made a beautiful bride, and by the way Joe looked at his new wife, Danielle knew Joe loved Kelly. She couldn't help but think of her and Joe's brief romance and how it had ended because of his lack of trust.

Danielle smiled again when she saw Kelly proudly showing off her new engagement ring setting to Joe's grandmother. By the elderly woman's expression, she approved. Silently, Danielle reached for Walt's hand and squeezed it. He gently returned the squeeze and didn't release her hand. Danielle sincerely hoped Joe and Kelly had found their forever kind of love, as she had found with Walt.

THE GHOST AND THE TWINS

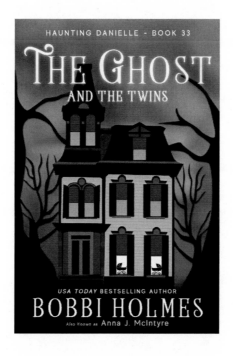

RETURN TO MARLOW HOUSE

THE GHOST AND THE TWINS

HAUNTING DANIELLE, BOOK 33

Return to Frederickport, Oregon, in the 33rd Book in the Haunting
Daniele series. Restless spirits invade Beach Drive with the arrival of the
twins and the stork's unexpected return.

BOOKS BY ANNA J. MCINTYRE